Built

Built

AMIE STUART
JAMI ALDEN
BONNIE EDWARDS

APHRODISIA
KENSINGTION BOOKS
http://www.kensingtonbooks.com

APHRODISIA BOOKS are published by

Kensington Publishing Corp.
850 Third Avenue
New York, NY 10022

All Kensington titles, imprints and distributed lines are available at special quantity discounts for bulk purchases for sales promotion, premiums, fund-raising, educational or institutional use.

Special book excerpts or customized printings can also be created to fit specific needs. For details, write or phone the office of the Kensington Special Sales Manager: Kensington Publishing Corp., 850 Third Avenue, New York, NY 10022. Attn. Special Sales Department. Phone: 1-800-221-2647.

Aphrodisia and the A logo Reg. U.S. Pat. & TM Off.

ISBN-13: 978-0-7582-1923-7
ISBN-10: 0-7582-1923-7

First Kensington Trade Paperback Printing: August 2007

10 9 8 7 6 5 4 3 2 1

Printed in the United States of America

Contents

Kink

Amie Stuart

1

I was in hell. The black and gold hell that was Glorious Creations, and escape was at the top of my list.

I flipped the thermostat on, praying this time it would work. Repairing the salon's older-than-dirt air conditioner had meant spending most of the morning in the thick Houston heat, but I'd damn sure rather be out there than in here with all these women.

Four of the seven barber chairs were occupied, plus the two old women under the dryer and a couple more getting their nails done. I could feel all of them staring at me as I moved around to close the front door. Posters in the reception area settled into place on the walls, and the sound of female chatter immediately picked up.

I turned toward the break room, ready to make my escape when an elderly woman with snow-white hair lifted the dryer.

"D'Angelo, how's your mama doing?" She was tiny, with almost wrinkle-free skin that made guessing her age pretty much impossible. She looked familiar, but I couldn't place her.

I barely slowed my pace to answer. "She's fine, ma'am."

"D'Angelo—"

My aunt would have my ass if I was rude to her customers. I bit back a sigh and stopped directly under a vent, letting cool air wash over me. The woman sat up a little straighter and gave me a smile meant to charm. I did likewise and waited to see what she wanted. "Yes, ma'am."

"I want you to have my grandbabies," she announced— loudly.

I stared at her, a "fuck no" lodged somewhere in my throat, while every woman in the salon cackled or expressed their own desire for me to father their child or grandchild. If I had a nickel for every time some woman, old or young, had said the same damn thing to me, I'd be a rich man.

Rubbing the whiskers on my chin, I turned and glanced at my aunt in the mirror. Apparently, not shaving wasn't the deterrent I'd hoped it would be. Aunt Glo shrugged, a smile on her face. *What the hell could I say?* "Thank you, ma'am."

"I'm surprised anyone wants his babies with that fuzzy head of his," my cousin Vivi practically shouted from the far end of the shop. She stood behind her chair, in the middle of a weave, her own tiny braids held back from her face by a rubber band. Vivi was a looker, she knew she was a looker and made sure anyone within a fifty-mile radius knew it too.

"Nothing a haircut and a shave wouldn't cure," a busty blonde announced from her nail station.

I'd noticed her on an earlier trip from the A/C unit, located out back, to the thermostat by the front door. But then, how could I miss her?

She tucked her long, tanned legs underneath her seat and winked at me. Her tiny pink bandana-print skirt barely covered her ass and matched a pair of painfully high-heeled shoes the same color. Pink and blue and blonde; in her own way, she was as out of place in the salon's black and gold surroundings as me.

My aunt sauntered over and planted a kiss on my sweaty cheek. "You should put that poor woman out of her misery," she said. One penciled-in eyebrow crested, dipped, and crested again while she spoke.

"Her granddaughter would scare a Rottweiler," I murmured.

She snorted with laughter and rubbed my cheek. "You so pretty, D'Angelo," she teased in a singsongy voice. "That's what they *all* say about *you*."

"I know." I sighed in resignation. I wasn't conceited; I'd heard all my life how *pretty* I was, and I hated it. Not that my brothers were ugly—far from it—but my light skin and green eyes had always attracted a lot of attention, and not always the good kind. I got down to the business at hand. "You need a new compressor, Aunt Glo."

She waved off my bad news and turned her back to me, prepared to finish up a wrap on the woman in her barber chair. "Come see me Saturday morning for a haircut, young man."

Bubble gum and rubber bands would probably have been just as effective as anything I could do with a wrench and a prayer, but Aunt Glo was cheap. We'd just have to baby it along until Dad could convince her to shell out some real dough for that compressor.

"Thanks for waking me up, Aunt Glo." Looked like I'd just have to wait until Sunday to catch up on my sleep.

I settled in the chair, coffee clutched in one hand, as my aunt whipped a silver cape out, covering my jeans and T-shirt.

"My pleasure." Smiling serenely in the face of my sleepy glare, she dug out a wide-tooth comb and her clippers.

I lurched forward and turned to look at her. "Just a trim—please."

"Trim my ass, boy. You're not gettin' out of my chair until

you let me do something with that nappy-ass head of yours. Now turn back around."

My hair wasn't nappy, just curly, but Aunt Glo wasn't a woman you argued with. Sighing, I did as she'd instructed.

"If you're a good boy, I'll give you a manicure when she's done."

"Che-rise!" My aunt's shout ended on a laugh. "Girl, you are shameless!"

"I was just kidding," Cherise drawled from her spot behind us.

Smiling to myself, I turned to face the mirror again, focusing on the blonde in my line of sight. Today her hair was pulled up in a funky ponytail like something out of *I Dream of Jeanie*. Even though her ass was covered by a pair of capris and her cleavage was hidden by a sleeveless turtleneck, she still looked hot enough to make me need to adjust my jeans.

Now that was something to wake up to.

"Don't even think about it, boy," Aunt Glo practically growled.

"'Bout what?" I knew damned good and well who and what she was talking about. The first tug of the comb at the top of my head made me wish I hadn't given in quite so easily about getting a haircut, though.

"You know what!" She pulled again, harder this time for emphasis, almost driving the vision of Cherise giving me something more than a manicure right out of my head.

I could practically hear my aunt's foot tapping as I tried to take a sip of my coffee. "She talked to me first, Aunt Glo."

"Boy, I worked hard to get that girl out here." She scowled at me through the mirror. "Including *five* trips to Baytown to see her, and I sure don't need you mucking things up."

"Would I do something like that?" I bit back a grin, then winced, praying she'd finish torturing me soon.

"What are you into now, D'Angelo?" Vivi asked, appearing at my elbow. The smell of warm sugar and grease from her bag of donuts teased me as she sank into the empty barber chair beside us. She popped a donut hole in her mouth.

"You could share those," I said.

"Cherise," Aunt Glo hissed again, interrupting my bid for breakfast.

"Oh, *no!*" One eyebrow shot up as Vivi leaned forward and crumpled the now-empty bag. "You don't want to hit that."

"That was rude," I said, pointing to the bag she was holding. It looked like breakfast would have to wait too.

"Who said I wanted to mess with her?" I whispered, hoping Cherise couldn't hear us from where she sat just a few feet away.

"*That*"—Vivi tilted her head in Cherise's general direction—"is bi-sexin-*all!*"

I nearly dropped my cup of coffee before I regrouped and took another look at Cherise. "She's bisexual?"

"I don't care what she's doing as long as she's here when she needs to be here and paying me my money on time." Aunt Glo's voice was low and firm as she added, "And neither should you."

"You're full of shit, Vivi," I muttered.

"Go ask her yourself," she challenged, arms crossed over her tiny chest. Vivi's smirk and the knowing look in her pale brown eyes convinced me she might be telling the truth.

I slid into the chair across from Cherise, still unsure if Vivi had been yanking my chain or not. Up close her eyes were a clear, pale blue with just a little gray to them. Despite the curves, the full lips, and the occasional freckle, I got the feeling she was more spice than sugar. My eyes drifted a bit, finally landing in the vicinity of her hidden cleavage. *Dayum! No woman should be that fine.*

Her lips twisted into the tiniest smirk. She knew exactly what I'd been doing. "You don't exactly look like the manicure type."

"It's been a while," I lied with a shrug.

"Cherise, he's trouble with a capital *T*," my aunt said loud enough so every woman in the salon heard.

Ignoring her, I said, "Funny, Vivi sorta said the same thing about you."

"I'm sure she did." Her lips thinned briefly. "Your hair looks nice."

I ran a hand over my too-short hair and thanked her, feeling a little self-conscious. At least she hadn't said I was pretty.

"So . . . D'Angelo." She crossed her arms, resting them on the table, her blue eyes twinkling.

Cherise might end up being the first blonde I ever dated, but she wouldn't be the first white woman. Now, before you go throwing rocks at me, you have to know my mom's Puerto Rican and my dad's black. I was raised in a middle-class home where the fact that we were mixed was just that. A fact. And at twenty-seven, I'd dated all kinds of women. So far, the only person who'd put up a fuss about it had been Vivi, which was no huge surprise.

Of course, first I had to get Cherise to go out with me.

"D. Everyone calls me D," I said, offering her my hand.

"Nice to meet you . . . D." She took it, her soft skin and strong fingers registering somewhere in the vicinity of my dick. "I have a client due in ten minutes, and you look like you'd take a lot longer than ten minutes."

I bit my lip but couldn't hold back my laughter. "Maybe some other time, then?" Standing, I crossed to my aunt's work station, pulled a twenty from my wallet, and dropped it next to her cell phone.

Aunt Glo stepped out of the break room and leaned against the door frame, her arms crossed over her gargantuan chest. It stuck out from her round little body like a shelf, all of her accentuated by a vivid turquoise top that gaped open at her chest. "Give my best to your mama and daddy, D'Angelo."

That was my cue to leave. Like I said, she wasn't a woman you argued with. "Yes, ma'am." From the corner of my eye, I watched Cherise head up front, the globes of her heart-shaped ass swinging from side to side. I felt as if I'd been sniffing relaxer . . . or air-conditioning coolant.

2

As the only unmarried son within cooking-for distance, my mom insisted I eat dinner with them on the weekends. Considering I wasn't the world's greatest cook, I didn't put up much of a protest.

But tonight I escaped as soon as good manners, and Mom, would allow and headed to my best friend's for a night of beer and the type of advice I could only get from Kevin.

He might live in a questionable neighborhood and his car might not be new, but all the women at the club told me he was fine. Usually while they were crying on my shoulder about getting dumped. Kevin lived simple to keep the female predators off his back and still managed to get more pussy than a tomcat.

Most women thought Kevin was the womanizer and I was the nice guy. Truth be told, I was just a nicer womanizer than Kev.

Outside his tiny apartment, someone drove by, their bass rattling the windows. On the coffee table in front of us sat an open bag of chips, at least a half dozen empty beer bottles, and a jar of picante sauce. On the thirty-seven-inch television in front of us, the Astros were getting their asses kicked. Kevin couldn't cook either, so I'd given him the care package from my mom. Not that Mom would ever find out where her care package ended up. She didn't like Kevin much.

"We can still hit the bar if you feel like it," he offered, handing me a fresh beer.

"Nah," I said thoughtfully, "maybe later." Once he sat down again, I made myself bring up the subject that had been bugging me since I'd met Cherise on Thursday. "Yo, Kev?"

"Huh." He grabbed the remote and muted the television. It wasn't like we were paying a whole hell of a lot of attention anyway.

I laughed self-consciously. "There's this chick up at Aunt Glo's—"

"She hot enough to piss Vivi off?" he asked, laughing along with me. Kevin had been in love with Vivi since high school. She didn't feel the same. And she didn't like competition.

"Blond, blue-eyed, and built like a brick shithouse." I nodded.

"Then go for it."

I'd dated a lot of women—black women, Mexican women, even a Korean girl, but . . . "There's just . . . she's kind of a freak."

"Huh? What exactly do you mean by 'freak'? 'Cause you know there's freaks and then there's *freaks*!" He sat up on the fake leather couch, then we both laughed when it made a farting noise. Blame it on the beers.

"Vivi says she likes women." I took another swig of my beer.

"You got the hots for a lesbo?"

"Nah, uh-uh"—I waved the beer bottle—"she likes men too. She's . . . bisexual."

"I know men who would pay to have that problem." He burped, then continued, never missing a beat. "Here's how I see it. You got your uptight hos like Vivi. Wouldn't know a good fuck if it walked up to her and said, 'How do you do'."

More laughter sent beer through my nose.

"*Then* you got your regular, garden-variety skank hos looking for a welfare ticket. Or a daddy for their six dozen kids. Bitches will lie every fucking time about the birth control or get your ass so drunk you forget it." Kevin punctuated the high points with his beer bottle. "Last, but not least, you got the hos that just can't make up their mind. Dick. Pussy. Dick. Pussy. Like your chick . . ."

"Cherise."

"Cherise . . . You sure she's white? 'Cause that doesn't sound like a white girl's name."

"She's fuckin' got *blond* hair," I reminded him, laughing.

"Doesn't mean shit. She could be mixed . . . like you."

"Just trust me on this." I shook my head and reached for another chip.

"I'm surprised Vivi hasn't run her ass off."

"Me too."

"So, you gonna get you some bisexual ho pussy, huh?"

I nearly choked on my chip, coughing and ending up with hot sauce burning my throat. Kevin stood up and reached in the space under the television stand. He fumbled around for a few minutes before holding up three DVD cases.

"Your assignment, if you should choose to accept it, is to watch these porno movies. All girl, all the time. And don't forget to return them when you're done."

I raised my head and glanced in the bathroom mirror.

Fuck shaving.

I knew I shouldn't have gone out in the middle of the week, but after blowing off the bar on Saturday night, Kevin had given me shit until I'd finally caved. Only to end up hooked up with some Wednesday Night Special I'd regretted almost as soon as we got back to her place.

Freaks I could handle, no problem, but *she* had four kids. A one-night stand wasn't what she'd been looking for. Definitely one of Kevin's garden-variety hos.

I settled for brushing my teeth and a quick, chilly shower to help clear my head, then headed for the shop where I swapped my car for the work van.

Aunt Glo had gone in at the crack of dawn's ass to do paperwork and discovered there was no getting out of that new compressor I mentioned the previous week. I couldn't complain too much, not after spending the last five or six days looking for an excuse to go back to the salon.

I stuck my head in the back door, ready to give Aunt Glo shit for holding out for so long only to stop dead in my tracks at the sight of Cherise in shorts, flip-flops, and a tank top. She was folding towels, a mountain of white stacked on the dryer in front of her.

She turned and gave me a tired look, her curls already looking limp, and it was just after 8:00 AM. "Sugar, please get that damn thing fixed." Sugar came out sounding like 'sugah.' A very different sound from my mother's Puerto Rican accent.

Replacing my auntie's air compressor took most of the morning. Once I'd finished up and refilled it with coolant and tested the system, I packed up my gear.

I stood at the thermostat, my shirt stuck to my back, eyeing Cherise and guzzling Gatorade.

I'd never in a million years considered dating a woman who *dated other women*. What exactly did a bisexual woman do anyway? Where did they meet other women? How the hell did it all work, and could I really do this? More importantly, did I really want to do this?

By the time the place began to cool down (the way it should

have if Aunt Glo had let me fix it right the first time), Cherise was finished with her client, and I was finished with my job. Time to head back out into the heat. But not until after I caught her eye and gave her a long, lingering look. Despite the possible complications and my own reservations, I was interested. Real interested, and I wanted her to know it.

I stood reloading my tools into the van when the back door slammed. Turning, I smiled at the sight of Cherise heading my way.

"You're too pretty to be a boy."

My shoulders tightened at the word *pretty*. I hated being called pretty. Growing up, being the lightest-skinned kid in the neighborhood had gotten me beaten up more than once. Usually while my brothers watched. "I haven't been a boy in a long-ass time."

Her eyes crinkled at the corners in obvious amusement.

I slammed the sliding door, pleased that she'd followed me outside, despite the unintentional insult. "You think that's funny? Calling me pretty? Calling me a boy?"

"Baby boy, I've seen more in my thirty years than you can imagine."

"So I heard," I said, smirking. I shoved my hands in my pockets and leaned against the side of the van.

"What *exactly* did you hear?" Her closed face and the arms she crossed over her lush chest told me that maybe I'd crossed some sort of invisible line.

"That you like women?" I answered, almost embarrassed to even say it.

"I like men too—all kinds." She slowly moved closer, her hips swaying, her shoes slapping against the pavement. "That bother you?"

"No," I lied. I forced my breathing to remain even and steady as her hand rested on my belly before slowly sliding higher until it stopped at my left pec. Just over my heart. Could she feel it? Did she know the effect she had on me? My cock swelled, strangling slightly on my briefs and jeans.

"I don't believe you, D'Angelo."

"It's D," I corrected with a nod. No one but my parents called me D'Angelo (which rhymed with *tangelo* if you said it just right).

"They give you a middle name, D?"

My eyes focused on her full, pink mouth, I licked my parched lips and answered, "William."

"So how come you don't go by Will?"

I shrugged and watched her from behind my sunglasses, wondering why my name was so important. "Dunno."

"You think you can handle me . . . *D?*" she asked, switching gears. She gave my pec a squeeze and my dick responded.

"Why don't you go out with me Saturday night and we'll find out?" I wanted to reach up under the edge of her shorts and see if she was as turned on as I was, but the white steel door that led into the back of the shop reminded me that any minute now my auntie could come out and check on me, check to see if I'd left, haggle over the huge-ass bill I'd dropped on her desk, whatever.

If Aunt Glo—or worse, my mom—found out I was even thinking about messing around with Cherise, I'd be in deep shit. Really, *really* deep shit. It was trouble I didn't need, but the kind of trouble I couldn't resist.

"What's the kinkiest thing you've ever done?" She was skeptical. Her hand drifted between the buttons of my work shirt, tickling my chest even through the wife-beater I wore underneath. "Gone down on a girl?"

"Yeah," I said with a snort.

"*That's* the freakiest thing you've done?" Her arched eyebrow left me feeling inadequate, and I didn't like it.

"I've never gotten any complaints," I said defensively.

"But did you *like* it?"

"It was okay." I didn't hate it, just figured it was all part of the process.

"You should love it. You should love *everything* you do to a woman."

The weight of her words settled low in my gut, and I stayed silent, unsure of how to respond. The early-afternoon sun beat down on us, making my skin slick with sweat and reminding me I had a schedule to keep. I dug for my keys, stalling while I searched for the right words that would get her to go out with me.

"Would you fuck another woman for me?"

"Yeah." So maybe I was lying, but damned if I wasn't willing to try. I'd never talked about sex like this with a woman. "So how does the whole bisexual thing work?"

I winced at her howl of laugher.

"However the hell I want it to, honey," she said, letting her hand fall to her side. "You don't want to play with me."

Oh, yes, I did. "Yeah, I do."

She shook her head, lips pursed.

"Yeah, I do," I insisted, nodding my head vigorously. I was in way over my head and drowning fast.

"Then meet me at the diner on the corner at nine tonight . . . and don't be late."

3

I spent the rest of the day barely able to focus as I worked my way from replacing leaky drip pans to a rewiring job, courtesy of someone's dog.

I should have gotten Cherise's phone number. Should have told her to meet me outside the diner—the owner of the café was a friend of my auntie's. Next time I'd be sure and get her cell phone number. If there was a next time.

I climbed out of my Acura and brushed away imaginary wrinkles from my favorite green plaid shirt, ironed just for her. I hadn't been this worked up over a first date since high school.

She appeared at the corner of the diner, striding down the sidewalk toward me, her hips swinging full tilt.

She'd changed into a short skirt and heels. Did she ever wear anything that didn't show her legs?

Grinning at the thought, I circled the car and opened the door for her, eyeing her long, tanned legs as her skirt rode up. She got settled in the passenger seat but never fixed it. Just let it lay there, hugging the tops of her thighs.

Thank God my jeans were loose enough my dick wouldn't strangle. It was gonna be a long night.

"Where to?" I asked once I was behind the wheel again. I kept my eyes firmly focused on the road as I followed her instructions to a club she knew.

I wasn't comfortable at all with the dimly lit parking lot behind the Manor. Not that the neighborhood was seedy. Far from it. For the life of me, I would never have guessed the type of place someone like Cherise would hang out would be located on the edge of River Oaks. Just a stone's throw from some of Houston's oldest mansions.

On the outside, the club could have almost passed for someone's house—and might have been at one time.

Cherise greeted the hulking doorman by name, giving him a pat on the chest as she passed by. He grinned and held the door while she dragged me inside, as excited as a kid on the last day of school.

The air was thick and heavy and smelled like sex. Like someone had bottled it and then sprayed it everywhere. I followed Cherise through the crowd toward the bar, almost unable to take my eyes off the three women on the makeshift stage, which was draped on either side with red velvet curtains. They were naked except for their thongs and the neon body paint they were smearing on each other as they wriggled around like happy puppies to some techno house jam. Techno was probably my least favorite music, but right then, they could have been dancing to opera.

Two more women stopped in front of me and gave me a once-over. They were dressed almost identically in super-short vinyl skirts, their matching vests barely covering their tits. They could have passed for sisters, or at least cousins. I nearly choked on my tongue when they French-kissed each other. Make that kissing cousins.

I had a feeling that, after tonight, I wouldn't need to watch those pornos Kevin had loaned me.

"What do you think?" Laughing, Cherise pressed against me and handed me a beer.

I draped an arm around her waist, letting my hand settle on the curve of her ass, and took a long pull off my beer, glad for the distraction.

"They're all right." They were more than all right. Kevin would shit when he found out about this place.

With a knowing grin on her face, she clinked her bottle against mine and I took another long drink, hoping the cold beer would help clear my head. When I looked up again, the girls were gone, lost in the dim light and thick crowd.

"Don't worry," Cherise assured me with another squeeze, "I'm sure we'll see them again."

She shifted, nodding to her left at the couple—er trio—on the couch beside the bar. Some very slick-looking white dude had an arm draped around a tiny black girl, and he was fondling her tit while a brunette straddled his lap. Every once in a while he'd smack her bare ass.

Okay, so it wasn't completely bare. She *was* wearing a thong, but her miniskirt was pulled up to her waist, exposing every inch of a mouthwatering, heart-shaped ass.

I turned away, trying to distract myself from the tiny patch of fabric that covered her pussy, the heat that almost suffocated me, and the hard-on growing more uncomfortable by the minute.

Most of the people around us were just as raunchy as the group on the couch. The bar was packed with people who were fairly normal-looking, beautiful, ugly, thin, or fat. I took it all in with a critical eye, trying to absorb the fact that I could have passed any of these folks on the street, or even fixed their air conditioners and never had a clue. The voice in my head kept chanting "holy shit" while the rest of me just felt sort of happy.

It wasn't just the sex and the groping and the naked women. It was the fact that nobody cared what anyone looked like, what anyone did, or how anyone acted.

"Don't stare."

I blinked and focused on Cherise, who'd been slowly leading me through the crowd. "Staring is rude. Watching isn't, unless someone acts like they don't want to be watched."

We made our way through the rest of the bar, traveling from room to room. Occasionally we'd find people sitting and talking, but that seemed to be the exception, not the rule. The *rule* was couples and trios and more, doing things I'd never seen *live*. The bordello-like couches and drapes fit. I felt like I'd stepped into another world. One I hadn't even imagined—except for maybe in my wildest wet dreams—ever existed.

"So, what do you think?" Cherise asked once we'd made a circuit of the bar. "Too rich for your blood?"

Rich had nothing to do with money. "I'm not sure." At that point, I was too fascinated and overwhelmed to make any decisions.

We stood just inside the last room, the pulsating flicker of a black light highlighting two bodies on a sofa in the corner, a woman straddling a man's lap, her tiny dress pushed up to expose a set of perfect C cups, a slightly rounded stomach, and what looked like a butterfly tattooed on her naked pussy. She stopped riding him and crooked her finger, motioning me over.

"That is fucking hot." And nasty. Dirty. Nasty. Hot.

Cherise's hand on my back, pushing me forward, set me in motion, and I slowly crossed the room, unsure of what to expect. The woman's tits were heaving from the exertion, a smile on her face. The man behind her gave me a wink as she tugged at my shirt, pulling me down.

I was gonna drown for sure. It was nasty, kissing her like that, with another man's dick up in her, but I liked it.

Yeah, I did, and I couldn't even blame it on being drunk.

I finally came up for air and glanced over my shoulder at Cherise, who stood with an arm around the French-kissing duo from earlier. They looked like they were cuddling, and the idea of watching Cherise with another woman went from being something I couldn't imagine to being something I wanted to see. *Badly.*

Suddenly, all I could think about was gettin' the fuck out of there, gettin' Cherise somewhere alone, and gettin' rid of the ache in my balls. I crossed the tiny room and wrapped my hand around her upper arm, dragging her away from the duo who now stood laughing. "Let's go."

She looked amused as I led the way outside and through the parking lot. After being inside the bar the evening was amazingly quiet, cool, and damp with the humidity that Houston was famous for. Our footsteps echoed off the asphalt.

"You know, we could have—"

"I'm not ready for that," I said, practically dragging her to the car.

"Did you like that?" she asked once we were safely back in the car.

I shoved the keys in the ignition and turned on the headlights before answering. "You knew I would."

"Actually, no, I didn't. Men's sexual tastes vary as much as their preference for blondes or redheads or even girls with big asses."

Laughing, I backed the car out. "Your place?"

"For what?" she asked softly.

Okay, now she was just being a fuckin' cock-tease. I stopped and leaned over, covering her lips with my own. Her mouth was still cold from the beer, and she was soft and a lot more submissive than I thought she'd be. I let her up for air long enough to bite at her lips, before diving back in and sucking her tongue into my mouth. Her soft moans grew louder and finally insistent enough that I released her, sagging in my own seat, my dick even more painfully hard than it had been when I'd left the bar. I thoughtfully wiped my mouth and said, "We can't go to my place."

I didn't take anyone to my place if I could help it. At least not the first time.

A very subdued Cherise stroked my cock through my jeans while she gave me directions to her tiny efficiency a couple of blocks from the salon.

"What about your car?" I asked as I parked directly in front of a green door with peeling paint. I pushed her hand away, desperate for a break from the intense friction or I wouldn't last thirty seconds.

"I walked. Now come on, sweet cheeks." Grinning, she shrugged out of her seat belt and climbed from the car.

I followed her up the tiny walk, pushing her inside before she could even get the key out of the lock. Her soft protest slowed me down, and I made myself content with running my hands up and down her thighs and burying my face in the nape of her neck. I couldn't keep my hands off her. "Hurry," I growled, wondering how much longer I could hang on.

We made it as far as the couch. And we never got the lights on. I barely let her go long enough to let her fish a condom out of the end table drawer.

"You keep condoms in your living room?"

She giggled and shimmied out of her top. "For some reason, my dates never seem to make it upstairs."

I glanced up at the darkened loft as I tossed the condom wrapper aside and forced myself to slow down. This wasn't a race, but watching her shimmy out of her skirt and panties made my mouth water. I slowly lifted each of Cherise's feet and took off her shoes, giving the arch of each foot a nice deep rub with my thumb before sliding my hands up the length of her long, smooth legs.

"I'm gonna have to get you to give me a foot massage sometime." Smiling in the dim light, she used her leg to pull me closer.

Not that I needed a lot of encouragement.

She yanked my shirt over my head, and I shivered as a cool breeze from the fan overhead drifted across my back.

"You need to finish getting naked." I had her upright and her bra off before she could protest. Not that I thought she would.

She stretched out on the couch, fingers playing with her nipples while I kicked off my Timberlands.

Fucking with my shoes on just didn't sit well with me.

Then it was just me and her all soft underneath me, her tits crushed against my chest, her long-ass nails occasionally digging into my back as I slid home inside of her. She was hot and tight and slick enough to take my breath away, to pull a moan of satisfaction and frustration from the back of my throat.

She met every thrust, her body arched against mine, her legs wrapped around my waist, and her lips moving nonstop. "Such a pretty baby," she whispered, running a hand through my hair.

The tug of my hair being pulled ever so slightly sent a spike of need to my balls and made me throb. I buried my face in her neck and gave it up, promising myself I'd make it up to her in round two. Something soft and slow that wouldn't make me feel so greedy.

I barely made it home in time to shower, change, and run through Jack in the Box for breakfast and coffee. The day was another busy one, and I didn't surface for air until late in the afternoon when my cell phone rang. I stood in a backyard that hadn't seen a lawn mower or rake in weeks, if not longer, slapping away mosquitoes and adding coolant to another air conditioner.

"What are you doing tonight?" Cherise obviously didn't believe in wasting words.

"Gettin' some rest," I said with a smile. The crick in my back from sleeping on her couch had been worth it.

"Why don't we go out instead?"

"How about Saturday night?" I countered. I was so tired, I'd be lucky if I made it through the rest of the day without screwing anything up.

"Aw come on, it's Friday! Just for a little while! I promise I'll be good," she purred.

The sound of a screen door slamming nearby made me anxious to wrap it up. "No sex clubs tonight?"

"Girl Scout's honor."

Laughing, I knew there was no way I could turn her down despite the fatigue that permeated every inch of my body. "An hour, then."

Jimmy Z's looked like the kind of place Kevin would bring businessmen from out of town looking to have a good time, and maybe get laid, but not spend as much as they would at a titty bar.

In other words, very, *very* white collar.

Good thing I only promised Cherise an hour.

The bar reminded me of my aunt's salon but more expensive and with chrome instead of gold.

With Cherise's directions in mind, I wandered up to the second level, searching for a table near the stairs where she'd said she'd be sitting with some friends. On top of being in a strange bar, meeting her friends wasn't exactly something I was up for. Meeting friends was such a chick thing, but then, she wasn't exactly a "normal" chick.

Grinning at the thought, I wound my way through the crowd, still wondering what to expect when I finally located Cherise.

She turned and said something to the waiter who nodded and disappeared into the thick crowd, then she slid off her stool and dragged me over by the hand so she could introduce me to her friends. She actually looked excited. Not sure if it was for my benefit or not, though.

Who the hell knew black could look so good?

Hell, Cherise was obviously the reason someone had invented black. Her pants hugged her hips, and she wore a snug black top that barely kept her tits under cover. It might have stood a chance if she'd been wearing a bra, but I'd bet my last paycheck she wasn't. Not the way she nearly popped out of that flimsy little shirt. *Damn, that was nice.*

And her friends weren't hard to look at either.

With her dark blond hair and tall, athletic build, Carlotta was sexy in an exotic, supermodel sort of way that made me look twice. Lexi, on the other hand, was smaller with a slighter build and red hair. She reminded me of the girl next door—if the girl next door had been white.

I'd barely gotten settled and snagged a sip of the beer she'd ordered me when a remix of Nellie Furtado's "Promiscuous" had Cherise coaxing me out onto the dance floor. I ended up in the middle of a girl sandwich with her and Carlotta.

No complaints, not a one.

Later, back at the table, another man joined us, and judging from the enthusiastic way Carlotta greeted him, they were a couple. As dates and evenings went, it didn't get much more normal than this. We danced, we drank a little, and we laughed a lot between Lexi's construction job stories and Cherise's travel adventures.

After I stayed longer than I'd intended, Cherise walked me out to my car and gave me a searing kiss good night.

"Get some rest," she whispered, her lips against mine, "'cause tomorrow night, I'm gonna wear you out, baby boy."

4

By the time "tomorrow night" arrived, I'd nearly driven myself crazy wondering what Cherise had in store for us.

I picked her up after dinner and a grilling from my mom. *That woman always knows when I have a date. Or maybe she just knows when I'm up to something.*

Cherise stepped outside and stopped to lock the door. She had on some tiny pink halter dress with swirls all over it, and her hair was pulled up on top of her head.

I should get out of the car. I should hold the door for her. But I can't move. So, yeah, I'm a man and we're dogs and we think with our dicks, but when the woman you've spent all day thinking about comes out dressed like that, it just hits a man low. Okay, fine, right in his crotch.

She turned around, and I opened my door to get out, but she waved me off, insisting she had it. Instead, I leaned over and opened the passenger door for her.

She snapped on her seat belt and leaned over to kiss me, her eyes blazing. Something wasn't right.

"Bad day?"

Staring straight ahead, she blew out a heavy breath. "Tell me about Vivi."

If she was asking about Vivi, then "bad day" was probably an understatement. My mouth dropped a bit in surprise before I spoke. "Aw shit . . . you hungry? Did you eat?" I asked, thinking we could talk over food.

She glanced down at her hands before focusing outside the car again. "Not really . . . no . . . I'm good," she replied, shaking her head.

"Vivi," I drawled, backing out of the parking space, "is a bitch." Lips pursed, I pulled out of the tiny complex and into the heavy evening traffic.

"No shit? Three of my clients were no-shows, and two more showed up at the same time."

It wasn't hard to make the logical jump. "You think Vivi—"

"I KNOW Vivi did it! Fucking vicious bitch!" She shook her head in obvious frustration, but refused to look at me.

"It's okay." I checked over my shoulder and changed lanes, prepared to pull into a Denny's parking lot so we could talk.

"No, it's not okay! You don't fuck with someone's living."

I pulled to a stop and killed the engine. "I didn't mean it like that. But I can't talk to you when you're upset, and I can't help you when you're upset when I'm driving."

"Sorry." She sank into the seat, eyes on the dashboard, like she was no older than one of Vivi's kids.

"Did you talk to Aunt Glo?"

"She left early . . . D'Angelo, I never double-book, *ever*!"

I leaned over and tapped her chin, forcing her to look at me. "You have every right to be mad, and if there is anything I can do besides listen, you tell me. Unfortunately, you're not the first person she's tried to run off. Hell, I remember when she was a teenager, she ran off a couple of Aunt Glo's boyfriends— even tried to run off my brother's wife," I added, smiling in the dark.

"Tried?" She sniffled the tiniest bit, like she was trying not to, like she didn't want me to know how upset she really was.

"My sister-in-law, Shondra, kicked her ass."

"The idea has merit." She nodded slowly.

Chuckling, I leaned in closer until we were nearly face-to-face and took her hand. "If there is anything I can do, all you have to do is ask."

"Thanks." She stared up at me in the dim light. I couldn't tell what was going through her head, and now she looked more confused than mad. "What did your aunt do . . . about Vivi and Shondra?"

"Chewed Vivi's ass out. Told her to mind her own business. The problem is, she thinks everybody's business is her business."

"Well, she'd better stay the fuck out of mine, or I'm gonna do a lot more than chew her ass out."

"What now?"

"Now we party," she said with a smile.

Cherise hadn't been kidding when she'd said she'd wanted to party. We'd left the bar shortly after one in favor of something more private. I'd had my reservations, but she'd brushed off my protests, assuring me I was more than ready to get into trouble.

About twenty people mingled around, making themselves at home in the loft of one very rich dude. The owner in question was nowhere to be seen. He'd disappeared with his wife and another couple after ordering everyone to make themselves at home. We'd taken him at his word.

I sat slumped on the couch, watching Cherise flirt with another woman, wondering if anything would come of it. Especially since this was the third one tonight. Cherise had her fingers hooked in the deep V of the other woman's shirt. They were both laughing and checking each other out. And every once in a while, they'd touch, fingers in each other's hair, hips accidentally brushing up against each other, lips to ears, saying things no one else could hear.

Men had nothing on women when it came to flirting. The way they flirted made me want to see them kiss, to see them naked, see them touch each other. I was enjoying the living hell out of it and had the hard-on to prove it.

A pretty Cuban girl with tiny breasts and a tiny waist and built thick from the hips down came and sprawled across my lap. We'd done a shot together earlier in the kitchen. "Elise, right?"

"Want to go upstairs?" Elise smiled up at me, showing off straight white teeth.

She didn't waste any time. Apparently she'd noticed my hard-on, and even though the party reminded me of some of the ones I'd gone to back in high school, the kind where someone's parents are out of town, I didn't feel like saying no.

I glanced at Cherise again, who wiggled one eyebrow at me as if to say "go ahead." She hadn't been kidding when she'd stuffed those condoms in my pocket earlier and suggested I put them to good use—if I wanted.

What the fuck . . . I wanted.

I nodded and helped Elise up. I was just drunk enough to not care, but not so drunk I didn't know what the hell I was doing.

I patted Cherise's ass on the way by and let Elise lead me upstairs, down the hall, and into someone's bedroom where we found a threesome going on; but I turned down their invitation to join them. I couldn't hold back a grin, though.

With a tug of my hand, Elise led me through the adjoining bathroom to what looked like someone's office. She never hesitated, just stripped off her long red dress and matching panties and bent over the desk. The view was heavenly.

No sooner had I gotten the condom on and slid into her

than the door behind me opened, a soft purr of laughter assuring me that it was Cherise.

She cupped my bare ass and squeezed, then pressed herself against me, her hips moving with every thrust I made, as if we were fucking Elise together. Her fingers slipped under my shirt, digging into my shoulders and the soft material of her dress pressed against my bare skin, pulling a moan from the back of my throat. This was good. This was *very* good.

Underneath me, Elise arched up on her toes, pushing her ass higher. My fingers itched to smack it and watch it jiggle like it did every time I slammed my cock home inside her.

Cherise moved away with a soft order to not stop. Trust me, the thought never crossed my mind.

She circled the desk, collapsing in a chair and propping one long leg on the desk, her skirt pulled up around her waist. Legs spread, she watched us and played with herself. Her eyes at half mast, her lips curved in the tiniest hint of a smile.

My balls twitched and tightened as I moved that much closer to my climax. The sight of her sitting here watching me didn't intimidate me at all. It turned me on a lot more than I thought it would, even more than watching her flirt earlier had. And, apparently, it turned Elise on too.

"You like watching me fuck your man?" she panted, and then squealed when I thrust extra hard.

Cherise swung her leg down and leaned forward, holding out a wet, red-tipped finger to the other woman. "I like it a lot."

"He's got a big dick." She laughed, then groaned, a loud happy sound that registered somewhere deep in my gut.

I smiled at the compliment.

"I might have to steal him away from you."

Now was not the time for a damn cat fight. I stopped smiling.

"You don't have to steal him. I'll share."

Elise drew Cherise's fingers into her mouth and sucked them clean. Then Cherise did what I couldn't; she leaned over and kissed Elise.

The sight of their lips locked while I was still fucking Elise pushed me over the edge and I felt as if I were being turned inside out. As if it were more than semen I was filling that condom with. Something that, once lost, I couldn't ever get back.

Hands propped on either side of Elise's hips, I tried to catch my breath while offering up a silent thank-you for the condom. For the protection from more than just the obvious.

Feeling a little overwhelmed, I pulled out, smacked her on the ass, and yanked my jeans back up. Ducking into the bathroom, I leaned against the counter, almost afraid to look at myself in the mirror. Instead, I glanced at the the threesome going on in the bedroom.

A sultry brunette with smeared red lipstick lifted her head from between her partner's thighs. "Join us?"

"No thanks," I said with a shake of my head, closing the door behind me.

Knowing my latest fuck was bisexual, that she'd flirt with women, that I'd seen her kiss women, that she'd have sex with women was completely different from seeing it in action. And watching two strangers was different; it gave the sex a definitely pornish quality.

Back in the office, the green lampshade on the desk illuminated the two women who didn't even notice my return.

I knew Elise hadn't come but hadn't really cared. And here was Cherise, taking care of business for me. Elise lay sprawled on the desk, her heels propped on the edge, her fingers playing with her smallish breasts. Tight nipples just a shade or two lighter than milk chocolate stood at attention.

I stopped just above her head to watch and listen. All I could see of Cherise was the top of her blond hair and the occasional twinkle of her bright blue eyes. Her lips were buried deep in

Elise's pussy, and judging from the other woman's sighs and wriggling hips Cherise knew exactly what she was doing.

"I might have to steal her from you," Elise sighed, her head rolling from side to side in pleasure.

I leaned over and sank my lips into hers, the taste of pussy, Cherise's pussy, filling my mouth. I kept kissing her while watching Cherise in fascination. She liked it—obviously. And something about watching the two of them really turned me on, deep and low in my gut. Something twisted, tightened. I didn't really understand the why of it all but didn't particularly care at that point either.

5

Sinking deeper in the bed, I stretched and flexed my legs. After we'd left the party last night, I'd brought Cherise back to my place. I hadn't been up for another crick in my neck or a night on her couch.

I checked the time, slammed the clock back down on the nightstand, and rolled onto my back, one arm thrown over my eyes against the early morning sun coming through the windows. It was just after nine, and I didn't have anything to do or anywhere to go today.

I needed sleep, especially after last night. I smiled at the memory, then immediately frowned when it hit me that I was alone in bed. A noise penetrated my hungover brain. Footsteps, and I'd be damned if that wasn't toast and coffee I smelled. I knew I couldn't have done that—I never set the coffee's automatic timer. It was some sort of perverse punishment for needing caffeine in the first place.

More footsteps. It had to be Cherise. A day in bed with her sounded like a great way to waste a Sunday. I threw back the sheets and sat up, wincing slightly as my feet made contact with the bare wood floor. Standing and stretching again, I worked out a few more kinks before stepping out from behind the divider that separated the loft's living and sleeping areas.

Apparently, I wouldn't be dragging Cherise back to bed anytime soon.

Dressed in one of my wife-beaters and her tiny black panties, Cherise sat on the couch surrounded by all my photos—and I had a lot. Baby pictures my mom had given me, photos of me and my brothers J. J. and Marcus, growing up, my parents. All of them lined up on the coffee table and the floor at her feet or laid out on either side of where she sat in the middle of my couch.

"What the fuck are you doing?" I crossed the floor and stood at the foot of the couch. I wasn't angry as much as baffled and a little irritated. Some of them had been stored under the coffee table with my photo albums, all four of which were also scattered around her.

"Eatin'," she muttered around a mouthful of toast. "Nice do."

She sat happily chewing on her toast and rearranging photos like pieces on a checkerboard.

I scrubbed at my head and turned toward the kitchen, aware but uncaring that I probably looked like I'd stuck my finger in a light socket. I fixed myself a cup of coffee and liberally doused it with brown sugar and creamer before practically collapsing on the countertop. *What the fuck was Cherise doing with my pictures?* "You gonna put all that shit back?" I asked, pointing at the mess she'd made.

"Is that the Eiffel Tower?" she asked, ignoring my own question as she flipped the photo album around and held it up.

"Yeah."

"You don't really look like the Paris type."

"Thanks," I drawled. I crossed the room and sank into the

easy chair across from the couch, propping my feet on the coffee table and silently watching her flip pages.

"Switzerland?"

"Yup," I replied before she could even show me the photo. "Italy too."

"You like to travel?"

"My dad's older brother lives in Italy; guess I got it from him."

"Italy. You like Italy?" She finally looked up at me, but for the life of me, I couldn't figure out what the hell was going on with her.

"Go every two years," I said with a smile. "Ever been?"

"Never made it out of the States."

"At least you made it out of Texas, though, huh?"

"How do you figure?" she asked, returning her attention to the photos.

"Your stories from the bar, remember?"

"Oh, yeah. I get around a little. Nothing like this, though." She put the album back and started rearranging the photos again.

"You *are* going to put all those back, aren't you?"

"Sure, sure. Is this Shondra?" She held up a photo of my brother Marcus and a pregnant Shondra, taken on Mother's Day.

"Yup."

"She's pretty."

"Shondra's a sweetheart. Puts up with my brother's stupid ass." I laughed.

"Your brother travels too?"

"Used to. Not so much now with the baby on the way." Standing, I crossed to the couch and cleared a spot beside her. After I shoved the albums back under the coffee table, I pulled her onto my lap. Even with no makeup and crumbs on her face, she was pretty. I brushed a few of the crumbs away and kissed her, teasing her tongue until she pushed me away.

"What about the pictures?" she whispered, pointing toward the table.

"You can put 'em up later."

Laughing, she wrapped her arms around my neck and pulled my head down.

The weeks after my mid-July hookup with Elise were crazy. I started blowing off Kevin and even my weekly dinners with my parents. I felt bad, but I couldn't seem to stop myself.

Every date with Cherise was a trip to the bar or another private party in some unspoken agreement to find a third, so I wasn't surprised when she called and said that Elise would be meeting us for dinner at P.F. Chang's.

I opened Cherise's car door and offered her a hand. "So what exactly is the plan?"

"The plan?" She stood up and hooked an arm around my neck, a smile on her lips. "We have dinner, we talk, and afterward we see if she's still interested in going back to your place—"

"*Your* place," I corrected, leaning down to nuzzle her bare neck.

"You don't want Elise at your place?"

"I have rules, babe."

Laughing, she slipped away. I slammed the door, set the alarm, and hurried to catch up with her. I had a feeling I'd spend a lot more of the summer trying to catch up with her.

We joined Elise in the bar for drinks while we waited for a table. It was crowded and loud, but they still managed to find a way to flirt with each other. I'll be honest and tell you it was a little intimidating knowing I wasn't the only interested party at that table. Once we were seated, I sat there watching two pretty ladies laugh and tease and flirt with each other over lettuce wraps and Mongolian beef.

That's when I realized how little it was about me. Not that I wasn't wanted or needed, but if I hadn't been there, they still would have ended up in bed together. Only I wouldn't have gotten stuck with the bill.

Trust me, no complaints.

"So, D'Angelo"—Elise leaned forward and Cherise scooted around so they sat next to each other—"what do you think?"

I sat there, trying to look relaxed. To be honest, I wasn't sure I knew the answer to her question. Distracted at the sight of their pretty faces pressed cheek to cheek, I laughed. Cherise was almost darker than Elise. And where Cherise looked smart, I almost wanted to say *cunning*, Elise just looked like your average party girl out to have a good time. "I think we need to get the hell outta here."

I stood up and offered them both a hand, then followed them out, watching, assessing. Halfway to the car, it finally clicked what had been bothering me.

Cherise was in charge. Elise and I were just participants. Talk about performance anxiety.

The girls stopped at Elise's green Accord and stood hand in hand.

"Her place or mine?" Cherise asked.

Smiling, I wrapped an arm around both of them. "Whatever makes you ladies happy is fine with me." What the hell else could I say? We weren't going to my place, and I wasn't running the show.

"Follow us." Cherise sounded giddy as she kissed Elise on the cheek, then dragged me away by the hand.

I've never heard Cherise talk as much as she did on the way to her place.

"You're excited," I said once I could squeeze a word in.

"Well, yeah. It's been a while." She turned in her seat to face me and ran a hand up my thigh. "Aren't you?"

"Yeah." I flipped on the turn signal, then checked the rearview mirror to see if Elise was still behind me. She waved.

"You nervous?" Cherise leaned over so her chin rested on my shoulder.

"A little." I turned into the complex and parked, leaving the spot in front of Cherise's door for Elise.

"Why are you nervous?" she teased, laughing softly. "Just relax. We're gonna have a good time."

Inside, Cherise poured everybody wine, then kicked off her shoes, letting them land somewhere under the stairs. She leaned against the bar while I sat on the couch, one arm draped around Elise's shoulders.

"D, do you want to watch or just jump right in?"

"Why don't I let you two get comfortable and then come watch?"

"You don't have to do that." Elise leaned against me, smiling in a way that should have tempted me, but I stuck to my guns.

"Suit yourself." Cherise laughingly pulled Elise from her seat, and the two ran upstairs.

I heard the thump of Elise's shoes hitting the floor, more giggles, and then silence. I finished off my wine, then picked up Elise's wineglass and drank it a little slower while I kicked off my own shoes and sat back to listen, my gut twisting in anticipation. I'd give 'em ten minutes.

More laughter and Cherise or Elise, I'm not sure who, telling me what I was missing, convinced me to knock it down to five. Standing, I poured another half a glass of wine for courage and sipped it slowly while unbuttoning my shirt.

For a few minutes, I couldn't hear anything, then, "Hurry up, D'Angelo!"

Smiling, I headed for the stairs, taking them two at a time until I reached the top. They were stretched out on the bed, lips locked, Elise's face hidden by Cherise's hair. The sound of them kissing and the sight of those two naked, pretty bodies in bed convinced me watching was the way to go—for now. I slid my shirt off and sank into the room's only chair.

Despite her natural tan, Elise wasn't much darker than me, while Cherise had obviously spent a lot of time in the sun, topless. The two of them wrapped around each other had to be one of the most beautiful things I'd ever seen.

Elise shifted so that she lay stretched out on top of Cherise and buried her face in her tits. Cherise looked over at me and smiled, and I adjusted my legs to accommodate my growing hard-on. I sat there rubbing it and watching them, waiting to see what would happen as Elise worked her way lower. Cherise's hands were in her hair, and she kept talking, rambling on like she did when *we* fucked. I almost felt jealous, and the thought made me smile. There wasn't really anything to be jealous about.

I stood and stripped off my jeans and briefs, while never taking my eyes off the girls. Elise had her face between Cherise's thighs, and I couldn't see anything, but I could definitely hear the wet sound of her tongue in Cherise's pussy. She had her eyes closed, her legs spread, her hips arched off the bed as she moaned.

Moving closer for a better view, I wrapped my hand around my dick and stroked myself slowly. I wasn't about to blow my load on a hand-job. Not with those two waiting.

But I wanted to watch just a little bit longer.

Elise had her ass in the air and her knees tucked up under her, her pussy spread wide; for a minute I considered just ramming into her. Instead, I sat down, lifted Cherise's leg so it was propped on my shoulder, and smiled down at Elise. I pushed her hair out of her face and watched her tongue stroke and suck the soft pink folds of Cherise's pussy. Her chin and the tip of her nose were wet.

There's something beautiful about watching two women together, beautiful and soft and feminine in the way they know each other's bodies. Ways a man could probably never understand.

I tucked her hair behind her ear and then ran a hand down the length of her back, over the curve of her ass to her pussy. Her hips shifted, and I slid two fingers inside of her, happy to watch and play despite my own painful erection.

"You like that, D?" Cherise asked. She was smiling, arms stretched over her head grasping the headboard, eyes half closed, her hips shifting, riding Elise's tongue.

"Very much." I kissed the inside of her thigh and smiled back at her. "Very, *very* much."

Elise's pussy clenched around my fingers, and I decided it was time I did more than watch. I pulled my fingers out, licked them, and gave Cherise a wink before moving behind Elise. The girls shifted so there was more room but never missed a beat. I spent a long time admiring Elise, who'd shaved *everything*. Her pussy was smooth and very, very wet. I planted a soft wet kiss on one cheek of her ass, then the other, then slid lower, letting my tongue tease the tender skin just below her puckered little hole. She started to hum, and Cherise started to laugh, and I dove in, using my fingers to keep her lips spread apart.

I didn't stop until I heard Cherise shouting that she was gonna come. I pulled back to watch, wiping my chin and stretching out alongside them, one hand hanging on to Elise's ass, kneading it. Cherise's hips were arched off the bed, her face buried in the pillow as she thrust, hard, against Elise's mouth a couple of times.

She collapsed against the mattress and pulled Elise up by the hair, and they were kissing again, their mouths open and their tongues teasing each other. I wanted to come so bad my dick had started to leak, but I wasn't ready for this to end. Not yet.

Cherise purred and then giggled some more as she rolled onto her side, her hand between Elise's legs. "You have a job to finish," she said, looking my way.

"I know." Smiling, I stretched out on my back and flicked my tongue at Elise, who giggled.

She straddled my face, and I wrapped my arms around her legs, pulling her down so I could reach her pussy with my tongue.

A drawer opened, then closed. I felt the cold wetness of a condom being slid on, and then Cherise was riding my dick. Moaning, I shifted, almost unable to concentrate on Elise. She was moaning, too, her hands wrapped around the headboard above me. They were almost in sync, Cherise's hips lifting and falling in time with Elise's while my tongue dove in and out of her. I sucked at her clit and nibbled at it. She squealed, grinding hard against my mouth and crying louder and louder.

I closed my eyes and let myself drown in complete sensory overload until Elise finally slid off my face and collapsed next to me. I kept an arm wrapped around her, listening to the sound of her trying to catch her breath. She wiped my jaw off and whispered something about me smelling like pussy. Smiling, I pulled her mouth to mine and let the climax that had been building below finally erupt.

I felt like I had been sucked dry by the time Cherise finally collapsed on my chest, her head next to Elise's.

"Who's ready for round two?" she asked, laughing softly.

"Not yet," I whispered. I could feel my heartbeat in my dick. It was almost painful, especially with Cherise's pussy still contracting around me.

She finally slid off me and took the condom off. I opened my eyes enough to watch her disappear down the stairs. I turned and smiled at Elise who lay curled up beside me, her head on my chest.

"Y'all do this often?"

"This is my first time," I confessed.

"How long have you two been together?"

"Almost two months." *Technically, six weeks was almost two months, right?*

"Seems like longer." She smiled, then gave me a soft little kiss.

She was right, though; it did seem like longer.

The rest of the night passed in a tangled daze until I couldn't move, and they went downstairs to shower together. By the time I woke up, Elise was gone and Cherise was downstairs frying what smelled like bacon.

I grabbed my clothes and eased down the stairs, slipping into the bathroom for a quick shower. Cherise had breakfast on the table by the time I came out.

"What time did Elise leave?"

"Early. She had to go to work." She set a cup of coffee on the table in front of me and kissed the back of my neck.

Somewhere in my sleep and sex-fogged brain, it registered that she'd put sugar and cream in it for me.

"You okay?" She tilted my head back and let her hands slide down my chest. There was no missing the worried expression on her face.

"You mean last night? That was some pretty amazing shit."

Laughing, she forced me to scoot my chair out and fell into my lap. All she had on under her tiny robe was a pair of white panties, and she smelled sweet, like oranges.

"Think you might want to do it again sometime?"

"Hell yeah." I reached up under her robe, part of me amazed I could even think about sex after the way we'd gone at it last night.

"Why, you nasty boy," she said, grinning.

"I'm *your* nasty boy, though."

She practically purred with pleasure at that, and breakfast

got cold while we had a quickie in the kitchen. Afterward, she hopped in the shower again while I stood at the counter, eating my reheated eggs.

The first time I'd been in Cherise's apartment, I'd been too busy trying to get her panties off to pay attention to my surroundings. Then we always seemed to end up at my place, so I hadn't been back over here since that first time.

This time I took stock, carefully.

The neutral, apartment-grade carpet.

The worn navy couch we'd fucked on the first time. It still had a little life left in it, and it matched the chair upstairs.

The television and the table it sat on, both spotlessly clean. Frowning, I double-checked to make sure my first impression had been right. Not one picture decorated the walls; not one photograph sat propped in a frame on the television; and the homey touches, the silk flowers on the end tables, seemed generic and almost disposable.

There were no photos. Not upstairs, or I would have remembered. Not downstairs. None. Anywhere.

6

"What are you doing on Monday?" I stood at the door, ready to leave. After putting Mom and Dad off for weeks—no mean feat when you work for your dad—he'd cornered me, insisting I come for lunch today and plan on spending the afternoon.

Even though I'd suggested she come with me, Cherise's good mood had vanished when I'd told her why I had to go. And she'd said no. "Working." She adjusted the framed 5 X 7 photo on top of the TV stand.

I'd given it to her last night for our two-month anniversary. She'd tried to act like she didn't care, but she didn't fool me. Not the way she kept looking at it and messing with it. Her reaction had convinced me that I was on the right track with her—at least as far as figuring out what made her tick. Even though I still hadn't figured out why she had no pictures and why she had an aversion to family.

"Monday's a holiday," I reminded her. "I'm pretty sure neither of us has to work, 'cause Aunt Glo does a huge-ass Labor Day barbecue at her place and invites like half of Houston."

"Oh . . . oh, yeah. She mentioned it." She finally finished adjusting the photo to her liking before turning to face me.

When she didn't say anything else, I pushed on. "Want to go with me?"

"And, like, meet your family and shit? No thanks. Besides, I'm supposed to go to Lexi's I think."

"'K, then." Swallowing my disappointment, I crossed the room to give her another kiss good-bye. Before I'd even taken a step, she asked if I wanted to go with her. "You do realize missing Aunt Glo's barbecue is punishable by death in my family?" I teased.

"Would it kill you to do something different?" Her shoulders were stiff under my hands.

"No." But I'd have to think about it. Blowing off a major family event could have serious repercussions and involve a shitload of nagging. "What do you have against family get-togethers?"

"I just don't want to spend my day off with Vivi." She shrugged off my arms and took a step back, forcing me to release her.

Fair enough, but I didn't believe for a minute that's all there was to it.

"So, you're not coming with me?"

"I might. I might not." I didn't like being pushed, not even by Cherise.

Cherise had been wrong; the barbecue was at her friend Lanie's.

Okay, so I didn't *exactly* blow off Aunt Glo's barbecue. I just left early and ignored Vivi's demands to know where I was going. She'd have a complete and teetotal bitch fit if she knew about Cherise. Just for her, I made up some BS about meeting Kevin, knowing she'd drop the subject immediately.

Leaning back in the patio chair, I glanced through the

kitchen window to where Cherise and her three friends were getting the last of dinner together. The sun was almost gone, but the pool light made up for it.

"You do know what they're doing in there, don't you?" Devon asked. Carlotta's boyfriend was a riot. Even in Dockers and a polo shirt he looked like a computer geek, which made the occasional observations he threw out even funnier. As couples went, he and Carlotta probably looked like they went together about as well as Cherise and I did.

"Huh?"

From my other side Wade snickered. "Getting the dirt on you."

"Oh, shit," I muttered, and took a sip of my beer.

Both men laughed, and inside, all the women did, too, almost as if they'd heard Wade. He was Lexi's boyfriend, and they both worked construction. Lanie, apparently, was the only one solo tonight since her boyfriend was out of town on business.

"Speaking of dirt, the rumor is you and Carlotta are moving in together," Wade said.

"I *should* neither confirm nor deny that rumor," Devon began when Wade and I both interrupted him laughing. "But, yes, it's true."

"Congratulations," I murmured, still laughing to myself.

The women trooped out, their hands loaded with bowls and paper plates. Wade pulled the steaks off the grill, and Cherise collapsed in my lap before I could even offer to help.

"How am I supposed to eat with you blocking me?"

Turning, she wrapped an arm around my neck. "I'll feed you, honey."

"What are you gonna feed me?" I gave her an evil grin and ogled the cleavage almost directly under my chin.

"Now, now, none of that," Lanie said. "If I can't get lucky in my own house tonight, no one else damn sure is."

* * *

"My place or yours?" I asked once we were back on the 610 Loop.

"Yours." She put the seat back and closed her eyes.

My thoughts and John Mayer for company, I left her alone most of the way home except to occasionally glance at her out of the corner of my eye. Cherise had a smudge of barbecue sauce on her white tank top.

"Why do you keep looking at me?" she muttered, lowering her sunglasses.

"When's your birthday?"

"December." She sighed.

"What day?"

A semi blew by on my left-hand side, blowing its horn.

"Why?"

"Because I don't want you gettin' all pissed at me if I forget. I can't forget if I don't know. . . . You know what I mean."

"All right." She put the seat up and ran a hand through her hair. "My favorite color is pink, which is a no-brainer even for a guy. My favorite flowers are zinnias. I wear a thirty-six D bra and size six panties. I sunbathe topless, usually at Lanie's house on Sunday afternoons with the girls, and I don't know when my birthday is. Happy now?"

Shock forced my foot off the gas. "Hap—how the hell can you not know when your birthday is?" I frowned at her, then forced myself to focus on the heavy traffic again as I took the exit for my apartment.

"I wasn't born in Texas." She sounded matter-of-fact but angry, like she could start an argument with me any second. And maybe even wanted to.

"What the hell does that have to do with . . . If I was smart, I'd drop it," I said, almost to myself.

We eased up to a red light, and I glanced at her out of the

corner of my eye. Her jaw was twitching, and she had her arms crossed over her chest again. She licked her lips and glanced out the passenger window just as the light turned green.

With a monster truck behind me, I had no choice but to go. Once we were in the elevator on the way up to my loft, I cornered her. "Look—"

"Drop it, D."

"I care about you, and whether you like it or not, that means I want to know about you."

"Maybe I don't want you to know about me." She stood in the corner, glaring at me.

The elevator eased to a stop, and I went to stand next to her.

"You want me to take you home?" I asked as the doors slid open. My gut twisted. I hoped like hell she'd say no.

"That's okay. It's late." She stepped out of the elevator and I followed.

Cherise didn't speak again until she'd stripped down to her thong and climbed into bed. She had all the pillows tucked behind her head and the sheets pulled up to her chin. "I was in foster care."

I sank down on the bed beside her. "I'm sorry—"

"Fuck your pity."

"Fuck you! I was apologizing for being nosy, goddamnit!" I yanked my T-shirt over my head and threw it in the corner, then headed for the shower, hoping she'd calm down by the time I got out.

The bedroom was dark, and Cherise was curled up on her side, a fist tucked under her chin. I stood beside the bed, water dripping down my back, and stared at her, trying to figure out if she was really asleep or not. The air conditioner kicking on forced me to finish drying off and get dressed. I curled up next to her and kissed her bare back.

If someone had told me back in June that this was going to be the longest, hottest summer of my life, I would have laughed at them or thought they were just talking about the weather. But as the weeks had flown by, piling up on each other, I'd found myself sucked deeper and deeper into Cherise's world. At the same time, I never seemed to get any closer to her, and that bothered me . . . a lot.

But at least now I knew why.

Rolling away, I stretched out on my back and watched the lights from an adjacent building play across the ceiling.

"You're awful quiet." She rolled over to face me but couldn't seem to look at me. Her forehead pressed against my arm.

"So are you." Matter of fact, she'd been quiet all day. Not that she was normally a talker to begin with, but today was different in a way I couldn't quite put my finger on, and our mini-fight hadn't helped.

"You want me, you're gonna have to take me as I am, D'Angelo."

I'd already figured that out. "Just give me a chance, okay? That's all I'm asking."

She snuggled against me, naked, warm, and sweet. "Hungry?"

"Hell no. Between Lanie's barbecue and Aunt Glo's ribs, I'll be stuffed for a week."

"You too stuffed to fool around?" she asked, running a hand up my leg.

"Never."

7

Whoever was lying next to me didn't feel or smell like Cherise. I forced my eyes open, my belly clenching in fear at what I'd find.

On the contrary, she was a tiny black girl. I knew her name but couldn't quite wrap my head around it.

When Cherise said I had to take her as she was, I didn't realize that meant things would get progressively crazier. Here it was, not even two weeks after our Labor Day spat and I'd let her talk me into what could only be called an orgy. The details were sketchy but there had been five of us last night.

I shifted my legs, then tried to roll over and realized I couldn't. There was another body wedged at my back, and I hoped like hell it was a woman.

Trista . . . Tawny . . . Whatever her name was, the girl in front of me wriggled her bottom against me, but my poor dick didn't even twitch.

My arm was stuck under the pillow cradling her head. *How the hell am I going to free myself? Get out of this bed?* Panic set in quickly, but I forced it back, forced myself to stay calm. I shifted the tiniest bit, relieved to see Cherise on the far edge of the king-size bed. I was in a hotel room, and pieces of the previous night came drifting back in a way that made me wince.

Besides the black girl, there was a couple separating Cherise and me. A young, very good-looking couple we'd met up with at the bar last night. And the first time we'd ever just gone with strangers.

I'd spanked her, the pretty redhead curled up against her husband now. I'd spanked her last night, and then, at her husband's encouragement, fucked her in the ass. Never mind that she'd liked it, or that, at the time I'd liked it, too, the thought that I'd fucked a married woman while her husband had watched and gotten off on it made me slightly queasy now.

I tiptoed across the floor, which was littered with clothes and condom wrappers, and finally located my clothes and shoes, except for my underwear, which was nowhere to be found. Movement from one of the bodies in the bed propelled me out the door without them and without Cherise. Easing the door closed, I winced at the chill of the wet concrete under my feet.

It had rained last night, the type of rain that left everything fresh and clean, or as fresh and clean as Houston ever got. That only made me feel worse. Hell, from the sound of it even the fucking birds were happy.

I eased down the stairs to the sidewalk while rubbing my aching head and wondering where the hell I'd parked my car. Disengaging the alarm helped me find it. I gave a prayer of thanks I hadn't wrecked it or killed someone, because I'd been in no shape to drive last night.

I'd never been so relieved to be home. I locked the door and turned off the phone's ringer, then stripped and showered. I'd have to take my clothes to the basement laundry room later today. I didn't feel right washing those clothes in my mother's washer. I was too embarrassed to see her right now anyway, or my dad.

By the time I climbed out of the shower, all the hot water was gone, but I didn't feel much better. I brushed my teeth three times, gargled twice, then threw on some pajama bottoms Mom had gotten me for Christmas. Under the cool, clean sheets of my own bed, I stretched out and tried to force myself to sleep. It was almost impossible with the scratches on my back stinging and a raging hangover. It only got worse as more bits and pieces of last night came back to me, and I realized just how far down I'd let Cherise drag me. Yeah, I knew I'd let her. I was just as responsible as her.

And no, hell no, I didn't feel bad for leaving Cherise behind. She was a big girl and could take care of herself, probably better than I could. Okay, I felt a little bad after the fact, but all I'd been able to think about was getting the hell out of that hotel room.

I'd just dozed off when a pounding at the door had me grumpily sliding from the bed. In my disoriented, half-asleep, blind-from-late-morning-sunshine state, I hadn't even figured out who it was when they pushed their way inside, hollering at the top of their lungs. "Man, where the fuck you been? You don't call, you don't write? What's a brother gotta do?"

Kevin.

Fatigue, a hangover, and remorse weighing heavily on me, I slumped against the wall and pushed the door closed. Rubbing my eyes, I forced myself to focus on my friend.

Kevin headed for the couch, his mouth working nonstop. "Fuckin' even your mama don't know where you are anymore. Not that she'd tell me if she did. She hates my ass." His grin slowly disappeared as he looked me over.

I shuffled into the living room behind him and pretty much fell into the leather easy chair, at a loss for words. "I think I'm in trouble," I muttered.

"Well you look like shit. What'd that white chick do to you?"

"She's a fucking freak. A major freak," I croaked, sinking deeper in the chair, "and, apparently, so am I."

"Aw hell," he drawled. He sat up and propped his elbows on his knees, ready to hear every dirty detail.

"Be right back." I got us both a Coke from the fridge and three ibuprofen for my head, then filled him in on just how far I'd sunk. By the time I finished, it even sounded bad to me. Worse than bad. Though I wasn't really sure what qualified as worse than bad.

"You had sex with three other people? With *another man*?" Seeing Kevin speechless was almost worth my misery.

"Four," I said hoarsely, part of me glad I couldn't remember everything that had happened the previous night. "And technically I just had sex with another man *in the room*." With another man's wife and probably another woman.

Kevin burped, excused himself, and then scrubbed at his forehead with the palm of his hand before smoothing it across his bald head. A sure sign of frustration. "I don't know whether to high-five your ass or chew you out! So you like this chick?"

"Yeah," I said thoughtfully. Right then, I wished I didn't like her so much.

"Doesn't sound good."

"I can't figure out how to get out of this shit-hole mess I'm in." As much as I wanted Cherise, I *didn't* want her life. Which didn't leave me with many alternatives.

"Dump her," Kevin suggested.

"Don't want to, that's the problem."

She was my drug now, my drug of choice, but maybe a few days away would help me put things in perspective.

8

Going cold turkey had been a sucky option, but it had also been my only option. I avoided Cherise for over a week, despite the fact I was jonesing just to hear her voice. I knew better than to talk to her until I had a plan and some fucking balls firmly in place.

More than anything, I needed a break from the sex.

Something I never thought I'd think, let alone say. And no, I didn't say it. If I had, Cherise would have blown me off like last year's lipstick.

Instead, I talked her into dinner with just the two of us, rather than another trip to The Manor.

"So what, uh, prompted this?" she asked when we reached the restaurant, her hand on the car door. The pale yellow wraparound dress she wore clung to every curve, and with her pale blond hair piled on top of her head, she looked classy . . . and damned sexy.

"I wanted to do something different." My hand on her bare back, I led her toward the restaurant's red double doors. "That okay with you?"

"Sure, but it's not our anniversary or anything."

"Does it have to be a special occasion for us to do something nice?" Something on neutral ground where I could keep the situation under control.

For the first time in all the months we'd been together, we got a look, a hard cool once-over from the maitre d'. I'd been here before with another woman and he hadn't even flinched. But then, she was mixed, like me. And the people we'd been hanging out with didn't give a shit about what you looked like.

For all of thirty seconds, I seriously thought about taking Cherise somewhere else. Then I muttered, "Fuck it" under my breath. Cherise frowned at me, obviously confused, and I shook my head.

"We have reservations." And my suit probably cost more than the older man's tux.

"You okay?" she asked once our reservations were finally located and we were seated.

"Yeah." I'd gotten looks like that my whole life, people who couldn't pigeonhole me, fit me in a box because my hair wasn't black and my eyes were green. And it wasn't just white folks doin' it.

Luckily our waitress was a lot more discreet—or just didn't give a shit.

We'd barely gotten our entrées—pork tenderloin in a ginger sauce for her and a steak for me—when Cherise brought up the subject of the club.

"Want to stop by The Manor later?"

Hell no! "I thought we'd go back to my place."

"Whatever." She shrugged, casually rolling her shoulders, but she wouldn't look at me for the longest time. "Sure."

I couldn't tell if she was mad because I didn't want to go to the club or because I'd left her behind last Sunday morning. That and the fact I'd avoided her phone calls for a week and a half hung between us, or at least it did for me. "About last Sunday . . ."

Cherise set her fork down and sipped at her wine, a guarded expression on her face. I got the feeling she wanted to be anywhere but here with me right now.

"I'm sorry for just up and . . . leaving you."

She waved it off, but her laughter was brittle, her eyes hard. "No sweat."

"You're not mad?"

"No." She shook her head, refusing to look at me again until after the waitress came and took our plates away. Then she leaned forward, her back ramrod straight as she gave me a hard assessing look. "Look, D'Angelo, I need to tell you something."

Oh, shit. Before she could speak, the waitress reappeared to fill our wineglasses and leave the check.

"Are you sure about that dessert?" I asked Cherise. "We could split some chocolate cake?" I was stalling.

"I'm positive."

I took a deep breath, forcing my heart to slow down. "Go on, then."

Eyebrows arched, she glanced down at the linen tablecloth, then back up at me. "I'm leaving."

Talk about out of left field. "Leaving?" I whispered.

The bottom fell out of my stomach, and I wished she'd said something before dinner instead of after. "Why?" I frowned, my face suddenly hot. "I . . . I thought . . . why?"

"It's . . . time. It's just time for me to move on." She shrugged and her eyes slowly drifted around the almost empty dining room. No wonder she hadn't been able to look at me all night.

Around us the few remaining diners continued eating, silverware clanking on plates, people laughing. I pulled my wallet from my back pocket and threw my AmEx on the tray with the check, desperate to get out of the restaurant before I caused a scene.

"*You think?*" I sighed, unable to catch my breath. "You think it's time?"

"That's what I do." She said it so casually we could have been discussing how she polished someone's nails, not the fact that she was leaving town, leaving me.

I glanced at the waitress, waiting until she was out of earshot before responding. "'That's what you do?'" I hissed, getting madder by the second. "Fuck 'em and leave 'em?"

"Yup." Her pink cheeks told me she was embarrassed despite her matter-of-fact tone of voice.

I scribbled my name on the receipt and stood up. A very subdued Cherise followed suit. She was more subdued than I'd ever seen her as I led outside.

A cool breeze washed away the humidity from earlier in the day. She shivered against me as we crossed the dimly lit parking lot, both of us lost in our heads.

"You're okay with me leaving, aren't you?" she softly asked. As if she had doubts.

"What if I said no?" As if I could influence her decision. I kept my eyes focused on the light across the street.

I wasn't okay at all with her leaving.

Her grip on my arm tightened and she leaned against me. "I'm sorry."

I believed her, but I still didn't like it. And I had the strangest feeling that, despite her insistence, she didn't like it either.

While Cherise was in the powder room, I hustled around lighting the new candles I'd bought just for tonight. I'd gone all out, putting them on the mantle, the coffee table and end tables, even the nightstands. The screen that separated the sleeping and living area glowed, and jasmine and vanilla slowly permeated the room.

I cracked open a Riesling I knew she liked and poured us both a glass as she rejoined me.

"You do all right for an air-conditioning man," she teased. "I always liked that about you."

Glass in hand, she crossed the room, and I followed. She was sitting on the edge of the bed, her legs crossed. I set my glass on the nightstand next to hers and knelt at her feet, letting my fingertips trail up the back of her calves. She hadn't worn pantyhose, but then, she never did.

I slipped her shoes off and filled my hands with lotion from the bottle I'd left on the nightstand.

"You had all this planned . . . for me?"

"For us, yeah."

Leaning closer, she ran her hand across my head and down the side of my face. It was a rare show of feeling, of tenderness, from Cherise, who wasn't the emotional type.

"What are you doin', D?"

"I owe you a foot massage." I slathered her foot with her favorite lotion and worked my way over each toe, across her arch to her heel. She sighed in pleasure, her eyes slowly closing. "That feels . . . *heavenly.*"

"Lay back," I whispered. I licked my lips and focused. This would probably be our last night together. I could ask her to stay. I should ask her to stay, but I wasn't going to. It wouldn't do any good. And the last thing I wanted was for us to fight— not tonight.

Tonight was about loving, not fighting.

Cherise didn't seem to have the strength to argue or to take the seduction I was pulling on her away from me. She did as I instructed, her thighs pressed tightly together. I smiled. When push came to shove, she wouldn't resist.

I stopped long enough to slip off my shirt, then went back to work. My fingers slid higher, massaging her calves until they relaxed. I gently pushed her thighs apart and moved between them so she couldn't close them again. Now they rested against my sides, the heat of her skin scorching me, distracting me as I worked my way up the back of her calves and crept under her dress. A small moan slipped out when I pushed her legs farther apart and worked at the tender skin of her inner thighs. She begged me to take her panties off and go down on her.

Instead, I untied her dress and pushed it open. "Not yet."

The candlelight played across her tanned skin, and her nipples puckered as a breeze strong enough to lift the sheers touched us both.

"Feel good?"

"Oh, yeah." She said it so softly I almost didn't hear her.

She hooked her thumbs in her thong and made to lift her legs, but my arms held her in place.

She groaned in frustration, her whole body tense under me again. "Damnit, D'Angelo, would you fuck me already?"

My fingers dug deep circles into the tops of her thighs. "No."

Love, lust, and the thrill of being the one in charge almost made me laugh. If all I had left was one night with her, we were doing it *my* way.

"No?" She struggled to sit up on her elbows and practically shouted, "What the hell do you mean, no?"

"I won't fuck you." I straddled her hips with my pants still on. They rubbed, lightly against her pussy, but not where she wanted it, not where it'd do the most good, and we both knew it. She was pinned so she couldn't arch her hips, couldn't find the friction, the relief, I knew she wanted.

"Then what the hell are you doing?" she whispered harshly, her chest heaving. Even in the dim light she couldn't hide her frustration.

I leaned down until we were nearly nose to nose, until I could see what looked like fear in her wide blue eyes. "Making love to you."

She swallowed hard, struggling to catch her breath, then sighed, relaxing when I latched onto one of her nipples and gave it a long gentle suck.

"Is that okay?" I moved higher, planting soft little kisses on her chest, easing toward her neck while she watched.

"What?"

"If I make love to you," I whispered, my lips pressed against her ear.

"If *I* say no?" she responded, using my own words from earlier.

"What are you afraid of?"

Her eyes drifted closed. "You can't change my mind, D."

Standing, I finished undressing. "I'm not trying to change your mind." I was a liar. I hadn't planned this to change her mind. I'd planned this to show her there was more to us than that damned bar and her sexual escapades. I wanted us to find a middle ground. It might be too late, but I'd take what I could get.

By the time I was done, there wasn't an inch of her that hadn't been licked, kissed, and touched. I buried myself deep inside her, so deep it felt like we were fused together.

She moaned, her eyes squeezed shut, and she seemed to pull herself together. I focused on her, on the feel of her lush body against every inch of me. On the legs wrapped around me, on the sweet, tight pussy contracting with every stroke. On her sighs and her nails digging into my back. I'd be damned if I'd come until she had again. She tightened her grip, her nails biting deeper into my back as she screamed and milked my cock until I couldn't hold back either.

"I don't want you to leave," I panted.

She licked her lips and looked at me, and I realized just how vulnerable we both were when she spoke. "Do you really want to talk about this right now?" she asked hoarsely, as if she were fighting her own tears.

I kissed her temple, then let my lips softly drift across her cheek to her ear. The lump in my throat grew until it was so large I thought I might choke. "I can't make you stay, but I don't want you to leave."

9

I knew it the minute I woke up. Cherise was gone. Her side of the bed was cold. The apartment was silent, and I didn't smell coffee. I lay staring up at the ceiling, thinking about the previous night, how I'd asked her to stay and how she'd never answered me.

After a shower and some coffee, I tried Cherise's home number, but it had been disconnected.

I had two choices. Sit and mope like a whiny punk or make it business as usual. I chose the latter, forcing myself to get out and run my normal Saturday morning errands—laundry, the dry cleaners, groceries, then collapsed on a bar stool at the counter when I was done. My fingers rapped a tattoo against the granite countertop before I grabbed my keys, finally giving into the urge I'd been fighting all morning and heading across town to the salon.

Inside, the chemical smell brought me up short, as did the crowd of women in the reception area, waiting their turn. The admiring looks made me uncomfortable, as uncomfortable as the overwarm salon. All the barber chairs were full, the dryers were full, all the nail stations too—except Cherise's, which looked like it'd been emptied.

Sighing, I crossed to where Aunt Glo was combing out an elaborate hairdo. "Can I talk to you?" I murmured.

The exasperated look she gave me made me almost regret coming. "Can you see how busy I am, boy?"

"I know, Aunt Glo. It won't take a minute. I promise."

"I'll be right back." Her happy cordial expression changed the minute we hit the break room. She turned to face me, grim and thin-lipped and tired-looking.

"Where's Cherise?" I asked softly. Not that anyone would hear me over all the hairdryers and such.

"She quit . . . Wednesday." Her eyes narrowed to thin slits. "Why are *you* looking for Cherise?"

"I uh . . ." I was still stuck back on "she quit Wednesday." "We've been seeing each other," I said, even as the bottom fell out of my stomach.

She pinned me down with a steady gaze that eventually softened. "Well, she and Vivi had World War Three up in here Wednesday afternoon."

Nodding slowly, I wandered to the break room door and snuck a look at Vivi. Sure as shit, she was sporting a black eye and probably deserved it. "Cherise mentioned a month or so ago that they were having problems," I confirmed with a small nod.

"This is the third or fourth time. . . . So, this has been going on *all* summer? *D'Angelo!* Do you know your daddy and mama have been worried sick about you? They thought you were using drugs or something!"

My face was so hot from embarrassment it was almost painful, and I couldn't look her in the eye. "I know."

"D'Angelo, honey, I have no right to get in your business—"

"So don't."

"You're grown," she continued after frowning at me for interrupting her, "but this nonsense you've been pulling with your parents is unacceptable. And besides, she's not the settling-down kind. You need to let her go."

Swallowing back the lump in my throat, I forced myself to look her square in the eye. "I know . . . I better let you get back to work."

I turned toward the door, then stopped at the sound of her voice. "If you need me, I'm here."

"Thanks."

Although I knew what I'd find even before I got there, I drove the few blocks to Cherise's apartment. Nothing. I peeked through the miniblinds, my hands cupped on either side of my face to diminish the glare of the late-afternoon sun. All her shoes were missing from under the stairs. So was the photo I'd given her, her few pieces of furniture, and her lone ivy plant. Her Mustang was gone too.

I looked around the run-down little complex, trying to hone in on a Plan B when my phone rang. At the sound of my mother's voice, guilt and resignation convinced me that maybe having dinner with Mom and Dad wasn't such a bad idea.

It took everything I had to make it through the evening before I could escape and head home. My cell phone hadn't rung the rest of the day, except for a call from Kevin trying to get me to go out.

When I got home, my last thought before I drifted off to sleep was that I'd have to track down Lanie. If that didn't pan out, there wasn't much I *could* do to find Cherise.

For the life of me, I couldn't remember Carlotta's last name, and information had no listing for a Lanie Daniels. It was just after eight in the morning, way too early to go to her house. Patience had never been one of my strong suits, but I didn't have much choice. I spent the entire morning cleaning the loft.

I was in the middle of scrubbing down the bathtub when the

phone rang. I rinsed my hands and ran for the bar, where I'd left my phone. "Hello."

"Hi, sweetie pie."

I nearly dropped the phone at the sound of Cherise's voice. At least it sounded like Cherise's voice. She'd never called me anything like *baby* or *honey* or . . . *sweetie pie.* I crossed to the couch and sank down in the cushions. "Wh-where . . . what?" I wasn't even sure what to ask. "Why did you just fucking walk out?" I finally demanded. "I would have helped you move or pack or something."

"No, you would have tried to talk me out of it."

"Did I try to talk you out of it the other night? No. I told you I didn't want you to leave, but I didn't beg. I didn't pick a fight or rant, did I?" I wanted to kick the coffee table.

"No," she said, sounding contrite.

"What do you want?" I demanded. "You quit your job; your apartment is empty. Where are you? Fucking California?"

"Why don't you come over? I'll cook and we'll talk."

"I thought you left town."

"I changed my mind. . . . Please say yes, D'Angelo . . . please." She was practically begging.

What else was I going to do with an empty Sunday afternoon? "Where the hell are you?"

"Carlotta's."

I scrambled for a pen and wrote down the directions, promising to be there as soon as I'd cleaned up.

I hated that sucked-in feeling that crept up on me, growing with every mile that took me closer to Cherise.

I could see why she'd moved. The condo was a world away from her tiny apartment. I stood at the door, waiting for her to answer. Here on the back side of the complex, there wasn't much to see, but the cars were nicer, the grass was neater, and I could hear kids laughing. They rode past on their bikes. It was almost too ordinary for Cherise.

She answered the door dressed in cutoff shorts and a faded tank top. Good thing I hadn't bothered to dress up.

"Come on in," she said, swinging the door wide so I could pass. She looked . . . good. Relaxed, happy even. "Hope you like roast chicken."

I silently followed her through the living room to the kitchen. Her ratty couch looked sad on the almost-new Berber carpet, but she'd added a few more plants, and the photo I'd given her sat on the mantle with some new black candle holders.

"Table new?" I asked, indicating the black oak kitchen table.

"Carlotta sold it to me. Want a beer?"

"Got tea?" We could have been having a conversation anywhere about anything, not about the fact that she'd fallen off the face of the planet, moved, and quit without even bothering to tell me. Not that I hadn't expected it, but her abrupt departure still stung.

She filled two glasses and joined me at the table.

"Why didn't you tell me?" I wrapped my hands around the damp glass and waited.

"I did."

"That's bullshit!" Frowning, I sat back in the chair and crossed my arms over my chest. "You didn't tell me you quit your job on Wednesday or about the fight with Vivi."

"I know . . . and you're right, it is." She looked contrite with her lower lip caught between her teeth. "I'd planned on leaving, really. I even told the girls I was leaving. They weren't happy either," she added with a chuckle. "I'm not very good at this."

"Practice makes perfect."

She nodded in agreement, then smiled. "I was all set to go. I met the girls Saturday morning, we packed up all my stuff, and then they took me to breakfast. They padlocked the truck and refused to give me the key to the lock until I agreed to sublet Carlotta's condo."

The thought of how furious she must have been made me laugh but didn't make me any less unhappy with her.

"I've never had friends like them before. I stayed as much because of them as you. D'Angelo, you can't change me; you do realize that?" she asked, suddenly serious.

"As often as you've said it, how could I not?" As often as she'd said I couldn't change her, it'd taken me a long time to figure out she was scared of someone changing her. Of someone forcing her to be something she couldn't or didn't want to be. I leaned forward and propped my elbows on the table. "You are the only person who can change you, Cherise. I don't *want* to change you, but I also don't want to go through this shit again. All you have to do is fuckin' talk to me."

"So where does that leave us? Do you not want to see me anymore?"

"You gonna stick around a while?" I countered, unwilling to give in just yet.

"Did I mention I was leasing with an option to buy?"

Down and Dirty

Jami Alden

1

Taylor pulled her pillow over her head, but the harsh mechanical whine pierced the thick down. She pulled the comforter up, willing to risk overheating if it meant she could get an extra hour of sleep. But it was useless. Why did her neighbor have to decide that this, of all Saturday mornings, was a great day to get up at the crack of dawn to do yard work?

Flinging back the comforter, she staggered to the window and inched aside the shade, recoiling as bright sunshine stabbed at her retinas. Okay, so perhaps it wasn't precisely the crack of dawn, but close enough. She squinted in the direction of her neighbor's house, and sure enough, a shirtless man expertly wielded a weed whacker along the other side of the fence that divided their lots. His head was bent, covered by a ball cap, and her annoyance waned momentarily as she admired the sleek muscles moving under acres of smooth, tan skin. The gardener from *Desperate Housewives* had nothing on this guy.

Still, after working until four A.M. this morning to put the finishing touches on a huge venture financing deal, she was in no mood to tolerate a noisy gardener, even if he did provide grade-A eye candy. Pulling a robe over her camisole and panties, Taylor slipped on a pair of rubber flip-flops and strode purposefully over to her neighbor's front door. Though the house had sold several months ago, Taylor had been so busy with work she hadn't met her new neighbors. Unlike most of the houses on her cul-de-sac, no toys littered the beautifully landscaped front yard, so she doubted a family had moved in. She took a moment to admire the pristinely trimmed hedges and planters full of bright flowers that bordered the front steps. Her own yard, she thought guiltily, needed only a car up on blocks to complete its Ma-and-Pa-Kettle, white-trash motif. But she'd barely seen her own house in the daylight for the past six months, so calling a gardener or landscaper was beyond her capability. Hmm. Maybe she'd hire the shirtless wonder working on her neighbor's yard, since he seemed to know what he was about. But only on weekdays, when Taylor wasn't desperately trying to put a dent in her perpetual sleep debt.

She rang the doorbell, aware of the warm morning sun penetrating the thin cotton of her robe. She probably should have gotten dressed, but if she had her way, after she spoke to her neighbor, she was crawling right back into bed in blessed silence. Several seconds passed with no answer. She looked around. The only vehicle in the driveway was a large white pickup with TIERNEY'S LANDSCAPING AND OUTDOOR DESIGN printed on the door in big green letters. But then, most people in the neighborhood parked their cars in the garage while they were home. She pressed the doorbell again, following it with several sharp raps.

"Can I help you?"

Taylor jumped as the speaker's deep voice sent an electric current down her legs. She turned and faced the gardener, her eyes locking first on his bare chest, then traveling covetously up the muscled expanse to a perfectly delicious-looking neck, and finally settling on a face so gorgeous that Taylor swore she heard angels singing as his ridiculously vivid green eyes crinkled in a smile. Her mouth went dry as she took in the most stunningly perfect man she'd ever seen. She mentally sighed, knowing that under the short, gold-streaked brown hair, his head was no doubt full of landscaping gravel.

"I was hoping to talk to the owners." Heat crept up her neck and face as his intense gaze raked her from the tips of her pink-painted toenails, up her bare legs, and over the thin cotton robe—the only thing standing between his frankly assessing gaze and her flimsy blue cotton camisole and panty set. She licked her lips and smiled as though it was perfectly proper for her to be standing on her neighbor's front porch in a robe that left most of her legs bare.

He cocked his head to the side as though confused. "The owners," she repeated, enunciating every word in case his grasp of English wasn't optimal. "Do you know when they'll be home?"

His thick brows furrowed, and his mouth quirked into a puzzled smile. "I am the owner."

Taylor couldn't keep the surprise from her face. "You are?"

His smile faded a little at her disbelief. "Yeah, I moved in almost six months ago. Joe Tierney."

Good Lord! All this time she'd assumed a childless couple or, judging from the neatly tended flower beds, a gay man had moved next door. Never in her wildest imaginings did she think that six foot three inches of sweaty male perfection had been living right next door. She was getting distracted by that chest again, which was rippling with muscle, little beads of sweat dampening the soft line of hair bisecting his perfectly chiseled abs. She suddenly realized he was standing there expectantly with his hand out. It was a big, tough-looking hand, with long fingers crisscrossed with tiny scars. A vivid image popped into her brain of her grasping that hand and flinging him to the ground to have her way with him.

Where in the world had that come from? Thank God her boyfriend, Steven, was coming home tomorrow. Clearly the lack of sleep—not to mention sex—over the past several months were conspiring to send her heretofore subdued libido into overdrive. All she knew was that if she let this hunk of burning love touch her, she couldn't be held responsible for the consequences.

Still, it would be rude to refuse to shake his hand. "Taylor Flynn," she said, and offered just her fingertips. Even that slight brush of her smooth, perfectly manicured fingertips against his callused ones was enough to send a jolt of pure electricity to a spot between her legs that had lain dormant for the past three months.

She snatched her hand back as quickly as possible, rubbing it against the side of her thigh in an effort to force the tingles she had no business feeling into submission.

"What can I do for you?" he asked, his businesslike tone snapping her brain back into focus.

Using all her flagging energy, Taylor schooled her face into a polite, beseeching smile, and summoning the sweet, cajoling tone that had convinced many a start-up CEO to hand over a significant percentage of his company to Taylor's venture capital firm, she said, "I was wondering if you wouldn't mind holding off on your yard work until a slightly more civilized hour."

His smile stayed put, but his eyes were flat as he squinted into the bright morning sun. "It's ten A.M."

Her own smile slipped. "Well, that may be, but I had a very late night and—"

"I'm sorry if you can't be bothered to drag yourself out of bed after a night of partying, but I have a lot to get done today."

"I was working," she said, tired frustration melting her smile into a tense glare, "until four A.M. And if you can't bring yourself to be courteous enough to stop with the heavy machinery, I'm not above calling the police."

His only reply was a rude snort.

"I'm serious," she snapped, realizing somewhere in the back of her mind that she should maintain some hold on her temper, which had grown progressively shorter as she'd worked herself nearly to death in recent months. But his rudeness, combined with the unwelcome sexual sparks that were flying between them, sent her headlong over the edge. "I'll lodge a noise complaint—"

"And they'll tell you that it's past eight A.M. and that I'm abiding by all the noise ordinances of the city of Menlo Park, California. Trust me—Taylor, is it?—you don't have a leg to stand on."

Rage coursed through her, hot, unbridled, and so intense she actually felt the prick of tears. All she wanted was a little sleep. Was that too much to ask for? Instead she said, in her most withering, icy manner, "I suppose I shouldn't expect basic manners from someone like you." She whirled and stomped away as he muttered something under his breath. Something that sounded suspiciously like, "Needs to get laid."

Though that same little voice warned her not to engage, to retreat to her house before she ended up in an all-out feud with her neighbor, she whirled around. "What did you say?"

He sucked his bottom lip in and crossed his arms over his chest. His eyes narrowed and his lips pursed for a moment, as though he was debating whether or not to speak. Honesty won out. "I said, somebody needs to get laid."

Taylor's mouth opened and closed like a dying carp. She couldn't believe he was not only rude enough to think such a thing, but to say it out loud. "I don't see what that has to do with anything!"

"Maybe if you had a boyfriend to take the edge off every once in a while, you wouldn't be so uptight. And maybe," he continued, leaning in closer so she could smell him, all salty sweat and clean man skin, "he could mow that disaster of a lawn of yours and help bring up your neighbors' property values."

His scent washed over her in waves, making her nipples harden under the smooth cotton of her camisole and distracting her from the fact that he'd just insulted her landscaping in addition to her sex life. She shook her head. He was a dirty, sweaty, laborer—not the kind of man who should make her nipples tighten and her panties moist! Summoning up the icy hauteur that had become second nature, she snapped, "I have a boyfriend—a rich, successful man who has more important things to do than mow my lawn."

"No kidding. Your lawn obviously hasn't been mown for a long, long time." There was no mistaking the lascivious note in his voice.

She closed her eyes and sighed. "Obviously you're working some double entendre there, but I'll have you know my relationship with Steven is just fine. What we have goes far beyond sex—"

"Bingo, exactly as I thought," he interrupted. "'Beyond sex' is code for no sex."

Taylor snapped her mouth shut, embarrassed to have revealed so much. She'd never been the type to share intimate details of her sex life, even with her closest friends. What in the world possessed her to have a conversation like this with a man she just met? "I don't see that it's any of your business," she said lamely. "It hasn't been that long." *Only four months, but who's counting?* "He travels a lot," she said in response to his knowing smirk, then mentally slapped herself. Why was she making excuses to him, of all people?

"Let me tell you something, Taylor," he said, and leaned in closer. Close enough for her to see every dark, ridiculously long eyelash surrounding his stunning green eyes. Close enough to see that the dark stubble of his beard was interspersed with gold strands. Close enough to smell the scent of his shampoo coming off his sweat-dampened hair.

She resisted the urge to flick her tongue out to catch a stray bead of perspiration sliding down the dark column of his throat. "What's that?"

"A man doesn't go without sex if he can help it. So trust me, if he's not getting it from you, he's getting it from someone else." He turned and left her sputtering in his front yard, almost too angry to notice that he looked just as good from the back as he did from the front.

From his vantage point around the corner, Joe watched Taylor as she glared at the spot he'd recently vacated, her jaw clenched as though holding back a rage-fueled tirade. After several seconds she whirled around and stomped back to her own yard, offering him an excellent view of sleek thighs and nicely toned calves. He licked his lips, wishing her robe was several inches shorter so he could get an unimpeded look at her tightly muscled ass.

Unlike his neighbor, who clearly had been clueless about him until this morning, Joe had been fully aware of Taylor from the first week he'd moved in, when he caught a glimpse of her coming back from a run at some ungodly early hour. Which was ironic, considering this morning she was complaining about his working at a civilized hour like ten A.M. Even from a distance, he'd seen she was beautiful, with clean, classic features and Nordic goddess coloring. And unlike most women who looked sweaty and mussed after a jog, her hair was still neatly slicked back in a ponytail, her cheeks faintly rosy from exertion, but otherwise she was neat and . . . tidy. That was the word for her.

Since then, he'd found himself watching for her in the mornings when she left for work, always perfectly put together in a suit or other business attire. He didn't know what it was about her, but he loved watching her priss in and out of her car, so cool and self-contained in her own little world. Obviously she was some kind of high-powered executive type, with her shiny black five-series BMW, not to mention the house she lived in—alone.

He wondered about this alleged boyfriend, the one whose car was never in her driveway, as far as he could tell, and who clearly didn't give Taylor what she so obviously needed. If ever there was a woman in need of a long, hard fuck and about a half dozen or so orgasms, it was prissy little Taylor Flynn. His groin tightened at the thought of being the man to help her out. Close up, she was even better-looking, her skin pale and flawless without a stitch of makeup, her mouth rosy and delicate, even when pursed in an angry pucker. For once, this morning her hair was loose, hanging in silky blond strands that made his fingers itch to thread through them. But even though she was obviously just out of bed, she looked cool and composed, like one of those icy blond heroines in the Hitchcock movies his mother used to watch.

At least she had been cool and composed until he brought up her sex life, he thought with a smirk. He wasn't a rude person by nature, and under most circumstances would never consider speaking like that to any woman, much less one he was attracted to. But he had the same reaction to Taylor that he'd had to Jennie Douglas in the third grade. Jennie with her perfectly matched designer outfits and neatly braided hair, who had looked down her tiny perfect nose at him when he'd offered to share a package of powdered donuts with her and wrinkled her nose while staring in disgust at his hands, dirty from digging for worms during recess.

The next day, Jennie had found one of those worms in her lunch box and had been "accidentally" shoved into a mud puddle as Joe ran by her to catch a football.

When Taylor had refused to shake his hand, offering just the barest tips of her fingers, he'd felt a surge of the same childish, irrational anger. But instead of pushing her into the mud, he'd insulted her sex life.

Real mature, he thought, resisting the urge to do further damage by running the weed whacker for the rest of the day. He'd been obnoxious enough already, and he'd be lucky if Taylor didn't come up with some way to make his life a living hell. Fortunately, she seemed to work a lot, so she probably didn't have much time to devote to petty revenge.

He sighed and picked up his garden shears to finish pruning the hedge that bordered his back patio. He'd been trying to figure out a way to introduce himself to his beautiful neighbor for months, but this was hardly how he'd envisioned it going. He clipped his way over to their shared fence and peeked over. No sign of her in the backyard, which was no big surprise since it was basically a big overgrown weed patch with some beat-up lawn furniture and a crumbling concrete patio that fairly cried out to be torn up and replaced. He wondered if the inside of her house looked any better, or if her physical person was the only thing she kept in any sort of order.

Not that he'd ever find out. Even if he hadn't been completely obnoxious and pissed her off, it was obvious she was a total snob who would never consider lowering herself to date a man who actually worked with his hands.

Too bad, he thought with a pang of regret as he imagined Taylor's long, lean legs extending from the hem of her robe. If given half a chance, Joe bet he could show a woman like Taylor a damn good time.

2

"How dare he?" Taylor asked no one in particular as she briskly folded a dozen pair of brushed cotton bikini underwear. Though compelled by rage, she didn't allow herself to rush, knowing if she didn't take the time to fold each piece of lingerie into perfect thirds and separate them by color, she'd waste precious time Monday morning when she reached without looking into her panty drawer and pulled out the wrong shade.

"How dare he tell me I need to get laid?" she said to the panties, her shoulders tensing with rage all over again. So what if it was a little too close to the truth? What kind of man was so rude as to say something like that to a woman he'd just met?

Her lips tightened in distaste as she remembered her mother's last boyfriend—at least the one she'd had the last time Taylor had been home nearly fifteen years ago. Herb, with his beer-stinking breath and sweaty, grabby hands. Supposedly he worked in construction, but the only thing Taylor had ever seen him build was a pyramid of beer cans on the coffee table that occupied the middle of their double-wide's living room. Herb spent most of his time on the couch, yelling at the TV—that is, when he wasn't yelling at Taylor, telling her not to be so uptight, to be nicer to him, to come over and sit on the couch with him so he could give her what she needed.

Her skin crawled at the memory, and she looked down to see a pair of black bikini briefs wadded in her right hand. Carefully, she smoothed them out onto the bed and folded them. Her neighbor Joe was just like Herb, just like her mother's other boyfriends. Callous, rude, the kind of guy who thought the solution to all the world's problems could be found at the tip of his dick.

She heard a rustling and snapping outside and abandoned her lingerie to look out the window. Joe was back in his yard, trimming his bushes with a pair of lethal-looking hedge clippers. Okay, maybe he wasn't *exactly* like Herb and his ilk. The only six-pack Herb ever saw was in the refrigerator, and Joe's perfectly chiseled cheekbones and jawline were a universe away from Herb's mean, piggy eyes and puffy, ruddy face.

Still, he was the same uncultured, crude jerk, but in a much better-looking package. As though he'd felt her looking, Joe straightened up and glanced up toward her window. Taylor jumped to the side, watching as he pulled a bandana from his back pocket to wipe his face. Something like lust curled in her stomach as she watched his big hand wrap around a bottle of water. She licked her lips, watching the muscles of his shoulder and arm flex as he brought the bottle to his lips.

Yes, he was a jerk, but he was just about the sexiest jerk she'd ever seen. She allowed her eyes to skim down his sweat-slicked chest, to his muscular calves and big feet covered by heavy work boots. Her fingers itched to slide down his torso, to undo the fly of his shorts and see if his cock was as big as the rest of him. Maybe she could take him up here, to her room, tie him to her wrought-iron bed frame and punish him for his rudeness. . . .

He lowered the bottle, his mouth quirking in a half-smile as he raised his hand in a quick wave. Oh, God, he'd caught her staring! She flung herself back from the window, as though that would help matters. Hopefully at that distance, he hadn't been able to see the lust-crazed light in her eyes and the blush she knew had suffused her face. What in God's name was wrong with her? She rarely fantasized about sex, and if she did, it never entailed tying a gorgeous naked man to her bed so she could straddle him and take his long, thick, cock deep inside. . . .

There she went again! Taylor grabbed a stack of panties and took them to her dresser to put away. As she pushed aside a stack of beige panties to make room for the black, she caught a glimpse of ice-blue satin, pushed all they way back in the left-hand corner. She pulled out the blue satin garter belt, along with the matching thong and demi-cup bra. She'd bought them last spring for the romantic weekend she and Steven had planned in Big Sur. It had been over a year ago, and even then, Taylor had sensed something was missing, had felt compelled to do her part to spice up their rather bland sex life.

But Steven had spent the previous two weeks on a grueling overseas sales trip and had spent nearly the entire weekend sleeping off his jet lag.

Needless to say, the garter, the thong, and the bra all still bore their original price tags.

Where had her libido gone? Where had Steven's? As she'd admitted to Joe, sex had never been the most important part of her relationship with Steven, but she certainly hadn't been asexual. She simply hadn't been trying hard enough. That was the problem. After two years together, of course their sexual attraction had waned a bit, and she'd been working so hard she hadn't really put much thought or effort into rekindling those fires.

Well, no longer. Regardless of what Joe Tierney thought, she could be a sexy, sensual woman who kept her man satisfied. She looked at the clock. Eleven twenty-two. Steven was arriving later this evening from a trip to New York, but they didn't have plans to meet up until brunch tomorrow.

She quickly showered and dressed in a knee-length linen sundress. She had just enough time to get waxed, smoothed, and polished to perfection before Steven came home and found her ready, waiting, and wanting on his big California king.

Joe propped his hands on the end of his shovel and let out a low whistle. Taylor's pale blond head whipped around. "Do you have something to say," she asked, arching one perfectly groomed eyebrow, "or are your communication skills limited to catcalls?"

He straightened up like a chastened schoolboy. Maybe this was a chance to undo some of the damage from earlier. "You look very nice, Taylor." Which was an understatement. She looked phenomenal. Simultaneously sexy and classy, in a pink sleeveless dress made out of some kind of floaty material that hit her right at midthigh, showing off her amazing legs. As he looked more closely, he could see that she wore nylons, even though it was still about ninety degrees out. He thought she'd looked hot earlier today when she'd hightailed it out of the driveway, her hair in a prim bun and in another more casual dress.

But now she looked incredible. Though the V-neck of her dress wasn't cut particularly low, it called attention to the ripe curves of her breasts. Her pale shoulders gleamed in the late-afternoon sunlight, making him wonder how it would feel to trace his tongue along the silky line of skin and muscle. He wondered what she would do if he walked over and pulled the flimsy strap of her dress down her arm and slid his hand inside her dress to close over her tit.

Probably smack him in the face and look at him like she was looking at him now—like he was so far beneath her it was a wonder she even noticed his existence. Which really pissed him off. "Got a hot date?" He smirked. "Just so you know, the uptight-bitch look isn't much of a turn-on." Her eyes narrowed, but he refused to flinch. Hey, he'd tried to be nice, to give her a compliment, and she'd given him a look like he was lower than dog crap. As far as he was concerned, if there were a mud puddle around, Taylor would be facedown in it.

"Not that it's any of your business," she said as she opened her car door, "but my boyfriend is coming back tonight from a business trip, and I have a very nice surprise for him."

Something about the snooty way she tossed her head made him grin. "Good. Maybe he can help you get the stick out of your butt."

She muttered something about an immature bonehead, slammed the door, and peeled out of the driveway.

Joe watched, laughing as her car disappeared around the corner. Damn, what he wouldn't give to throw Taylor down and dirty her up a little bit.

Taylor reapplied her lip gloss, checking her reflection one last time in the rearview mirror. Did she really look like an uptight bitch? She'd really tried to look a little sexier, a little more casual this evening. Maybe Joe was right. *Why do you care what he thinks? His idea of sexy is probably too much makeup, a skirt that could double as a belt, and an IQ that matched a woman's bra size. Steven thinks I'm attractive—sexy even. We've just fallen into a bit of a rut.*

She smoothed the skirt of her silky chiffon dress and ran her fingers through her hair one last time before letting herself in the front door of Steven's town house. The air-conditioning hummed, the startling cold making the skin of her arms prickle and her nipples tighten against the satin of her bra. Built in air-conditioning was one perk, she conceded, of living in a cookie-cutter town house. While Taylor loved her old two-story craftsman home and her quiet cul-de-sac, it, unlike Steven's two-year-old town house, needed several upgrades. Flaws and all, she'd adored it from the moment she'd first laid eyes on it. Cozy, cute, with its own fenced yard, it was the kind of home she'd always dreamed of. One that was a universe away from the double-wide she'd shared with her mother in a dusty trailer park in southern New Mexico. When she'd bought her first house, she felt like she'd put her past behind her once and for all.

In the year and a half since she'd moved in, she'd spent a lot of money on making it her dream home but hadn't gotten around to installing AC before the warm weather hit. Steven seemed to have left it on while he was out of town, which was good since Taylor didn't want to start sweating until they got to the really good stuff.

She started up the stairs to the second floor, pausing at the sound of the stereo playing. Had Steven left it on while he was out of town? That was so unlike him. Come to think of it, so was the air-conditioning. Even though he probably made over a quarter-million dollars a year, he was completely anal when it came to household expenses. No way would he be so careless as to leave the air-conditioning, not to mention a major electronic appliance, on to suck the power grid dry. His cleaning service, which came once a week, must have left it on.

She stopped in the kitchen to put the bottle of champagne in the refrigerator to chill. As she turned, a tight sensation pulled at the back of her neck, telling her something was off, something she couldn't quite put her finger on. She did a slow sweep of the kitchen. A water glass, half full and marred by a thumbprint, sat on the counter. But the cleaners would have washed it when they came Thursday. . . .

A bump and a muffled voice came from the master bedroom. Burglars? The same moment that thought popped into her head, she saw the keys to Steven's Audi on the kitchen table. And she knew she hadn't interrupted a home invasion in progress.

Knowing, dreading what she was about to see didn't stop her from going to the master bedroom and turning the knob. Still, when the door swung open, she wasn't quite prepared for an unimpeded view of Steven's squarish, somewhat flabby ass as he stood at the foot of the bed heaving and groaning over the woman on all fours in front of him.

All of the restraint, the composure, the impeccable manners Taylor had spent the last fifteen years cultivating flew out the window. "I don't fucking believe this!" *If he's not getting it from you, he's getting it from somewhere else.* Apparently, that someone else was Annemarie, a barely legal junior sales associate Steven had hired last winter. Taylor recognized her as soon as Annemarie's head whipped around at Taylor's entrance. "Son of a bitch." Taylor wasn't sure if she was referring to Steven, for sleeping with another woman—girl!—under her nose all this time, or to Joe, for being right about the dismal state of her relationship.

"Taylor!" Steven gaped at her over his shoulder. "What are you doing here?"

She threw her hands up. "Well, I was hoping to get laid, but it looks like I'm a little too late to the party." She took in Steven's sweaty, naked body with distaste. From the neck up, he was a good-looking man, but it had been so long since she'd seen him in the full light of day, she'd forgotten what he looked like naked. Though he wasn't overweight, love handles had taken prominent places over his hips. And his butt—Taylor never knew men could have cellulite! His arms were scrawny, his hands pale as they still gripped Annemarie's hips, too shocked to let go.

Taylor realized with cold, cutting clarity that although Steven was the perfect boyfriend for her on paper, she had absolutely no desire whatsoever to have sex with him ever again. And even if she could summon a kernel of sexual attraction, she would never, ever forgive him for cheating on her.

Turning in disgust, she made it halfway down the stairs to the front door before he caught her by the arm. She turned, bracing herself for a full-frontal view, relieved to see Steven had wrapped a towel around his waist. It emphasized the soft pudge of his belly beneath a nearly concave chest, but at least she wouldn't have to see the part that had most recently been stuck inside another woman.

"Taylor, I'm sorry," he said as she jerked her arm away and ran down the last few stairs.

"Oh, please, you're not sorry," she spat. "You're sorry you got caught, and probably sorry that you won't have an inside contact at our portfolio companies anymore, but you're not sorry you slept with that . . . that child."

"Annemarie's twenty-five," he sputtered, gripping the knot of his towel as it started to slip.

"Clearly too dumb to realize that sleeping with you won't get her anywhere," she sneered, her hand on the doorknob. "I can't imagine she'd do it otherwise, since she probably doesn't enjoy it any more than I did."

His lip curled in a sneer as he met her attack with his own. "That's where you're wrong, Taylor. Unlike you, Annemarie actually knows how to relax and have fun. She's sexy, and funny—"

"And I'm not?"

He rolled his eyes and snorted. "You're about as sexy as a burlap sack, Taylor. It's no wonder I went somewhere else, since sleeping with you is like trying to fuck a bag of ice."

Ouch. Even though she had no interest in sleeping with Steven anymore, it stung to realize how little *he* wanted to sleep with *her*. The satin garters itched against her legs, and she suddenly felt very, very foolish.

She ran out of the house, nearly breaking an ankle when her high heel caught in a crack in the sidewalk. Tears of humiliation stung the backs of her eyes as she slammed her car door behind her and slipped the gearshift into reverse. *Look on the bright side: At least you didn't have a chance to go through with your ill-fated attempt at seduction. Think how much worse you would have felt if you'd tried and he'd rejected you.*

Cold comfort, even to a "bag of ice" such as herself.

She turned down her street, stomach clenching when she spotted Joe, still shirtless, his back muscles rippling as he stooped to pull weeds from around a hedge of flowering bushes. For God's sake, it was nearly six o'clock! Didn't the man ever stop working?

Maybe she could sneak by without his noticing. The last thing she needed was for him to rub her face in it. She pulled into her garage, wishing she could use the connecting door into the kitchen and bypass her front walk altogether. Unfortunately, she'd lost the key to that particular lock, and with her hectic work schedule, hadn't taken the time to get it rekeyed. She sighed. Having to haul groceries in the rain had nothing on facing a smug, arrogant neighbor.

"Must have been a quickie."

Taylor's shoulders tightened at the sound of his voice, and it took every ounce of restraint not to turn on him and tell him to shove his giant hedge clippers straight up his perfectly sculpted ass.

Instead, she took a deep breath and turned around, doing her best to keep the rage and hurt from bubbling to the surface. "I'm sure you'll be pleased to know you were right." She strove for a smile, feeling like her skin was cracking around the bones of her face. "Steven was indeed 'getting it somewhere else,' as you so quaintly put it. In fact, he was 'getting it' from his new sales associate when I walked in. Go ahead, say 'I told you so.'" She drew her shoulders back, bracing herself for yet another round of humiliation.

Joe's smirk melted away, concern clouding his green eyes. "Taylor, I'm sorry."

She didn't want his pity, but the sincere kindness in his voice started a warm glow somewhere in her belly. She held her hands up. "Don't be. Better I find out now before it's too late. Besides, we obviously weren't terribly . . . compatible in that regard anyway." *As if I've ever been sexually compatible with anyone,* she thought morosely. She turned and started up the cracked flagstones that constituted her walkway, freezing in her tracks when he called out.

"Hey, do you want to come over for a drink or something?"

Great. Now he felt sorry for her. "You don't have to console me, Joe. Besides, I'm sure you have better things to do on a Saturday night than entertain your—how did you put it?—frigid bitch of a neighbor."

"I think I said 'uptight bitch,' actually." His grin made her toes curl in her high-heeled sandals. "I don't have any plans, other than to maybe watch a movie and get to bed early." Was it just her imagination, or did his eyes momentarily focus on her breasts when he said "bed"? *Oh, come on, Taylor, I think we've just established that you're not the type to incite instant, wild lust in anyone, much less a young stud muffin like Joe.* Not that she would want to anyway, she reminded herself fiercely, as Joe, while gorgeous, was emphatically not the type of guy Taylor would ever go for.

But what would be the harm in one drink? Her only other option was to go home and feel sorry for herself. And right now, the only thing more pathetic than taking him up on his pity-driven hospitality would be to go home and wallow in the death of what she had thought was a perfectly nice, stable relationship.

Pasting on her brightest smile, she said, "I could really go for a strong vodka and tonic."

3

Joe mixed her vodka and tonic and excused himself to take a quick shower. Taylor took the opportunity to look around his house. Like hers, it was a small two-story, with an open floor plan on the bottom level. The recently updated kitchen opened onto a great room, which boasted a comfortable-looking ultra-suede couch and matching love seat. Across from the couch, nearly an entire wall was dominated by a huge, flat-screen television. Tiny surround-sound speakers were mounted in the corners.

Though Joe suffered from the typical male syndrome of decorating with major electronics, the house was much nicer than she would have expected from an unmarried man. Framed black and white photos decorated the putty-colored walls in interesting arrangements. And it was clean, too, although the stainless-steel kitchen sink was crowded with soaking pots and pans. Unlike her, he obviously cooked.

All in all, very nicely furnished and decorated. But obviously masculine. No little knickknacks, no little feminine touches. *No girlfriend.* Not that she cared.

She sipped her drink, savoring the bitter bite of the vodka and the cold fizz of tonic on her tongue, the relaxing warmth that spread through her veins with each sip. As she admired Joe's beautifully landscaped backyard through the sliding-glass doors off the kitchen, the memory of Steven's betrayal and parting insults faded behind a foggy, alcoholic haze.

She drained her glass as heavy footsteps sounded on the stairway. Joe entered through the door off the kitchen, and her mouth went a little dry. How could he look so good in a faded T-shirt and equally threadbare jeans? "I was admiring what you've done with the backyard," she said.

"Thanks. I could do the same with yours." Her what? Between the vodka and the way the cotton of his shirt pulled across his chest, she was having a hard time focusing. "In fact, it would be a favor to me if you let me fix up your yard a little bit."

"Oh, right. My yard." She shook her head as his words sank in. "I'll think about it." But she could barely think at all, what with all of the blood having left her veins. She felt flushed all over, hot even in his cool, dark living room. The garters chafed her thighs, and her stockings clung to her skin. For a split second she wondered what Joe would do if she asked him to peel them off her legs.

"Can I get you another?"

She stared stupidly until he gestured to her empty glass. "Oh, sure. But maybe you could go a little lighter this time, since I drained that one so quickly." And the alcohol was clearly scrambling her brains, turning her into a horny, lust-crazed nympho. He smiled and came over to retrieve her glass. The aroma of soap and warm skin assaulted her, tempting her to lean in and bury her nose in the strong column of his neck. But he retreated quickly, going to the granite kitchen counter to fix them both fresh drinks. His hair was still damp, waving a little bit in the back. Taylor laced her fingers together before she did something stupid, like walk over and stroke them up his nape.

He turned, his smile a slash of white against his work-tanned skin. She took her drink and raised it up in a little toast. She took a sip and sucked in a breath. "I think this is stronger than the last one."

He waved her to the couch. "I figure after the day you've had, you deserve to get a little plastered."

Normally she didn't overindulge in alcohol. She'd been around enough drunks growing up to know firsthand how un-attractive it was. Plus, she didn't like the idea of losing control and saying or doing the wrong thing. In her profession, image was very important, and she would never let her colleagues see her in anything but a professional light.

But she seriously doubted Joe ran in the same circles as she, so it wasn't like he was going to run into her managing partner and tell him how she had spent Saturday night lolling drunk-enly on his couch. Besides, he was right. After a day like she'd had, she should be allowed to cut loose a little.

She plopped down onto the couch with little grace, half-heartedly rearranging her skirt as it rode up her thighs. "Thanks for taking pity on me. I just can't believe . . ." She stopped herself. She didn't want to talk about Steven, or the fact that she was almost thirty-three and a hell of a lot further from marriage than she'd thought only the day before. Or the fact that she'd been dumped for a woman nearly ten years younger, at least twenty IQ points stupider, but all the more appealing because she let Steven do her doggy style, a position Taylor had always hated.

She looked over at Joe, smiling at her from the other end of the couch. He lifted his glass to his mouth, his tongue coming out to catch a stray drop from his lush lower lip. An image popped into her head, of her bent over, naked in her bed as Joe drove into her from behind. Rather than repulsing her, the thought sent a bolt of heat pulsing between her legs. She shifted her legs restlessly, squeezing her thighs as though to contain the hot surge of moisture dampening the thin strip of her thong. "I just can't believe it's taken me so long to figure out who my neighbor is!" she said in a desperate attempt to distract herself. "I would have never guessed it was someone like you."

"Someone like me?" He raised a thick, dark eyebrow, as though trying to decide whether or not he was being insulted.

"Well you're so young. How old are you anyway?"

"Twenty-eight."

"That's pretty young to own a house in the Bay Area, especially in this area."

"Speak for yourself."

"I'm thirty-two," she said, reminding herself of a little girl insisting she was not five, but five and a *half.*

"Ancient." He chuckled. "Let me know if you ever need help with your walker."

"Besides," she said, eyes rolling, "this neighborhood isn't exactly a mecca for young, single men."

He inched a little closer, draping his arm across the back of the couch. Another inch, and his fingers could brush against her bare shoulder, if he were so inclined. "Or for young, single women."

"I'm not single." She corrected herself. "At least up until today I wasn't. And I bought this house thinking I would raise a family in it eventually." She frowned, not wanting to dwell on Steven but unable to quell the thoughts of all the hopes and expectations she'd so foolishly placed on him. No, he wasn't the love of her life—Taylor wasn't sure there was such a thing—but she'd been content and thought he'd been too. They'd had similar goals, both personally and professionally, and Taylor had been confident he would be able to give her the two kids, a dog, and a picket fence sort of affluent lifestyle of which she'd dreamed. The kind of life that was a universe away from the life of her mother, a single waitress who raised Taylor in a trailer park while supporting a never-ending string of unemployed losers.

Instead, she would have to start all over, two years wasted with nothing to show for it. Sudden, hot tears burned at the back of her eyes, and she pinched the bridge of her nose to hold them back. The last thing she wanted was to start sobbing uncontrollably in front of Joe.

"Hey, it's okay," he said, taking the drink from her hand and awkwardly pulling her into his arms. One big hand patted her back as the other pressed her face into his chest. She buried her nose against the firm muscle. God, he smelled good. Her hand rested lightly on his waist, the heat of his skin radiating through his shirt. She wanted to tug it up over his chest and run her fingers over his smooth tan torso, but it would be rude to shamelessly hit on him when he was only offering comfort.

Besides, she reminded herself, though she might be wearing the sexiest underwear she owned under her dress, if she couldn't tempt a man like Steven, Joe would certainly find her powers of seduction sorely lacking.

Finally, she pulled away with a sniff, thankful the urge to break down and weep seemed to have passed. "I'm not usually this emotional," she said.

"Your boyfriend's an idiot."

She shook her head and settled back against the cushions. "It's not his fault he didn't want to sleep with me."

Joe leaned over, resting his palm on the couch next to her thigh, close enough that if she shifted her leg one millimeter to the right, she would feel his skin against hers. "There's no man in his right mind who wouldn't want to sleep with you, Taylor." His tone was fierce and so was his gaze as he fixed it on her mouth. She licked her lips as his intent became clear.

She should move, she should get off this couch and run for the door. Because he was too young, too wrong . . . too good of a kisser, she realized as his mouth settled on hers.

His taste flooded her as his lips parted, his tongue sweeping inside her mouth, hot, sleek, and smooth as it tangled with hers.

Wet, open-mouth kisses melted together until Taylor's breath came in little pants. Long, rough fingers slid the strap of her dress down her shoulder, his tongue sending sparks down her spine as it followed. She'd never thought of her shoulders, her collarbones, her jaw as erogenous zones until Joe nipped and sucked his way across them. She heard the buzz of her zipper at the same time cool air hit the skin of her back, and then she was bare to the waist except for her ice-blue-satin strapless bra.

She didn't recognize the wild woman who arched and moaned against Joe's hands and lips, who practically tore his shirt from his body so she could feel him, skin to skin. All Taylor knew was she was starving for the taste of him, the feel of him, the scent of him. She was so turned on, the skin of her inner thighs was slippery with her own moisture, and he still hadn't touched her below the neck.

Her hands eagerly explored his back as he tugged at the satin cups of her bra. "Beautiful," he murmured as her breasts sprang free, her nipples dark pink and so hard they nearly hurt. She moaned in anticipation as his tongue sneaked out, barely grazing the tip of first one, then the other. A low, throaty groan emanated from her throat when his lips closed over the sensitive flesh. Heat flooded her belly as he pushed her back against the cushions and settled himself between her spread thighs.

The thick column of his erection pressed against her stomach, his size evident even contained as it was by the fly of his jeans. Then again, everything about him was big, from the broad, work-toughened palm closing over her breast to the immense shoulders blocking everything from her view as he leaned over her. The mere thought of his long, thick cock sliding in, of her slick flesh stretching to accommodate him, sent a shudder coursing through her.

He kissed her again, harder this time, his breath fast and shaky as his hand slid over the curve of her hip, down her thigh, and back up again, taking her skirt with it.

His fingers froze on the strap of her garter. As though he couldn't quite believe what he felt, he leaned back, a slow, delighted smile suffusing his face as he pushed her dress up for an unimpeded view. "Well, well, Miss Taylor Flynn, aren't you just full of surprises?" His hand was dark against her thigh as he traced the strap of the garter, skirted the edge of her nude stocking, and slid up the smooth skin of her inner thigh, coming to rest along the baby-blue lace edging her thong.

His thumb, resting along the crease of her thigh, drifted lightly over her mound, stroked the flesh swelling against the silky fabric. A hot flush crawled all the way up her body, until the pale skin of her breasts was splotched with pink. Another gentle circle, a bare whisper of his thumb brushing over her clit had her arching her hips and digging her fingers into his arms.

She'd never experienced anything like this, the desperate need to feel his hands on her, the desire so fierce it was almost painful. She could chalk it up to skill, but she'd been turned on even before Joe had laid a hand on her. No, there was something about him, the rich scent of his skin, the way his green eyes narrowed and his mouth quirked when he looked at her. But really, none of that explained her ridiculously intense reaction.

His fingers tugged aside the now-drenched satin of her panties, and she nearly jumped out of her skin at the first brush of his bare fingers against the swollen folds of her sex. She was so wet she could hear the moist sounds his fingers made as they spread her wide so he could pluck and tease at her clit. Taylor bucked against his hand, needing more pressure, a firmer touch. But he seemed intent on getting to know every crease and furrow, sliding down to tease at her opening but stopping short of pushing inside.

She yanked his head down, sucking and biting at his lips, sliding her tongue inside at the same moment he slid two long, thick fingers inside her. She moaned into his mouth as his thumb traced rough circles around her clit, finally, finally, giving her the kind of touch she craved.

Her hips ground against his hand, fucking his fingers as his mouth made a scorching path down her chest, lapping at the sweat beaded on the skin between her breasts.

Suddenly, his hand was gone. "No," she cried out as she found herself shifted, repositioned until she sat upright on the couch. Joe ignored her protest as he knelt in front of her, pausing only to jerk the crotch of her panties all the way to the side before hooking her knees over his shoulders. Light exploded behind her eyelids as his mouth closed over her, sucking and lapping at her like he was a starving man and she was ambrosia. His fingers delved back inside, thrusting deep, stretching her wide, pressing up against a bundle of nerves as his tongue stroked against her clit.

Every muscle and every nerve pulled taut as she arched against his mouth. She looked down, saw his dark head buried between her legs, his mouth wet with her juice. He looked up and met her gaze, his so dark and *wanting*, it was enough to send her hurtling over the edge. The tight knot of her orgasm exploded, starting low in her belly and radiating out in pulsing waves. Relentlessly, he pushed her on, his fingers pressing high and hard inside her, his lips never ceasing their soft sucking until one orgasm turned into two, then three, until she was nothing but a boneless, panting heap.

Taylor could feel her heartbeat pounding between her legs, in the tips of her fingers, making the skin of her belly quiver. Joe slowly withdrew his fingers and pressed a soft kiss to her thighs as he sat back on his heels.

Her eyes popped open as the sucking sound of his mouth brought her starkly back to reality. She looked down, assaulted by the sight of her bare breasts illuminated by the evening sunlight, the sheen of wetness on her thighs, sprawled wide and still halfway over Joe's shoulders. Her stomach bottomed out as she realized what she had just done.

Oblivious, Joe rose up and put one knee on the couch, moving over Taylor with the look of a hungry wolf after a juicy steak.

She needed to get out of there before things got completely out of hand. *Like letting him go down on you in his living room doesn't count?*

He reached out for her hand, pressing it to his fly as he leaned in to kiss her. The heat and size of his erection pulsed against her palm, and as much as she craved the feel of the hot, thick, length inside her, some force of common sense propelled her off the couch. She hurriedly yanked her dress up to cover her breasts and down to cover her legs as Joe sat back, looking so bewildered that Taylor nearly hurled herself back down on top of him. "What's wrong?" he asked, reaching out as though to pull her back down on the couch.

She jumped back as though scalded, nearly falling on her backside as her high-heeled sandal twisted under her. "Nothing. Nothing's wrong. I just remembered I have a"—she wracked her brain for a plausible excuse—"a meeting tomorrow. Early."

"Tomorrow's Sunday," he said with a sexy little flick of his eyebrows that made her nearly lose all resolve.

She started backing toward the door. Joe got up to follow her, slowly, like a killer in a horror movie who has every confidence he'll catch his prey. "Yeah, but you know these high-tech executives, always trying to cram everything in." She was nearly to the door of his kitchen.

His hand slid down his bare stomach, coming to rest as his thumb hooked into the belt loop just to the right of his zipper. Drawing Taylor's gaze inexorably to the bulge that didn't seem to have diminished in the least.

Her eyes widened and moisture flooded her mouth, and suddenly all she wanted to do was get down on her knees and spend the evening finding out what Joe Tierney tasted like. She swallowed hard and took another step back, knocking her shoulder into the door frame. "Anyway, gotta go. Thanks for the drinks and the . . ." Her cheeks felt like they were erupting into flames as she waved her hand in the general direction of the couch.

His eyebrows raised in disbelief, and she could tell he was a millimeter away from writing her off as a crazy bitch.

She made a break for it before she could make matters any worse.

4

Not wanting to get caught in a lie, Taylor got out of bed at seven A.M. on Sunday and took off for her "meeting." Though she had no idea if Joe was even paying attention, she took her briefcase just in case. She filled the rest of the day with unnecessary errands, waiting until well after dark to return home, lest she run into Joe and his massive garden weasel. Not exactly how she'd planned to spend her weekend, but she had found some gorgeous matching bra and panty sets at the Stanford Shopping Center.

Not that there would be anyone to appreciate her sexy new lingerie anytime soon, even if she had imagined Joe's appreciative face as she carefully folded and put it away amid her more practical wear.

What in the world had she been thinking, letting things get so out of hand with him? Sure, he was incredibly hot, but Taylor was never the sort to let something like raw lust and alcohol overpower her good sense. Come to think of it, she couldn't remember the last time she'd felt anything remotely approaching raw lust, until she met Joe. Maybe that was her problem.

Well, now that she'd gotten it out of her system, she could simply go on as before and forget that she lived next door to possibly the hottest man in the entire universe.

Apparently her subconscious didn't get the memo. Sunday night she woke up sweaty and unsatisfied, her sex and nipples throbbing, her brain awash in scorching fantasies of Joe's hands, Joe's lips, Joe's cock easing the hot ache between her legs. That same lusty, sex-crazed being who had taken possession of her on Saturday night urged her to call him to see if he was still hard from the night before, but Taylor wisely resisted. It simply wouldn't do to hit Joe up for a booty call.

It was probably best to avoid him as much as possible. A strategy that got very old very quickly, as Taylor spent a good half hour Monday morning keeping their paths from crossing as she left for work. She was all packed up and ready to head out the front door when Joe appeared and put something in his truck. She paused, watching and waiting for him to get in and drive away. Instead he made something like a million trips into his garage for more landscaping equipment, until finally fifteen minutes had passed and he still seemed no closer to leaving. Was he messing with her? It seemed like a strange coincidence that after almost six months of never seeing him, suddenly Joe's departure time for work would so closely coincide with hers.

Taylor watched from her living room, admiring the way his muscles pulled against the thin cotton of his T-shirt even as she impatiently watched the minutes tick by. *Better enjoy it now. Nothing but flat butts and paunchy middles for the rest of the day.*

Mentally she scolded herself for her uncharitable assessment of her male colleagues' physiques. After all, ambition, intelligence, and a well-paying professional career were worth infinitely more than a perfect butt and ripped torso. *Steven had all those things, and look how he turned out,* an insidious voice whispered. She firmly pushed those thoughts aside. True,

Steven had turned out to be a thoughtless, selfish, unfaithful jerk, but that didn't mean she should throw away all of her dating standards. *But the ripped torso definitely has its merit. . . .*

Finally, Joe backed out of his driveway, allowing Taylor to make her short commute. Apex Ventures was located on Sand Hill Road where all the venture capital firms were clustered like a little cash colony at the foot of the Santa Cruz mountains. She murmured a polite hello to her assistant, Mary, as she walked in and started up her computer. Usually the second she walked in the door she was focused, knowing exactly what she had to get done, who she had to call, whose chops she needed to bust, whose ego she needed to stroke.

But this morning she was discombobulated and out of sorts, and by ten A.M. she still hadn't started on her update for the weekly partner and associates meeting. So when Jenna, Apex's entrepreneur in residence, popped her head in and invited her to get a cup of coffee, Taylor welcomed the distraction.

Since she was the only other single female under the age of forty in the office, Jenna had immediately latched on to Taylor when she'd started working at Apex. While Taylor had welcomed the opportunity to make a friend at the office, at first she'd tried to discreetly brush off Jenna's attempts to get closer outside of work. In the course of Taylor's career, she'd been careful to keep details of her past and personal life private, lest anyone identify any issues that might make them question her capabilities or commitment to her career.

But in the year that Jenna had worked at Apex, she'd slowly worn Taylor down, sharing her own confidences and slowly drawing Taylor from her reserved shell. It helped that as an entrepreneur in residence, Jenna was essentially enjoying a paid sabbatical as she awaited the right opportunity at one of Apex's portfolio companies. The fact that Jenna presented no competition in Taylor's quest to become the youngest partner in Apex's history made her that much easier to love.

"How was your weekend?" Jenna asked as she handed Taylor a mug of French roast.

"Fine," Taylor said as she poured in creamer—that is, if you counted catching your boyfriend cheating and nearly sleeping with your younger neighbor "fine." "Yours?"

Jenna pulled a face. "Nothing to write home about. Went to Spellman's for dinner on Friday. The usual. I really need to get myself a husband and kids."

Right. Marc Spellman, one of the managing partners, had invited Taylor to the dinner party, too, but she'd declined since Steven was going to be out of town.

"I wish you had gone," Jenna continued, "without Steven. At least then I would have had a partner."

Taylor picked up a spoon and absently stirred her coffee. "I hate going to those things alone. I always get a weird vibe from the wives."

Jenna sat down at one of the small café tables in the break room. "That's because they're intimidated by you."

Taylor rolled her eyes and sat down. "I think it's because we have so little in common."

"Or because you look like Grace Kelly's more beautiful twin. They don't like to think of their husbands working with someone beautiful, brilliant, and single, not to mention completely dialed into their husbands' daily lives. Most of them gave up their own high-powered careers to focus on little Jimmy's private school applications and Suzie's soccer practice. They're afraid you're going to lure their men away with your looks and intellect," Jenna said with a teasing wink. Much of Taylor's success depended on networking with her colleagues both inside and outside Apex, but she'd found that if someone's wife took a disliking to her, the husband became less enthusiastic to work with her. Taylor and Jenna had often commiserated on how difficult it could be as single women trying to negotiate the social demands of their careers.

But today Taylor was in no mood to joke about it. For two years, Steven had been her perfect social foil, the kind of man she could confidently take to business functions and know that he would reflect perfectly upon her. Of course, he was out of town more often than not and had been increasingly unavailable. It had nearly killed her to turn down Spellman's invitation, as Taylor knew it was a vital step in the direction of making full partner. Instead, she would have to continue to outperform the rest of the associates at the office, since she would be dateless for the foreseeable future.

"What is the matter with you?" Jenna asked.

Taylor looked up from her coffee, which had turned into a light brown whirlpool from the force of her stirring.

"You're distracted. Didn't you just close a big deal on Friday? Why aren't you talking my ear off about how significant it is in your quest to become partner?"

Taylor sighed. Where to begin? *I'm dejected because I caught my boyfriend doing his assistant in a sexual position that I particularly loathe, and less than half an hour later I found myself with my thighs around my neighbor's neck like a drunken sorority girl.* She blew out her breath and quickly filled Jenna in about Steven, leaving out the part about the sexual position and omitting Joe entirely.

"Oh, my God, why didn't you call me?"

Because I was too busy coming on my hot neighbor's face? Taylor felt her cheeks heat at the crudity of her thoughts. She finished her coffee and stood up. "I didn't want to dwell on it, and I still don't."

"Good riddance," Jenna said. "I always thought he was a pompous asshole anyway."

Taylor didn't have enough energy to argue, especially when Jenna was probably right. "Even so, I'm back to square one. Almost thirty-three and not a man in sight." An image of Joe, shirtless, sweaty, green eyes gleaming in a sexy grin popped into her head, making her thighs clench and her nipples peak beneath her silk blouse. An underage gardener didn't count, she reminded herself fiercely.

"Better no man at all than a man like Steven," Jenna said, emptying the dregs of her coffee into the sink.

Later, as Taylor stared at her computer screen and tried to focus on her status report, she wasn't so sure she agreed. Okay, infidelity aside, Steven was the perfect man for her. Ambitious, successful, and intelligent, he had understood the demanding nature of her career. Basically a male version of herself, Steven had seemed the perfect addition to her career-driven life.

Until, of course, she had found him naked and heaving over Annemarie.

She squeezed her eyes shut, trying to focus on committing the details of the latest series-B financing she had negotiated at a start-up medical device company. Never in her life had she let her personal life distract her from her work. And here she was, zoning out and completely unprepared for the meeting she had in less than forty-five minutes.

Worse, it wasn't even sadness over her breakup with Steven that had her fading in and out. No, it was Joe who tormented her, making her wish she hadn't stopped him in his tracks Saturday night. Making her wonder what he looked like naked, what he would look like when he came.

She put on her glasses and pulled out her profit-and-loss spreadsheets to get herself back on track. Never in her life had she been so obsessed with sex. Sure, she'd been known to enjoy it, but like one might enjoy a good steak. Every once in a while she really craved it, but it was so rarely done exactly the way she wanted it, the fantasy was usually better than the reality. But Joe, he'd done things with his hands and his tongue that she'd never even thought of.

Taylor shifted in her seat, her eyes drifting closed as she again felt the hot, wet tug of his lips around her clit, the firm thrust of his fingers against the knot of nerves inside her she'd never known existed. She felt like a molten chocolate cake, all hot and liquid at the center. She swallowed hard, knowing she should stop this fantasy in its tracks before it burned out of control, but she was unable to do so. Did Joe actually have a map to the elusive G-spot? And could he easily find it again, this time with his cock?

"Taylor, are you coming or not?"

Almost, she thought as Jenna's urgent voice poured a virtual bucket of cold water on Taylor's increasingly pornographic musings. Somehow she managed to muddle through the weekly meeting, providing a relatively cohesive update about her latest investment; she even managed to offer intelligible feedback on new prospects.

"This is ridiculous," she muttered hours later as she sat parked inside her garage, waiting for Joe to finish unpacking his truck. As luck would have it, he'd driven up about two seconds behind her, even though Taylor had purposely waited until well after dark before leaving the office. She'd figured that since Joe required light to do his work, he'd be home shortly after sundown.

She'd figured wrong, and so here she sat, trapped in her garage for the second time in two days, trying to avoid the only man to have appreciated her Brazilian bikini wax up close and personal. It was stupid, avoiding him like a child. She was an adult, fully capable of controlling her baser instincts. She'd never let herself get carried away by any irrational need or emotion, and she wasn't about to now. Best to get out of the car, face him like a grown-up, and prove to herself and him that what they'd done was no big deal. Just a random, meaningless, sexual encounter between two consenting adults.

An amazing, erotic, intense, sexual encounter. But meaningless. Completely meaningless, with no more significance than a handshake. And, she reasoned, the sooner she actually saw him again, the sooner she'd be reminded that though attractive, Joe was far from the man of her dreams. And the reason her orgasm had been powerful enough to make her nearly faint was that she hadn't had one in so long. So, really, nothing to do with Joe at all and everything to do with an obnoxiously long dry spell. Once she got that straight in her head (not to mention her other parts), she could stop fading into the lust-induced fugue state that had plagued her this afternoon.

So there was no reason she shouldn't be able to walk out of her garage, offer a friendly hello, and make it to her front door unscathed. Yet, just as she stepped out of her garage, she nearly wilted with relief as Joe entered his and lowered the automatic door.

Tomorrow would be soon enough to mend fences with her neighbor.

5

―――――

"So, you're done hiding from me?" Joe asked the next evening when he opened the front door to find Taylor on his porch. She wore slim-fitting black pants and a silky blouse that barely had a crease despite being worn all day. Her pale blond hair was pulled neatly back into a clip at her nape, not a single strand daring to move out of place. If Joe didn't have firsthand knowledge that Taylor was a natural blonde, he would have never pegged her as the same woman who had been half-naked, writhing desperately against his tongue and fingers as he brought her to peak after peak.

"Hide? Why would I hide?" she said, a polite, friendly smile pasted across her face. From her cool-as-a-cucumber demeanor, it seemed she had no memory whatsoever of her thighs wrapped around his neck. He wished he could say the same. Instead, the mere sight of her, prissily buttoned up though she was, made his cock surge from half-mast, where it had spent most of the past seventy-two hours, to full, aching hardness.

He put one hand against the doorframe and rested the other on his waistband. Her eyes drifted down, widening when they saw the conspicuous evidence of his arousal. She swallowed and licked her lips. Good. Maybe she wasn't so indifferent after all. "I don't know. Why would you hide? That's what I asked myself after you stayed in your garage for fifteen minutes last night."

"I was sorting through the recycling."

"Uh-huh. And yesterday, before you left for work, you weren't watching me from your living room window to see when I left?"

A rosy flush suffused her cheeks. "I had some things to do in there," she said lamely.

"I figured after the way you left the other night, maybe you were embarrassed." He, on the other hand, had first been flabbergasted, then pissed, then frustrated when she'd fled like a scared bunny rabbit with no intention of coming back. And through it all, he'd been hard enough to pound nails through drywall, left high and dry by the uptight little priss next door.

She started to squirm under his direct gaze, then seemed to force herself to reclaim her composure. It was a nearly tangible process, the way she drew herself up, straightened her shoulders, and leveled him with a cool blue stare. It was like she'd donned an invisible suit of armor, protecting her from all the messy complications of the outside world. "What's to be embarrassed about?" she said, so cool that ice wouldn't melt in her mouth. "We're both consenting adults. I mean, really, what's a couple of orgasms between neighbors?"

Simultaneously more irritated and aroused than he'd ever been in his life, Joe was more determined than ever to knock another crack into that shell. "Actually, I counted three," he said steadily. Her perfectly arched, light brown brows knit in confusion. "Orgasms," he clarified. "You had three of them."

He had to give it to her, the way she stood her ground, not betraying an iota of discomposure. The only evidence that he was getting to her was a rapidly beating pulse point in her neck, right above the ivory silk of her collar. He wanted to lean over and run his tongue across it. Bet that would set her off. Heat pooled low in his gut as he remembered the salty-sweet taste of her skin, the feel of her nipple hard against his tongue, the firm clench of her pussy around his fingers.

Jesus Christ, someone on this porch was about to lose composure, and it sure as shit wasn't Taylor.

"Be that as it may," she said sharply, arms crossed primly over her chest, "I see no reason why we can't just move on and forget it ever happened."

Forget how pink and tight her nipples got when he pinched them? Not likely. Still, he didn't interrupt as she continued.

"And in the spirit of maintaining good neighbor relations, I'd like to hire you to landscape my yard."

Taylor had concocted the plan late last night, and at the time it had seemed a brilliant solution. The way she saw it, there was no way she could completely avoid him for the next several years, and the longer she put off speaking to him, the more awkward their eventual confrontation would be. Yet she didn't completely trust herself not to throw him down and beg him to finish what they'd started Saturday night when she did see him again.

Which was when she'd come up with the perfect course of action: hire him. After all, she'd never had a problem keeping her distance from coworkers, and entering a business relationship with Joe would erect a much-needed mental barrier that would help keep her lust in check and her panties on.

"You want to hire me?" He straightened in surprise, his full, delicious lips flattening into a frown.

Amazing, she thought now, as the mere sight of his big, long-fingered hands made her nipples tight, how a plan that could seem so foolproof at three in the morning could be exposed as completely asinine in the light of day. She should have trashed the whole idea the moment he opened the door and she started to salivate. She should have run like hell for home when the sight of the unmistakably huge outline of his erection against the fly of his jeans made her sex swell and pulse. Clearly, being within five feet of this man was terrible for her sense of well-being. And yet her pride wouldn't let her run off again, like a little girl unable to handle the intense physical reaction this man for some reason evoked.

She was renowned for her self-control, damn it, for her cool head in all situations, for never letting her emotions supersede logic. And she wasn't going to let Joe Tierney change that. "Yes, I do. You said yourself my yard needs a lot of work and that it reflects poorly on the rest of the neighbors. I figure I'm doing us both a favor."

He stepped fully out onto the porch, rubbing his chin in contemplation. His scent wafted out on the early evening air, fresh soap and hot skin, tempting her to slide his T-shirt up his torso and bury her face against his chest. Instead, she clasped her hands behind her back, following at a safe distance as he walked to the edge of his porch to get a clear view of her front yard and driveway.

"I'll have to fit you in around other jobs," he said finally. "So, it could take quite a while."

"Okay."

He turned to face her. "I'm serious. We're talking several weeks."

She swallowed hard. Several weeks of him working in close proximity? Did he always take his shirt off when he worked, and if so, could she be held responsible if he found himself with his pants around his ankles and her on top of him? "No problem. I'm at work most of the time anyway, so you won't bother me." She smiled in genuine relief.

"That's another thing. If you want this done, you need to trust me and my decisions. I'll go over the initial design with you, but things will go much more quickly if I don't have to chase you down for every little decision."

"Obviously you do great work"—she gestured to his front yard—"and clearly I have no clue." She gestured to her own. "I'm sure whatever you come up with will be great."

"There's one more thing." He walked toward her, almost casually, but a strange, predatory light had entered his eyes, making him look like a lion about to pounce on a helpless gazelle.

"Price?" she said, wondering where that girlish, breathless tone came from. "Because I'm not really worried about it. I mean, I don't want to get ripped off, but I'm willing to make the investme—" She was cut off mid-word as his mouth closed over hers, his tongue thrusting inside in a kiss that was little finesse and all hunger. Instead of pushing him away like she knew she should, all she could think was, *Thank God I didn't have to make the first move like some desperate hard-up spinster.*

He broke away, pushing her against the siding next to the front door. "I'm not worried about money," he said, grabbing her hand and pressing it hard against his fly. "My problem is I don't think I can get much work done in this condition. Do you?"

Her fingers wrapped around the thick, hot length, and this time she didn't jerk away and make a run for home. Though she'd tried to deny it to herself, this was exactly what she'd wanted to happen. Offering an olive branch in the form of a job was all an excuse to see Joe again and hope he'd pick up where she'd so abruptly left off. "No," she murmured, her palm stroking him up and down through the worn cloth of his jeans. "I can see how this might present a bit of a distraction."

His hand cupped the back of her neck, holding her in place for the full force of his kiss. Taylor moaned, sucking his tongue into her mouth as her hands tugged his T-shirt up his back. "We better get inside." He broke the kiss, and it took her a moment to register what he'd said. The sight of her neighbor's Dodge Caravan barreling down the street snapped her partially back to her senses. Joe was right. It was probably best not to be making out like a couple of hormonal teenagers in full view of the neighborhood soccer moms.

Taylor's chest tightened momentarily as she realized how close they'd been to being seen. What would the neighbors think of her? Best not to ever let them find out. She let Joe tug her inside his front door, and they kissed, nuzzled, and caressed their way up to his bedroom. She was vaguely aware of a king-size bed with a heavy wood frame and matching nightstand before she was tumbled down on it.

He knelt on the edge of the bed, hovering above her as he stripped off his T-shirt and motioned for her to take off her blouse. Her fingers shook a little as she unbuttoned her blouse, baring herself to his hard stare. He smiled a little when her breasts emerged, barely covered in ivory lace so sheer her nipples were clearly visible. More proof that she'd wanted this to happen, she thought ruefully. She was wearing her fancy underwear.

Joe caught Taylor's hands and pulled her into a sitting position. From this position, it was a matter of inches for Taylor to lean forward and run her tongue down the ridged expanse of his abdomen. His skin jumped, muscles tensing in response as she followed with a series of soft, sucking nips around his navel.

"You realize," he said, capturing her hands and placing them near his waistband, "that I'm not going to let you run away tonight."

"I wouldn't dream of it," she whispered, flicking open the button of his fly. And it was true. Right now, at this moment, it didn't matter that Joe was completely wrong for her. It didn't matter that she'd die of humiliation if her neighbors and colleagues found out she was fooling around with her much-younger gardener like some character on a TV show.

Right now, she wanted Joe Tierney more than she'd ever wanted anything in her life, and she wasn't going to allow anything, not even her own better judgment, to prevent her from taking what she wanted.

Joe's breath tightened in his chest as Taylor unzipped his fly. He stood and quickly shucked his jeans and boxers. She knelt on the bed, staring hungrily at his naked body. He couldn't help the surge of pride that pulsed through him at her lusty, covetous expression. He pushed her back on the bed, quickly stripping her down to nothing but her lacy bra and matching panties. His cock hardened what felt like another inch as the silky, pale skin of her belly brushed against the tip. He grabbed her hands, pinning them to the bed as he stroked back and forth. Though she showed no signs of bolting, he wasn't about to take any chances.

Her legs wrapped around his hips as she changed her angle so he was rubbing directly against the wet satin between her legs. Moaning, she ground herself against him, pulling him down over her until the skin of his chest and stomach was glued against hers. Just like the other night, she'd morphed almost instantly from the sedate, buttoned-up executive to a wildcat, writhing and straining under him like she couldn't get enough.

That dichotomy drove him crazy, made him want to see just what Taylor kept hidden behind that cool, composed exterior. All that heat simmering underneath that she kept from bubbling to the surface. That heat was burning him, sending sparks through his skin, sizzling down his spine, making him worry that he was going to come before he even got inside her.

"Slow down, Taylor. We've got plenty of time," he whispered, even as his fingers hastily tugged at the closure of her bra. His tongue flicked a bead of sweat from one slope, finally managing to unhook the bra. He eagerly pulled the straps down her arms and threw the garment aside. "God, you've got great tits." As sex talk, it wasn't particularly eloquent, but it seemed to work for her, judging from the pink flush that crept up her belly and over the full swells. His big hands covered them completely, making him feel like some kind of conquering warlord. Her nipples were small and dark rose, a shade darker than her lips. The hard little peaks nudged between his fingers, begging to be pinched, licked, sucked.

She dug her fingers into his shoulder and arched against him. Her legs splayed wide, and he could feel the wet satin of her panties as she rubbed herself against his stomach. She was so wet, so ready, Joe could practically feel the hot clasp of her pussy closing around him.

She let out a feeble cry of protest as he pulled away to get a condom. He paused a moment to enjoy the sight of her sprawled across his bed. Her hair had come loose of its clip and haloed her head in a wild blond tangle. Her eyes were heavy-lidded as she watched him roll the condom down the length of his shaft. He pumped himself once, twice, watching the way her eyes lit up in anticipation. Coming down over her once again, he peeled off her panties. "Not planning on taking off again, are you?" Gripping his cock, he slid the head up and down her slit, spreading the slick moisture over her swollen flesh.

She moaned, arching eagerly against him, her short nails digging into his thighs as she sought to draw him in. "Not tonight, I swear."

Just in case, he gathered her wrists in one hand and pinned them to the mattress above her head. "Good." With his other hand, he guided his cock past the tight ring of muscle at her entrance and pushed himself halfway in before he had to stop and catch his breath.

"Jesus God, you have the sweetest, tightest pussy I've ever felt." Gripping her hip, he shoved himself the rest of the way inside, resting there for a minute as he struggled not to come.

"Do you have any idea," he muttered, drawing himself nearly all the way out, "how bad I wanted to fuck you the other night?" He eased himself back in, giving her a chance to get used to his size, feeling her soften and relax around him. "I've been hard like this for three days now." He ground himself deep inside her for emphasis, groaning in satisfaction as she responded with a sharp, high cry and wrapped her legs around his hips.

Unable to resist the hot pull of her cunt, he began a fast, pounding rhythm. Somewhere in the back of his brain, he realized he should slow down, that he should use a little more finesse before he completely lost control. But Taylor was unraveling beneath him. Her lips turned red as she tried to bite back her moans; the muscles in her arms stood out as she tried to free her wrists from his grip.

She likes it this way. He didn't think it was possible for him to get more aroused, but the sight of perfectly refined Taylor going crazy from his raw, lusty fucking made him swell even bigger inside her. She was so tight around him he could barely move, so wet he could see the sheen of moisture on his cock every time he pulled nearly all the way out and hammered back in. He threw his head back, grinding his teeth as he fought for control. Releasing her wrists, he hooked his elbows under Taylor's knees, pushing her thighs wide so he could go even deeper.

Her eyes were closed, lips parted as her moans increased in volume until she was practically wailing. With a harsh cry, she stiffened against him, thighs tensing as her pussy throbbed and clenched around him.

Joe came down on top of her, groaning into her mouth as he rode her through her orgasm, his own building at the base of his spine. As she arched and jerked against him, he finally let go, coming so hard he saw stars behind his closed eyelids.

She relaxed for about two seconds before stiffening up again, and this time not in a good way. Even though she hadn't moved a muscle, he could feel her pulling away. He propped himself up on his elbows, looking down into her face, but she wouldn't meet his gaze. The closed expression dropped into place, and if his dick hadn't been still semihard inside of her, he would have thought they'd just exchanged pleasantries on the street corner. Her body tensed, shifting almost infinitesimally. Any second now, she was going to make a break for it.

"I should go." Bingo. She tried to squirm out from under him, but Joe kept her pinned there with a flex of his hips. She gasped, fingers clenching involuntarily around his shoulders even as she tried to gently push him off.

"What's your hurry?" he whispered, using his weight to keep her pinned to the bed, rocking his hips against her, harder this time. Though he meant it as a tactic to keep her in place, to his shock, he felt his cock surge back to near full hardness as her swollen tissue involuntarily clenched around him. "I don't know about you, but I'm just getting started."

"I have work to do, and we really shouldn't . . ." Her protest petered out into a low groan as he moved in a slow, circular motion, grinding his pubic bone against the engorged bud of her clit.

"Come on, Taylor," he said, bending his head to trace one hard, rosy nipple with his tongue. "You don't really want to leave, and we both know it." He emphasized this last point by taking the firm little bud into his mouth, sucking hard, rolling it against his teeth. He knew he'd won when her fingers tunneled through his hair, and she surged up against his mouth.

He quickly retrieved a new condom and plunged back inside her. Her hips thrust eagerly up against him, but this time he held her still, determined to go slow and savor every stroke in a way he hadn't been able to the first, furious time.

"Please," she panted. "Faster."

"No," he said, holding himself deep as he gripped her hips, pinning them to the bed. He buried his face in her neck, breathing her scent in with deep, sucking breaths. Floral perfume

116 / Jami Alden

mingled with the aroma of aroused woman and sweaty skin, the smell of his sweat mingling with hers as he slipped and slid against her.

Her hands were everywhere, sliding down his back, tangling and pulling at his hair, cupping his ass as she tried to urge him faster, harder.

"Relax," he whispered, increasing his pace, but just barely. "I promise I'll give you what you need."

He didn't know why he was tormenting her this way, why he wouldn't give in and fuck her the way she wanted. Something about her tugged at his baser instincts, made him want to dominate her, make her cede the control she cultivated.

But Taylor had a few tricks up her sleeve, he realized as her pussy clamped down around him, kneading him like a hot, wet fist, sucking him deeper into her body, urging him to pump harder. His hips moved almost against his will, his breath hissing at the hot friction of thrust and withdrawal. He reared up onto his knees, looking down at the place they were joined. Her clit was shiny wet, peeking through the neatly trimmed patch of gold curls. He brushed his thumb over it, making her arch off the bed.

Pulling nearly all the way out, he fucked her with short, shallow strokes, his thumb flicking her hard little clit in a matching rhythm. As her orgasm bore down on her, he drove deep once more so he could feel every pulse, every flutter of her inner muscles.

His release followed hers, leaving him spent, boneless, and too weak to move.

This time she didn't seem inclined to leave immediately, which was good since he doubted he could stop her. He didn't know why it was so important to him that she stayed. He didn't even understand why the hell he was so attracted to her. But from the first moment he'd seen her, long before he'd ever spoken to her, he'd been fascinated. Mesmerized by icy beauty and lean, curvy body.

And then she'd opened her mouth, let fly with the queen bitch routine, and he'd been both irritated and amused all at once. Maybe he wanted her because she presented a challenge. He'd never had a hard time attracting women, getting them to go out with him. His relationships to date had been casual, easy, and relatively uncomplicated.

But Taylor seemed bound and determined to fight her attraction to him at every turn. He had to admit, he kind of liked throwing her off her game. She came off so cool and collected, it gave him a weird sense of power to know she couldn't fight her attraction to him, no matter what her head was telling her.

He usually gravitated toward confident, easygoing women who were comfortable in their own skin. But for all her obvious success and experience, it was clear to him that Taylor wasn't completely at ease with who she was. Somewhere under that perfect surface lurked the real Taylor, and the hellcat she let loose in the bedroom was just the tip of the iceberg.

She might have seemed like an uptight snob at first glance, but he sensed that the real woman was a lot more interesting and a lot more complex. He didn't know why, but somehow, deep in his gut, he knew he could spend a good, long time pulling back the layers until he discovered what made Taylor Flynn tick.

6

It could have been minutes or even hours later when Joe kissed her softly on the forehead and got up from the bed. Taylor rolled onto her side, feeling as though her brain was lined in wool.

"Here, put this on." A soft garment plopped onto her face. Dazedly she realized it was a T-shirt. "I'll make us some dinner." He pulled on a pair of loose gym shorts and offered her his hand.

In some vague part of her brain, she knew she should go home but couldn't for the life of her remember why. *So this is what it feels like to get your brains fucked out.* Obviously all of the blood was still between her legs, because Taylor couldn't string a coherent thought together if someone held a gun to her head. But Joe had mentioned something about dinner, and now that the edge of sexual desperation had softened, she was suddenly ravenous.

She pulled on the T-shirt and put her panties back on before following Joe downstairs. Slowly, the blood drifted back up to her brain, allowing for clearer thinking. Taylor almost wished for an extended period of idiocy, because frankly her realizations were scary.

She replayed what had just happened over in her brain, almost as though it had happened to another person. She didn't recognize the woman on the bed, grunting and moaning as Joe had driven inside her with all the finesse of a jackhammer. Her eyes followed him around the kitchen as he pulled ingredients from the refrigerator and put some sort of grill pan on the stovetop.

What in the world had happened to her? How could she have so completely lost control? Again? Saturday's incident she could chalk up to the breaking of a long dry spell. It had had nothing to do with Joe himself and everything to do with the fact that it had been a very long time since she'd had sex, and even longer since she'd experienced the delights of a man's skilled tongue between her legs.

But tonight, she had no excuse. She'd wanted Joe, wanted the taste of him in her mouth, wanted to feel his thick cock moving deep inside her. And he certainly hadn't disappointed. She'd never had sex like that in her life, never been so consumed with raw lust, eager and needy like she couldn't get enough.

Her chest got tight and her breathing shortened as she realized she had wanted this to happen all along. Her hand fisted in the loose fabric of the T-shirt, and she jumped, startled, at the sizzle of steaks as he dropped them on the grill pan. She had to get out of here, should have left earlier before he'd pinned her to the bed and heaved over her like some Neanderthal.

And she'd liked it!

She stood from her chair, but Joe, as though sensing her movement, put down his tongs and turned to catch her before she could leave the kitchen. Pulling her close, he kissed her ear, and in spite of herself, Taylor could feel the tension slowly melting from her body. "I can see you're getting yourself up a tree about something," he said, flashing her a grin that made her stomach bottom out. "We're having a good time here, Taylor. Why don't you just relax and let it happen?"

The next thing she knew, she had a glass of good red wine in her hand and she was admiring the way his back muscles gleamed under the kitchen lights. Still, she couldn't help protesting a little. "I'm not really a relax-and-let-it-happen kind of girl."

"No shit," he replied, his soft chuckle going to her head faster than the wine.

She watched him cook in appreciative silence. Funny, she'd never thought of cooking as sexy, but when Joe did it—half-naked to boot—it was practically an aphrodisiac.

"I can start the demolition work on your place tomorrow afternoon," he said, giving the steaks a quick turn and putting an entire bag of spinach into a sauté pan.

She didn't have the slightest idea what he was talking about, which must have showed on her face.

"Your landscaping project?" His grin turned wicked. "You know, the one you came over tonight to talk about before you dragged me upstairs and begged me to fuck you?"

She let out a startled laugh. "I hardly begged." She paused, thinking a minute, and conceded that maybe she had, just once. But it hardly counted. "And I think you were the one who did the dragging. But tomorrow sounds fine, if you still want to take on the project." So much for her brilliant idea of keeping her distance by making theirs a business relationship. "I mean, if it's not weird for you to sleep with one of your clients."

"I think I can keep business and pleasure separated," he said, sliding a plate full of juicy-looking steak and dark green spinach in front of her. A loaf of warm, crusty bread appeared seemingly out of nowhere, its yeasty scent filling her nostrils. Her stomach rumbled so loud it practically echoed off his ceiling.

He laughed at her blush. "As much as I'd like to indulge in more of that pleasure, I think I need to keep your strength up."

She closed her eyes at the first heavenly bite of steak, as good as any she'd had at a four-star restaurant.

"You're going to make me drag you upstairs again if you keep making that face with every bite."

She cut another bite, flicked her tongue out to catch a stray bit of juice, and laughed at the fierce light that surged in his eyes. He half rose in his chair, and she obediently popped the bite into her mouth, chewed, and swallowed properly. "Sorry. I've been living on Lean Cuisine and cocktail party fare lately."

He cut into his steak, and Taylor couldn't help but notice that his table manners were impeccable. "You look like the type who eats out a lot."

"I do," she said, tasting the spinach and nearly groaning in appreciation of its garlicky bite. "But it's usually for a meeting, and I'm always talking so much, I never get a chance to eat."

"What is it you do?"

"I'm a venture capitalist. I work up on Sand Hill Road."

"Ah." His mouth quirked in a half-smile. "I should have known."

She paused, fork halfway to her mouth. "What do you mean by that?"

"Nothing bad. But you definitely seem the type."

"How would you even know?" she asked.

"I've had several as clients," he retorted.

"Just because you've worked on their yards doesn't mean you know what they're like." She nearly winced at her snotty tone, reminiscent of a cocky thirteen-year-old. And besides, she worked hard to fit in, to portray the kind of successful, well-connected image her position required. So why was she insulted that Joe pegged her as the proud yuppie that she was? "I'm sorry, I didn't mean that the way it sounded."

He gave her a small smile that didn't reach his eyes. "You're right. Just because I do their gardens doesn't mean I know them well."

Her bite of steak turned to leather in her mouth as she struggled for something to say. He was different from any man she'd ever dated—if one could even call this a date. This was one reason she liked to date men with similar careers, men with whom she could easily discuss work-related topics. Somehow, she doubted Joe would be very interested in the trials and tribulations of taking their portfolio company down to three dollars per share for their latest round of financing, or how Taylor was recently invited to sit on the board of an up-and-coming technology company.

But he was different in other ways, too, besides having a career totally unrelated to finance or high technology. He had an easy confidence that, unlike in most men she knew, didn't seem to cross the line into unattractive arrogance. He emanated the aura of a man who was satisfied with himself, pleased with his accomplishments without being cocky. Most men she knew were eager to tell her about how they'd seen the potential for this or that company, known a particular industry sector was going to hit it big well enough ahead of time to cash in and buy the latest-model Mercedes.

But Joe, who was obviously successful, seemed to have no need to wear his accomplishments on his sleeve. She would have expected someone as young and good-looking as he was to be at least a little bit of an asshole. Then she remembered their first conversation. Right. He definitely had it in him. "What made you buy a house in this neighborhood?"

"You mean, how can someone like me afford to buy here?" His tone was mild, but she could tell he was still pissed at her earlier comment.

"That's not what I meant," she said testily, "but since you brought it up, I confess I have wondered."

"Oh, Miss Taylor, are you being so rude as to ask how much money I make?" He leaned back in his chair, crossing thick forearms over his chest.

She raised an inquisitive brow but remained silent.

"I'm fixing it to flip it," he said finally. "And I can afford to because my last house in Palo Alto increased in value by thirty percent by the time I was ready to sell. My dad went in with me on the first place, a tiny little shit hole in Mountain View. We bought it right after I left school—"

"School?" Now she was intrigued. Joe's career might not have been on her approved list, but a college degree would go a long way in making up for it. Now, if only she could do something about the four-year age difference. Her foolish pipe dreams about seriously considering Joe as boyfriend material were smashed to smithereens by his next words.

"I went to UC Berkeley for two years but dropped out after sophomore year."

"Were you failing?"

He frowned, spearing up the last bite of steak. "Not at all. It just wasn't worth my time."

Taylor knew her jaw was practically resting on the table, but she couldn't contain her shock. And dismay. In her world, education was everything. If she hadn't managed to get an academic scholarship, she would have never made it out of their trashy little trailer park. She would have ended up like her mother, killing herself trying to make enough money to care for herself, her children, and whatever loser boyfriends she collected along the way. "I can't imagine someone lucky enough to get into UC Berkeley quitting."

His brow furrowed. "I started working in landscaping in high school and knew it was what I wanted to do. All I needed were a few business management courses and some architecture classes, but after that, I thought it was unfair to waste any more of my parents' money. Helping me buy a house was a much better investment."

"But don't you want a degree to fall back on, just in case?"

"In case of what? I built my own business, and I'm doing pretty well." He gestured around his newly remodeled kitchen.

She forked the last bite of steak into her mouth. "No matter what you do, everyone benefits from a good education."

"And I say practical experience is more important, especially in my field."

"But aren't you intellectually curious? Don't you want to learn about things besides the latest mulching techniques?"

His jaw tightened and she realized she had again offended him. She didn't mean to, but it always annoyed her when people squandered great opportunities.

"Not having a bachelor's degree doesn't make me uneducated," he said, his voice sharp. He waved his hand over her head, toward the built-in bookshelves surrounding the television in the great room. "Those aren't decorative, Taylor."

She glanced behind her, unable to see the titles from this distance. Fine, so he was well read. But his reading list couldn't be used to pad a résumé.

Early on, Taylor had realized education was the only way out of her dusty, dead end town. Taylor had focused on getting the best grades and resisted the tide of boy craziness that had consumed her friends. Even in her teens she'd known that if she let herself be distracted from her goal, she'd end up like most of her friends—pregnant and working dead end, low paying jobs while fetching beer and diapers for their families.

Taylor had been bound and determined to never suffer such a fate. She'd always known she would get out. And when she did, she'd go to college, have a great career, and never settle for a man who was any less accomplished than she.

This long-held conviction only strengthened as she built her career and got her MBA from Stanford. It became clear that when she finally settled down, it would have to be with a man who was equally or more successful in his own right, a man who could navigate the social obligations her career imposed and who would be a strong partner in her professional and social life.

Essentially, everything Joe was not. *Why do you even care? It's not like you had him in mind for marriage going into this.* Unfortunately, Taylor still didn't know what she'd been hoping to achieve by sleeping with Joe. In her limited experience, casual sex with unsuitable partners—or even suitable ones—created more trouble than satisfaction. But one touch of Joe's hands and she hadn't been able to stop herself, even knowing that sleeping with him was a terrible idea. Still, there was no denying the slightly sick feeling in her belly at the realization that this really could go no further. They were destined to share a single night of hot raunchy sex, a friendly meal, but nothing more.

He took a sip of his wine, watching her over the rim of the glass. "There are a lot of ways to be successful in the world, Taylor. Not everyone follows the same path."

Easy for him to say. Obviously he came from a caring, supportive family that could afford to send him to college and give him cash for a down payment. She opened her mouth to tell him so but stopped. She didn't really want to waste any more time debating over whether a college degree was required for future success. Not when his long, thick fingers were stroking up and down the stem of his wineglass, making her shiver at the memory of them stroking against her skin.

His eyes crinkled at the corners as though he read her thoughts. He reached out and grabbed her forearm, pulling her off her chair and into his lap. He was hard again, prodding insistently against the backs of her thighs. His palm skimmed up her thigh, under her shirt, delving without preamble down the front of her panties. She moaned and shuddered, soaking his hand at the first slight brush of his fingers against her clit. "Now that we've discussed our philosophies on education, how about we shut up and move on to dessert?"

If she really was going to limit this to just one night, she might as well indulge.

7

"If you don't tell me what's going on, I'm going to pour this in your new bag." Taylor's head snapped up from her computer as Jenna plopped down into one of the leather armchairs on the other side of Taylor's desk, holding her coffee cup threateningly over Taylor's new Louis Vuitton. Jenna crossed one leg over the other and began impatiently bouncing her foot.

Calling Jenna's bluff, Taylor did her best blank look.

"Is it Steven? Did something happen with him again? Because Monday you were a little spacey, but yesterday you were fine. But now today you're all jumpy and . . ." Jenna relinquished Taylor's bag and flailed her arms around, perfectly capturing Taylor's rather spastic morning. "If it were anyone else, I wouldn't even notice, but you . . ."

She didn't have to continue. Taylor knew what she was going to say. Taylor was always perfectly composed. Taylor could pull an all-nighter in the office, shower and change in the locker room in the building's fitness center, and look like she'd had a full eight hours. Taylor could take a red-eye, spend the entire flight studying a business plan and due diligence documentation, and still negotiate killer terms without missing a beat.

Yet today, for the second time this week, Taylor was jumpy and absentminded, losing track of a task or conversation as soon as it began. And once again, it was all Joe's fault.

All because she was ferociously horny.

One would think that after last night's bedroom acrobatics, they both would be satisfied for at least a few weeks. But no. This morning, as soon as her breathing had changed, Joe had tried to put his impressive morning erection to good use. But Taylor had held him off, determined to stick with her regular routine of an early morning run before work.

"Great, I'll meet you out front in ten minutes." And there he'd been, dressed in running shorts that showed off the thick, well-defined muscles of his legs and a T-shirt that hugged the massive width of his chest. As she followed him on her usual four-mile loop around the neighboring Stanford campus, she'd been mesmerized by the flexing and rippling of his leg muscles, by the high, round firmness of his ass as his pace kept him slightly in front of her. Never had she regretted the end of a run more.

And even though the dampness of her own shorts wasn't entirely due to the run, she'd been determined to stick with her one-night plan. Last night had been a freebie, like the obscene sundae from Ghirardelli Square that she allowed herself once a year when she flew her mother out to visit. A succulent indulgence that was in no way good for her. So when Joe had pushed himself into her entryway and suggested a joint shower, Taylor had fended him off, at the time feeling very proud of her restraint.

But now she was starting to regret that decision, because all morning she'd been plagued by a tight throbbing between her thighs, an itchy restlessness that would either have to be satisfied or waited out. Taylor wasn't sure she could afford the lack of productivity that waiting it out would require.

"You're doing it again," Jenna snapped, pulling Taylor sharply from her fantasies of a soap-slicked Joe pinning her up against the wall of the shower.

"What?" Taylor asked.

"Totally spacing out. Where did you just go anyway?" She waggled her dark brows suggestively. "From the look on your face, it must be nice."

Jenna wasn't going to be put off. And truthfully, Taylor was dying to confide in someone. Normally, she would never divulge details of her love life to a coworker, but Jenna was known in the business world for being honest, discreet, and not playing politics. Taylor knew Jenna would never use any personal information against her. "You have to promise not to tell anyone."

Delight suffused Jenna's face at the realization that she was about to receive a particularly juicy tidbit. She finger-painted a cross over her chest and leaned forward in the chair as Taylor spilled, omitting most of the more intimate details.

"That's it?" Jenna had the nerve to look disappointed. "From the way you were acting, I thought maybe you were doing one of the partners."

Taylor's nose wrinkled at the thought. "Ew. Besides, they're all married."

"Doesn't stop most of them."

"But, Jenna, he's a landscaper. And now he's my landscaper."

"So you hired him to plow your yard and now he's plowing you." Jenna laughed at her own joke.

"I'm sleeping with the help. It's so tacky."

"This isn't Victorian England, Taylor, and he's hardly the 'help.' Personally, I think this is exactly what you need."

Taylor scoffed. "I don't see how that could be."

"You're always so worried about work, so worried about

dating a status symbol. Why not have a little fun with a guy who obviously knows how to push all your buttons?"

"But this can't go anywhere. Not only is he a gardener—"

"Landscaper," Jenna corrected. "He's redesigning your yard—long overdue, by the way—not dropping by once a week to blow your leaves and trim your hedges."

"Whatever," Taylor said. "He's also younger than me, probably likes to go to sports bars and pick up drunk girls. It can't go anywhere," she repeated.

"Why does everything always have to go somewhere? Why can't you live in the moment and have a little fun for once? You're right, it probably won't get serious. I doubt he wants to get involved with an uptight workaholic. But if I had a hot young guy trying to get in my pants, I'd let him until it stops being fun."

"Am I really an uptight workaholic?"

Jenna's mouth quirked in an apologetic smile. "Kinda. But that fun side you seem determined to hide shines through enough to make me like you." At Taylor's silence she said, "Why don't you let fun Taylor out to play for a little bit? Think of Joe as a guy aperitif, sent to you from above to cleanse your palate of Steven's nasty taste. You can worry about acquiring the status husband later."

"I'm already thirty-two. It's not like I have much time."

Jenna shook her head. "A couple of weeks won't kill you. Besides, I'm afraid if you don't get laid, you're going to kill this deal with Medigen. If you do that, I can't be their new CEO."

Taylor shook her head in combined amusement and frustration as Jenna left. She wished she had a little more of Jenna's pragmatism and a lot more of her confidence. Unlike Taylor, Jenna never seemed to worry about doing or saying the exact right thing, yet she was incredibly successful. But Jenna was also brilliant enough that people would forgive her any social gaffes or eccentricities. Taylor wasn't sure she could say the same.

Still, as the morning wore on, she couldn't get Jenna's words out of her head. *If I had a hot younger guy trying to get into my panties, I'd let him.* She had to admit, Jenna had a point. She couldn't remember ever having sex this good, and she probably never would again. Why not indulge, give her body a little more of what it had so clearly missed?

Inexplicably, the faces of her high school friends, holding the hands of toddlers though they were scarcely more than children themselves popped into her head. Girls who had no ambition, who had settled for the first guy who came along and fooled themselves into thinking they were in love. They'd been content to stay in their small town with their small lives, never imagining that they could be more, have more. *Be careful, Taylor. Love can trap you and keep you from getting what you deserve from life,* warned that ever-cautious voice, the one that always told her to keep her eyes on the prize, to never get distracted from her goals.

Taylor stifled it. What was she so worried about? It wasn't like she was in any danger of falling in love with Joe, so how could he possibly throw her off track? Jenna was right. After all these years of hard work and sacrifice, of always making the right choices in pursuit of success, she had the right to stop and smell the roses, if only for a moment.

She picked up the phone and buzzed her assistant. "Nina, if anyone needs me, tell them I've gone for an early lunch."

Joe swung the sledgehammer, landing it with a loud, satisfying *thwack* against the cracked concrete of Taylor's patio. If you could even call it that. Essentially a crumbling slab, it took up nearly two-thirds of her backyard, leaving the rest to be overtaken by crabgrass and dandelions. So far he'd managed to smash up about one-quarter of it, and after nearly four hours he was covered in sweat and concrete dust. The work would have gone faster with more help, but all of his crew were tied up with other clients who had tighter deadlines. Besides, he liked working alone at the beginning. It gave him time to get familiar with the space and think on what direction the design would take.

He grinned to himself as he looked around, taking in a chaise lounge, a single lawn chair, and the sad-looking plastic table that made up Taylor's outdoor seating area. Whatever he did, it definitely had to be low maintenance. He didn't understand how someone so clearly concerned with appearances would allow her yard to fall into such a dismal state. He shrugged, taking up the sledgehammer again. Her neglect was his gain, both personally and financially. There was another advantage to working slow: it gave him an excuse to hang around Taylor for a while longer.

He shouldn't need an excuse, he thought, frowning, but after this morning it looked like he'd need one. That panicked look, the same one she'd had that first night he'd made her come on his living room couch, appeared the second she'd opened her eyes. She'd been polite but clearly uncomfortable when he'd insisted on accompanying her on her morning run. Rebuffing his attempts to draw her into conversation, she'd run with a fiercely determined expression, as though the run was something to be tackled with each deliberate step.

She wasn't completely indifferent, however. When he'd kissed her in her foyer and tried to muscle her up into the shower, she'd definitely been tempted. He'd felt her nipples peaking even through the dual layers of her sports bra and T-shirt, heard the hungry little sounds in the back of her throat when he kissed her.

Taylor liked him all right, but for whatever reason she seemed determined to resist him. He whacked the concrete again, frowning as he remembered their conversation from the night before.

He was pretty sure he knew why she didn't want to get involved with him. She'd been shocked, scornful almost, of his decision to leave college. That, combined with her references to "someone like him" and "the kind of people he worked for" all added up to reconfirm what he'd known from the moment he first laid eyes on her.

Taylor was a snob. One of those women who had a very specific idea of what sorts of men she would and would not date. And men like Joe, who worked with their hands and didn't have a formal college education, were most definitely on the "not" list.

He paused to take a swig of sports drink. Though the patio was shaded, he felt like he was going to melt in the noonday heat. The real question was, why the hell was he so determined to change her mind? Joe wasn't vain, but he knew he was a good-looking guy. If Taylor wasn't interested in him, he could find plenty of women who were. But he couldn't help grinning as he thought about the way she tried so hard to keep her cool, while her blue eyes burned hot and practically ate him alive. Then there were those brief moments when she let her guard down; he caught a flash of something warm, something brilliant, that drew him in, left him feeling like he'd been sucker punched in the gut. It was crazy. Even before he'd met her, he'd been drawn to her, like she'd flipped some primitive switch inside him that instinctively knew she was perfect for him, despite all evidence to the contrary.

And then there was the sex. He closed his eyes, savoring the memory of her sliding off his lap, pulling his pants down far enough to free his cock and taking it into her mouth right there at his kitchen table. Prissy, fastidious Taylor, who looked like she would have wrinkled her nose in disgust at the thought of performing oral sex, had wrapped her plump baby-pink lips around him and licked him greedily with her tongue as though his cock was the most delicious thing she'd ever tasted. When his orgasm had hit with all its toe-curling force, she stroked him hard with her fist, sucked him deep into her throat until she'd wrung him dry of every drop of come.

Joe opened his eyes, trying to scour away the images that brought him to rock-hard, uncomfortable attention. Smashing concrete was a good way to work off sexual frustration, but in this condition he might actually do himself harm.

Then, as though he'd conjured her, Taylor emerged from the sliding-glass door off the kitchen. He rubbed his eyes, not entirely convinced that his brain wasn't plaguing him with an erotic hallucination.

Her pale, slender hands went to the buttons of her blouse, efficiently unfastening them to reveal an inch-wide swath of silky ivory skin. He swallowed hard, deciding that if this was a hallucination, he'd happily succumb to insanity. As she neared, he caught a whiff of her perfume, fresh and floral, reminding him that he was in sore need of a shower. The intrusion of reality was enough to jump-start his brain. None of this made sense. After the cold shoulder this morning, why was Taylor here, stripping in her backyard when she should be at work?

"What's going on, Taylor?" he asked bluntly. "After this morning, I expected to have to work a lot harder if I wanted to get you naked again."

Her hands faltered, the seductive curve of her mouth turned uncertain. Clearly she hadn't expected any questions. "I don't know about you, but after this morning, I found myself . . . unsatisfied." Her voice was low, husky, but he could hear the tremor of nerves underneath. There it was again, another glimpse of vulnerability that took his breath away, obliterated any questions about her motives he might have harbored.

Taylor was incredibly beautiful but obviously had—in his mind—baseless doubts about her sexual allure. He wanted to find her idiot ex-boyfriend and pound him for shaking her confidence. On the other hand, he should maybe thank him, since the idiot's rejection meant Taylor was using Joe to build up her sexual self-confidence. And Joe wasn't above being used, especially by a gorgeous woman who seemed to have an inner nympho begging to be set free. If she let him have her body, someday he might also have her heart.

Which, to his shock, was what he was really after.

Not allowing himself to dwell on that startling realization, Joe decided to play along with whatever game Taylor had in mind. "Unsatisfied?" He grinned, letting the sledgehammer drop to the ground.

She stepped closer, reaching out with one finger to snag his T-shirt and pull the hem up, exposing his stomach. "Distracted," she said, running her finger up and down his abs, which twitched and jumped as though hit with an electric current. His dick, already pressing against the fly of his jeans, surged to nearly painful hardness. Sweat that had nothing to do with the heat or physical exertion trickled down the small of his back.

"What were you thinking about?" he asked, resisting the urge to reach out and pull her blouse all the way open and bury his face between her tits. The ball was in her court. He wanted to see how far Taylor would go to get what she so obviously wanted.

She paused, biting her lip, and for a moment the confident seductress was replaced by a shy teenager. "You," she finally whispered. He cocked an encouraging eyebrow. "Naked," she said, a naughty grin appearing as she got back into her role. She moved closer, so close he could feel the heat of her skin, feel her breath against his chest as she pushed his shirt higher up his torso. Her tongue flicked out to catch a stray bead of sweat, and he groaned at the contact. Quickly he took off his shirt, flinging it somewhere in the direction of the plastic table. Taylor used one hand to exert gentle pressure to direct him, backing him slowly toward the single chaise.

He sat down, swallowing hard as she pushed her blouse open

and unfastened the front closure of her bra. Her tits spilled free, like two berry-topped mounds of cream. His mouth watered for a taste. "Taylor," he said, swallowing convulsively as she reached up under her skirt to reveal yet another garter belt—a black one this time. Jesus Christ, in all these months of watching her, he'd had no idea she was dressed like a porn star underneath her all-business attire. He reached out to her, realizing as he did so that he still wore his leather work gloves and the rest of him was covered in dirt and concrete dust. He started to stand up. "Let me get cleaned up."

She pushed him back down onto the chaise. "No, I want to do it right here, right now." She was a woman on a mission, her eyes glittering with lust and sexual power.

"But I'm filthy," he said, holding his hands up in emphasis. "I'll get you all messed up."

She licked her lips and gave him an almost evil smile. "Then I guess you better not touch me."

8

Somewhere during the short drive home, the dam holding Taylor's sex drive in check had ruptured. Every wild, lust-filled impulse she'd ever denied blazed through her, setting her on fire, filling her with a need so powerful her body nearly shook with it.

At first she was afraid that Joe, still annoyed by her cold treatment earlier that morning, would push back too hard. For a moment, all the lingering fears and insecurities threatened to overpower her desire to take him like some kind of conquering Amazon queen. But then he'd cocked his eyebrow, grinned that sexy grin that made her go all hot and throbbing inside, and she knew he was up for whatever she had in mind.

He was gorgeous, sweaty and streaked with dirt. Her primitive reaction shocked her. Taylor had always gone for "tidy" sex—with all parties showered and fresh before hitting the sheets. But she didn't want Joe like that. She wanted him covered in sweat from a hard day's work, a man's work.

"Take off your pants," she said, surprised at her own bold tone. She didn't know if it was the look in his eyes, so dark with a desire she could nearly feel, or the hard ridge of his cock, pressing so blatantly against the confines of his pants, or the fact that she'd never have to look across a boardroom table at Joe and see a knowing smirk. Whatever the reason, she was more confident, freer in her sexuality than she'd ever been. She barely knew him, and yet, on this level anyway, she trusted him more than any other man she'd ever been with.

"Well all righty, then," he said, his light tone belying the hungry look in his eye as he unlaced his work boots, unzipped his pants, and shoved them down his legs. He stood and her breath caught at the sight of him, naked and fully erect in the bright midday sun. His erection bobbed away from his flat stomach, the plump head flushed and swollen. Taylor unzipped her skirt. Catching it before it hit the ground, she stepped out of it, carefully folding it before placing it on the plastic table. She shrugged her blouse off her shoulders, goose bumps breaking out as the silk rasped against the skin of her arms. Which left her in her bra, undone in the front, her black garter belt and stockings that she'd felt silly donning earlier this morning, a bright red G-string that barely covered her mound, and her black pumps.

From the way Joe's cock flexed and bobbed, it was obvious he enjoyed the view. Taylor moved closer, and his hands reached toward her breast. "Uh-uh," she chided. "You'll get me all dirty." His jaw flexed, eyes narrowed, but he obediently clasped his hands behind his back. Reaching out, she closed her hand around his cock, stroking the thick length from root to tip. He was so big her fingers barely closed around him, and moisture pooled between her legs as she anticipated taking him deep. Leaning in, she traced the outline of his pectoral with her tongue as she pumped him with her fist.

"Kiss me," she demanded, tipping her head back as he bent his head. He was rough, demanding, thrusting his tongue deep in her mouth as he pumped against her hand. She gripped him firmly, pulling him close enough to rub the engorged head of his cock against her stomach. He moaned into her mouth, sucking on her tongue as her thumb swirled a pearly drop of precome around the head. "Taylor," he gasped, prodding insistently against her belly, "if you don't stop that and fuck me like you mean it, you're going to get a lot dirtier than you bargained for."

She released him, and Joe took the opportunity to catch his breath and tamp down the urge to bend her over the cheap plastic table. Taylor's hand reached out, and he shuddered in anticipation. Using one finger, she pushed him back toward the chaise. He happily complied, reclining on the padded lounger, dick pointing straight up like a flesh sundial.

Sun dappled her skin where it broke through the leaves, glinting off her almost silvery blond hair. He stared up at her, transfixed, still not entirely sure this wasn't all some lust-induced hallucination caused by the raging hard-on that had plagued him all morning.

If it was, he didn't want to stop it, so he lay there obediently as she dug something out of her skirt pocket. It took all his restraint not to pump his fist in triumph when, with a smirk and a small flourish, she held up a condom. She swung one long, lean leg over the chaise, providing him with a mouthwatering view of her silk-covered pussy. Her scent wafted into his nostrils, fresh perfume and musky, aroused woman. Keeping his hands clamped on the arms of the chaise, he sat up and buried his face between her legs, tongue licking against wet silk as he sought the firm bud underneath.

"Take off your panties," he whispered harshly. "I want to taste you."

She hesitated, her hands hovering over his shoulders as though to push him away. He nipped her through the silk, a gentle, light pressure of his teeth that made her startle and gasp. "Do it."

He licked his lips as her slim, pale fingers pulled the crotch aside, revealing damp blond curls and plump, slick flesh. Her pussy lips were as soft and pink as those of her mouth, swollen as though begging for his kiss. Her clit was a dark rose peak, pulsing and throbbing in the warm spring air.

His kiss was soft, loving, as tender as any he'd ever given a mouth. He savored her sweet, salty flavor, eliciting tiny moans that sent bolts of sensation directly to his cock. He could feel her climax building, feel it in the way she trembled against his face, in the way her cunt rippled around his tongue when he thrust inside.

But she pushed him away before he pushed her over the edge. "I want to come on your cock," she whispered. His gaze jumped to her face, and he saw that she was as startled as he by her frank language.

Uncertainty appeared in her eyes. Joe lay back and shot her a lusty grin, trying to put her at ease. "Then I guess you better suit me up," he said with a pointed look at the condom she held between her thumb and forefinger.

She smiled and lowered down until she sat on his thighs. Gripping him with one hand, she rolled the condom down with the other, smoothing it into place with such deliberate care Joe nearly came from the soft pressure of her hand.

Tugging the crotch of her panties fully aside, she held him in place as she guided him to the dripping entrance of her pussy. He almost lost it as he watched the thick head of his cock sink into her tight flesh. She threw her head back, tits jutting out as she sank all the way down.

She rode him hard, hands splayed against his chest to brace her as she rocked on her knees. He lifted his hips to meet her, groaning as his balls met the soft flesh of her ass with every pounding stroke. The chaise creaked under the onslaught, threatening to collapse under them, but Joe didn't care. His mind, his body, his very being was completely focused on the prissy bitch cum sex goddess riding him, this gorgeous woman, so full of contradictions, who in a few short days had touched him in ways that went so far beyond sex.

Every nerve ending in Taylor's body was alive, bursting with sensation. Every inch of skin seemed an erogenous zone as she rose and fell on the thick length of Joe's cock. Tiny details stood out in stark relief—the gold flecks in his green eyes as his gaze ran hungrily over her body; the veins and muscles bulging in his arms as he gripped the chaise almost desperately; the musky scent of their sex mingling with blooming flowers and leaves.

She spread her knees as wide as the chaise would allow, desperate to take him deeper, harder. A warm breeze wafted over her skin, making her nipples tighten to the point of pain. As though reading her thoughts, Joe raised his head and caught one tip in his mouth, sucking so hard it nearly hurt. Taylor's high, harsh cry echoed up to the trees, and she arched into his mouth.

With him sitting half-upright, her clit bumped against the firm ridge of his pubic bone with every stroke. Her climax, which had been hovering around the edges of her awareness, suddenly pulled into sharp focus. One stroke, two, and the explosion rolled through her. She stilled, holding him as deep as he could go, grinding herself against him as she wrung out every last pulse of pleasure.

"You're so fucking hot," he groaned. "Can you feel how hard you make me?" He lay back, his feet falling to the ground, using the leverage to thrust up into her still-pulsing core. His chest heaved like he'd been running hard and fast, until finally, with a groan that ripped from his chest, his cock jerked and pulsed inside her as he came.

Although Joe had done his best not to dirty her up, Taylor still required a bit of cleanup before returning to the office. Her stockings were ruined, shredded and snagged by her enthusiastic gyrations, and her panties were stretched beyond repair. No amount of powder could conceal the rosy flush in her cheeks. And the smile on her face? She didn't think anything could take that off.

Joe had followed her inside and washed his hands so he could wrap her in his arms and give her a "proper" kiss good-bye. Like anything they'd done up to then was anywhere near proper. Still, he'd cupped her face in his hands, the soft press of his lips tender, almost comforting. Unlike the carnal, ravenous encounter they'd just shared, this was a sweet caress that warmed her in a way no orgasm ever could.

By the time she'd left, he was back at work, demolishing her backyard with swings of his heavy sledgehammer. She didn't allow herself to dwell on him or what would happen going forward.

She only hoped whatever happened, it involved a lot of Joe, naked, telling her how hot she was as he made her come.

9

"I was thinking tonight we could meet up after work, maybe have dinner downtown or something," Joe said.

Taylor looked up from her paper, regarding Joe over the rim of her coffee cup. A burst of contentment coursed through her at the sight of him. And, as she'd done for the past three weeks, she nipped it in the bud, reminding herself that regardless of how great he was in bed, no matter how nice it felt to come home to his cooking every night, no matter how gorgeous he looked sitting across the breakfast table from her, sweaty and shirtless from their morning run, this thing with Joe was just temporary. A transitional, meaningless fling until she found someone she could actually get serious about.

Despite her determination to keep their relationship about nothing more than a few (hundred) orgasms between neighbors, Taylor was growing increasingly worried about her level of detachment. Which was understandable, considering that since that day several weeks ago when Taylor had attacked him like a crazed nympho in her backyard, Joe had taken on the role of the ideal boyfriend.

That evening, when she had arrived home, her phone had been ringing as she walked in the door.

"Are you coming over here or am I going over there?" he'd asked.

Her mind had swirled with all the reasons she should put him off. But when he'd said, "Never mind. You come here since I actually keep food in the house," she'd gone, muffling the voices in her head protesting that having sex with him in her backyard in broad daylight was perfectly acceptable between casual sex partners. But having dinner? That was crossing the line.

Yet Taylor had ignored the voices that night and every night since, until here she sat, sipping her morning coffee with her not-boyfriend as though they'd been together for years. And apparently Joe was ready to move their relationship beyond the confines of their respective houses.

Though she knew it was unlikely, she didn't want to chance running into one of her colleagues while out with Joe. They would take one look at him, gorgeous, younger, someone who moved in completely different social and professional circles, and think she was playing sugar mama to some hot young stud. And while she wished she could be one of those people who didn't care what others thought, right now, she couldn't afford not to. The local high-tech financing world was a small one, and she knew people gossiped. Especially about single, ambitious women like herself. She was so close to a promotion she could taste it, and the last thing she needed was to have rumors swirling around about who she was sleeping with, taking the focus off her professionalism and putting it onto her sex life.

Men in this business might be able to get away with their trophy wives and girlfriends, but Taylor had no doubt she would be mocked, especially since her recent behavior contrasted so sharply with the perfectly poised, professional image she cultivated.

"You don't need to take me out."

"Taylor, we've been seeing each other for almost a month, and we've never even made it out of the house. Let me take you on a real date for once." His tone was light, but his smile didn't quite reach his eyes.

"I'm not sure what time I'll be leaving the office, so why don't we stick to the usual routine?"

"Fine." He stood up and dumped the remainder of his coffee down the drain. "Speaking of work, I need to get going."

A not-so-subtle hint that she needed to get herself home to shower and head into the office. He stood at the sink, his back to her as he stared out the window facing her house. Tension knotted his broad shoulders. He shook his head and said almost to himself, "Are you embarrassed to be seen with me?"

She stood and wrapped her arms around his waist as guilt flooded her. "Of course not," she said, grateful he couldn't see the awful truth in her eyes. Joe was smart and perceptive. Over the past few weeks, he'd displayed a sometimes disconcerting ability to read her moods. He knew how important her professional image was to her and, though they'd never discussed it directly, had most likely inferred that he didn't exactly fit the mold of her ideal mate.

He turned and kissed her, not his usual soft peck good-bye, but a hot, wet, tongue-thrusting kiss meant to make her weak in the knees. As she showered and dressed back in her own bedroom, she wondered how something meant to be fun and casual had become so complicated.

She had no illusions of being with Joe long-term. But she couldn't deny that the past few weeks had been amazing, and not just because of the sex. It was scary how quickly they'd fallen into a steady routine. Regardless of when she got home, he either appeared on her doorstep or left a message on her voice mail telling her to get her ass over to his house as soon as she got home. On nights when she didn't have an after-work social obligation, he almost always had dinner waiting. Afterward they'd cuddle on the couch, watching movies or expressing mock disgust at reality television contestants, until one of them (usually Joe) oh so casually put a hand down the other's pants.

As she drove to the office, she marveled over how, for the first time, she knew what it was to be completely comfortable in someone's presence. She felt no pressure to impress him with her accomplishments or be on guard against saying the wrong thing. He teased her and laughed at her and called her on her bullshit, but never in a way that made her feel anything but cared for. He always seemed to be available to her, even though she never called him to make specific plans.

That was one area where she had held firm—she never called him to let him know her schedule. Though the rudeness of it chafed at her, for Taylor, double-checking plans and running her schedule by someone else implied an obligation to that person. In short, it turned a casual fling into a real relationship.

Which, she reminded herself as she settled into her office chair and pressed her computer's ON button, was not something she could have with Joe.

Somehow, she needed to find the resolve to cool things off, if not end it altogether.

Her stomach tightened at the thought.

"Who killed your puppy?" Jenna plopped down in her guest seat, coffee cup in one hand and an apple fritter as big as her head in the other.

"I don't have a puppy," Taylor replied blankly, her mind still wrestling with the suddenly abhorrent thought of ejecting Joe from her life.

"From the look on your face," Jenna said around an enormous bite of pastry, "I would have thought someone threw your puppy off a freeway overpass."

Taylor wrinkled her nose in disgust. Though thankfully, the

image of dead puppies distracted her from Joe for a few precious seconds.

"Is Lord of the Orgasm falling down on the job?"

Taylor couldn't help but laugh at Jenna's latest nickname for Joe. "Nope, everything's fine there," she lied.

"Will I get to meet him this weekend at Spellman's barbecue?"

"No," Taylor said, aghast. "Why would I bring him?"

"The invitation specifically said to bring your significant other," Jenna said slyly.

Taylor made a show of looking through her in-box. "Joe is not my significant other. Like you said, he's like my man aperitif, cleansing my palate until I'm ready to date again."

"From what I can tell, he's not only cleansed your palate, he's ruined it for anyone but him."

Taylor did her best not to show how close to home Jenna's comment hit. She tried but couldn't imagine doing the things she'd done to Joe to another man, letting another man touch her the way Joe had. She could barely remember what sex with Steven had been like. Their sex life, never anything remarkable, had faded into a vague gray blur.

In contrast, she could remember every touch of Joe's lips and fingers, every stroke of his cock inside her.

But, as she had told Joe the day she first met him, there were more important things than sex upon which to base a relationship. Good—okay, great—sex could only take them so far. The best thing to do would be to end this thing with Joe before she made the classic female blunder of mistaking great sex for true love. Because that's all there was between her and Joe, right?

Jenna plopped a bound copy of a business plan onto Taylor's desk. "Here's the idea I was telling you about. I think I've finally found my deal. Now, if you can tear your mind away from King Dong for a little bit, I want to run some numbers by you." As the entrepreneur in residence at Apex Ventures, it was Jenna's job to seek out promising technologies, develop a business plan around it, and convince Apex to fund the new venture. If successful, Jenna would become the new company's CEO.

Taylor pushed lingering thoughts of Joe out of her mind. If she helped Jenna pull off this deal, Taylor would be that much closer to making partner. All the more reason to quit wasting time mooning over Joe and put her focus back on her career, where it belonged.

Joe heaved Taylor's cheap plastic patio table into the Dumpster he'd rented. He'd completed the finishing touches on her new flagstone patio earlier today and decided he couldn't stand the sight of her sorry-assed lawn furniture in her beautiful new backyard. A brand-new teak set was scheduled to be delivered any minute, complete with a double chaise lounge. He grinned in anticipation of testing it out when Taylor got home.

Even so, he couldn't get rid of the nagging sensation that he was on borrowed time with Taylor. He'd have to be a complete idiot not to realize he was far from Taylor's ideal man. He'd never laid eyes on her ex, but he knew the exact type. A cocky exec in his late thirties, a lawyer or a venture capitalist or some other job where he made lots of money without actually making anything.

Despite all the time they'd spent together in and out of bed, he still didn't get her. Which was probably why he was still so fascinated, he thought wryly. Though he'd never really been into girls who tried to fuck with his head and played games. But that was just it—while he knew Taylor was holding herself back, emotionally if not sexually, it wasn't because she was trying to tease him or keep the mystery going. Something in her life had made her desperately afraid of making what she considered a wrong choice, and if he could only figure it out, he was sure he could break through all of her stupid hang-ups about who she should or shouldn't be dating.

He suspected it had something to do with her family. Every time he brought it up, she closed up, quickly turning the conversation back on him. He'd tried a million different ways to probe, but she never gave an inch.

Not that he was any better. So far, all he'd told her was that he had an older sister and a younger brother and that he'd grown up in the Bay Area in a comfortably middle-class family. Which was all true, though he'd left out facts he was sure Taylor would find important. Like that his sister was married to one of the most successful venture capitalists in the country, and he had no doubt Taylor had met him in the course of her career.

He'd been tempted to tell her that first day, when she was so shocked that a plebeian such as himself had known what a VC does. At the time, he'd stifled the urge, reminding himself that he didn't need to impress her with his family connections. Now he kept quiet because he wanted her to take him at face value, wanted to know that she'd fallen in love with him because of who he was and not how he could further her career.

He peeled off his gloves and tunneled his fingers through his hair, cursing himself for thinking like such a goddamn chick. But he was in unfamiliar territory, afraid he was actually in love for the first time in his adult life, but with a woman who seemed determined to keep their affair under wraps.

He wondered, not for the first time, why he was so worried about defining their relationship. He had a beautiful woman who loved fucking him and didn't care whether he bought her dinner first. A woman who didn't call him twenty times a day to consult him on how she spent every minute of her day. In the past, he would have called her the ideal woman.

But after nearly a month, Joe was more determined than ever to break down the barriers Taylor had erected between them and prove to her that while he might not be her ideal man, he was the only man for *her*.

10

Taylor breathed a sigh of relief as she pulled into her driveway and didn't see Joe's truck parked next door. Jenna pulled her black Saab in behind her as Taylor parked in her garage.

Even though Jenna knew all about Joe, Taylor wanted to avoid an awkward introduction. She could imagine it now. *Jenna, this is Joe, the guy who's been fucking my brains out for the past three weeks. Joe, this is Jenna, the only person I've told about this furtive little thing we're having.* When he called tonight, she'd explain she was having a working dinner with a colleague over at her house and that she'd be over later.

Or maybe she shouldn't. The fact that she felt she owed him an explanation was a red flag, yet another sign that she was allowing herself to get more deeply involved than she had ever intended.

"Your place looks gorgeous," Jenna exclaimed. She slammed her car door and paused to admire the freshly planted front lawn, slate walkway, and stone-lined flower beds. "Hot in bed and an artist too? If I ever get out of my condo and actually have any yard to speak of, I'm definitely hiring Joe."

Inexplicably, Taylor felt a surge of pride in Joe and his work, and couldn't help but brag. "You think this is nice, you should see the back. He completely rebuilt and redesigned the patio to look like it's part of some Tuscan villa."

As Taylor unlocked the front door, Jenna continued to ooh and ahh over little details that Taylor herself had missed, like the way Joe had alternated red and pink azaleas in the stone-lined flower beds.

"Something smells amazing," Jenna said, sniffing the air as she stepped into Taylor's foyer.

Taylor shrugged off her blazer and hung it in the front closet. "The neighbors must be barbecuing. We're going to have to do waiters on wheels, I'm afraid."

She led Jenna into the kitchen and started riffling through the stack of takeout menus next to the phone.

"Uh, Taylor, I think someone might have taken care of dinner for us."

Taylor looked up, taken aback by the downright ravenous expression on Jenna's face. "I know you said he was hot," Jenna said, drool practically dripping down her chin, "but you didn't do him justice."

Taylor turned to look where Jenna was staring out the sliding-glass doors, and even through her irritation, Taylor had to admit that the sight that greeted her was indeed drool-worthy. Joe was on her new patio wielding a spatula as something cooked on a grill she hadn't owned earlier that morning. A similarly unfamiliar teak table and chair set was laid out with plates and silverware, along with a platter of vegetables and a bowl full of salad.

"He cooks too?" Jenna sighed. "Taylor, are you sure you only want him for sex?"

Until that moment, she didn't realize she had been asking herself the exact same thing. That realization, combined with Joe's presumptuousness, galvanized her into action. "What are you doing here?" she hissed as she stepped out onto the patio, Jenna close at her heels.

"Hey." He turned with a smile so sweet and sexy it would have melted her into a puddle if she hadn't been so irritated. "I finished your patio," he said with a gesture of his spatula, "and I thought we'd christen your new grill and deck furniture."

"I didn't buy a grill," she said as tension knotted her shoulders.

"I did," he said. "And I couldn't let you ruin your beautiful new patio with that plastic crap." He deftly flipped a succulent-looking steak and reached out his hand. "I'm Joe, by the way."

Jenna practically mowed Taylor over in her haste to shake Joe's hand. "I figured," Jenna said. And *giggled*, for God's sake. "Taylor's told me *all* about you," she said with another titter.

Taylor looked at her friend in shock, wondering what annoying sorority girl had overtaken her usually level-headed friend.

"I wish I could say the same," Joe said as he turned to Taylor, an odd look in his eye, "but she doesn't tell me much."

"You'll have to add the grill and furniture to your final invoice," she said tightly.

"They were a gift, Taylor," he said softly.

Something like shame curled in her belly at the momentary flash of hurt in his eyes. "I can't accept them," she replied. His eyes narrowed and she blundered on. "I know you went to a lot of trouble, but Jenna and I have a lot of work to get done tonight, so . . ." She trailed off.

He released the spatula with a clatter. "All you had to do was call me and tell me your plans." The anger in his voice spoke of weeks of pent-up resentment, and Taylor realized he had not only noticed her refusal to make plans with him, but it had also obviously pissed him off.

"You two clearly have something to discuss." Taylor had actually forgotten her friend's presence for a moment until Jenna spoke. "Taylor, we can finish up tomorrow. There's no reason we have to finalize the draft tonight."

Taylor shook her head. "Jenna, we have so much momentum, we should really finish the business plan while it's still fresh in our minds."

Jenna glanced at Joe, admiration mixing with wariness as she took in the way his every muscle vibrated with tension. "No offense, Taylor, but somehow I think whatever momentum we had is pretty much gone." Without so much as a "see ya," Jenna made a beeline through the house, heels tapping a rapid rhythm across Taylor's kitchen floor.

Hands on her hips, she whirled to face Joe. His lips were tight, and a muscle flexed in his jaw as he clenched and unclenched his teeth. "What do you think you're doing, Joe? You can't just come over to my house and start cooking like you own the place."

He took the steak off the grill, shaking it onto the platter with such force it nearly slipped onto the ground. "I was trying to do something nice for you, Taylor. If you had other plans, you could have picked up the goddamned phone."

"You're not my keeper," she said, hating that she sounded like a petulant adolescent and hating that deep down she knew he was right.

He flipped the gas knobs off and slammed the grill's lid down so hard, Taylor was surprised it didn't break apart. "What the fuck am I, then, Taylor?" He turned to her, his stance mirroring hers. "I'd say I was your boyfriend," he continued before she could speak, "but that usually implies going out in public together, which we never seem to do."

She shook her head and looked down, the rusty color of the flagstones blurring as she blinked back tears. The hurt and justifiable anger in Joe's eyes made her want to weep, even as she knew she couldn't give him what he wanted. "Why do we have to label it?" she said lamely, not wanting to enter a discussion that would bring the end to whatever it was they had.

"Because I don't like feeling like your boy toy or your fuck buddy," he said sharply. "Especially when we could have something really great, but you're too goddamned stubborn to see it."

Maybe he's right. So what if he's not well educated and doesn't fit in with my world? He makes me happy.

For now, she reminded herself. What about later, after the sexual urgency died down? When the demands of her career required her to attend endless social functions, work late, and travel? Joe, with his nine-to-five life, would grow to resent her hectic schedule. Not to mention he would hate having to give up his evenings to accompany her to parties where he knew no one and had nothing in common with anyone.

Nothing had changed. It could never work. But Taylor wasn't ready to say good-bye just yet. So she decided to distract Joe the best way she knew how.

Joe braced himself as Taylor slid her hands up his chest, steeling himself against the flash of heat that erupted in his groin at the first brush of her fingers. "I know what you're trying to do," he said through tightly clenched teeth as he wrapped his fingers around her wrists, "and we're not finished with this discussion."

She stood on her tiptoes, leaning close until the soft weight of her breasts rested against his chest and her stomach cradled his suddenly raging hard-on. Her bullet-hard nipples peaked the thin fabric of her blouse, nudging his chest with the evidence of her need. She may have been using sex to distract him, but at least she wasn't faking it.

"Please, Joe," she whispered, her hot breath wafting against his neck, followed by a little flick of her tongue that nearly brought him to his knees. "I'm sorry I got mad at you for cooking dinner. You just caught me off guard, and it's been a really long week. I don't want to argue." Freeing her wrists from his grip, she wrapped her arms around him and slid her hands down to cup his ass, pulling him more firmly against her.

"I don't either," he breathed against her cheek, meaning it. But he also didn't want to blunder along in this relationship purgatory, endlessly trying to pin her down as he fell deeper and deeper in love.

His head snapped up. It was the first time he'd admitted it, even to himself. It made him feel a little sick as the undeniable truth hit him like a gut punch.

He must have looked a little dazed, because Taylor cupped a hand over his cheek and asked, "What?" with a concerned look on her face.

He stared down at her eyes, icy blue yet hot with passion, her hair so pale it was almost silver in the late-evening light. Her lean curves were covered by her stylish but conservative work wear. On the surface, Taylor, with her prim, tidy, ultra-professional appearance, was nothing like the kind of woman Joe had imagined himself falling in love with. She was different from every woman he'd ever dated, taking her life, her work, *herself* way too seriously. Yet over the past few weeks, he'd discovered her dry sense of humor, her sharp intelligence, not to mention her almost insatiable sex drive.

Seeing her had become the highlight of his day, the moment she would let him strip away the uber-career woman façade to reveal the funny, sexy woman underneath.

Now if he could only convince uptight, workaholic Taylor that being with a man who appreciated her funny, sexy side was worth a lot more than one who appreciated her Stanford MBA.

A wave of frustration hit him, warring with the desire that made him so easily distracted. Damn her, why wouldn't she give in, admit they were great together, and stop trying to pretend this was nothing but sex?

And damn him and his randy cock, which was rapidly drawing all the blood away from his brain until he couldn't remember what he was supposed to be pissed off about.

"Let's test out the big lounger," Taylor said, grabbing the front of his shirt in her fist and tugging him toward it.

Joe took one step forward, then stopped, wrapping his hand around Taylor's fist as something dark, something primal twisted in his gut. He was sick of waiting patiently for Taylor to come around, of being led around by his dick. "You decided you wanted to fuck instead of talk," he said, pulling her almost roughly through the sliding-glass doors. "That's fine with me, but we're going to do it my way."

11

A quiver of fear raced down Taylor's spine, followed immediately by a hot rush of moisture between her thighs. Joe was all but shoving her up the stairs, his shoulders bunched tight with tension, every muscle standing out in stark relief against the thin fabric of his T-shirt.

When they reached her bedroom, he quickly stripped off his clothes, then hers with ruthless efficiency. Once he had her naked, he pushed her down on the bed and wrapped her hands around the rails of the wrought-iron headboard. "Don't move or I'll tie you up," he said, his voice dark and commanding in way she'd never heard before. Taylor felt a tiny tremor of unease as his hot green gaze scorched a path down her naked body.

Joe was an earthy, dominant lover, a man who loved women and loved sex, and always ensured that she had as much or more fun than he did. Even though he was a big man, he was never rough, his touch incapable of bringing anything but pleasure.

But now his face was set in hard lines, his eyes stormy with desire and anger. He looked capable of anything.

He bent his head and took her mouth. It wasn't the rough, lip-mashing kiss she expected. Instead, Joe sucked first her upper, then her lower lip between his, nipping her just hard enough to send a thrill of sensation between her legs. Her fingers gripped the headboard tightly as he flicked his tongue down her neck, between her breasts, tracing a scorching path over her silky, pale flesh. His mouth closed over her nipple, sucking hard, closing his teeth over her with a pressure that stopped just this side of pain.

His fingers pinched her other nipple hard, and to her shock, Taylor's pussy clenched at the small hurt.

"You like that, don't you," he murmured, biting down again as she jumped against his mouth. This was a new side to herself, and she didn't like it.

She released the headboard and pushed at his shoulders. "Let me up."

He lifted himself off her, but instead of letting her move out from under him as she expected, he grabbed her wrists and pinned them to the pillow. "Don't make me tie you up," he warned, urging her hands back around the headboard.

Taylor swallowed heavily as her state of complete vulnerability hit her. He could do whatever he wanted to her. And she could do nothing to stop him.

His eyes softened as he looked down at her, and he leaned in for a soft kiss that couldn't help but reassure her. "I would never, ever, hurt you, Taylor," he said, and she believed him wholeheartedly, despite the fact that he still had her pinned to the bed. "You'll like everything. I promise."

"I'm not so sure about that," she snapped, "if what's happened so far is any indication."

"Oh, really?" he said, eyebrow cocked as he shifted his

weight to lie beside her. He reached his hand down to cup her mound, his middle finger dipping in to verify that she was drenched.

She opened her mouth to protest, uttering a high, startled cry as he gave her nipple another almost punishing nip. At the same time, he thrust two fingers deep inside her, and to her shock, she found herself pressing up into his mouth, urging him without words to suck her harder, to give her that little taste of pain that made her pussy shudder and ripple around his pumping fingers.

"That's what I thought," he said, the arrogance in his tone almost enough to make her try to nail him in the groin. But not quite. "See, Taylor," he said between firm sucks, "you have all kinds of ideas about things you should and shouldn't like. You need to be a little more open-minded."

She knew he wasn't merely talking about sex, but before she could analyze his comments further, his finger surged deep, making her arch off the mattress. She wanted him inside her so badly she could taste it, but she resisted the urge to release her grip on the headboard and yank him to her. Something about pretending to be helpless, allowing him to do whatever he wanted, spoke to some deep, dark part of her she hadn't even realized existed. A part that reveled in his unabashed lust and the slightly unhinged look in his eyes. From the first night with Joe, she'd felt nothing but pleasure from his touch. She wondered if it was even possible for him to go too far. As she moaned and writhed against his hands and mouth, she didn't think so.

Abruptly he withdrew his fingers, forcing a cry of protest from her throat. Ignoring her, he pulled her by the hands into a seated position, guiding her to the foot of the bed. He quickly donned a condom and moved behind her. Positioning her on her knees, he placed her hands on the wrought-iron footboard.

Her stomach clenched as she felt the tip of his cock brushing against her buttocks.

"Just relax, Taylor," he murmured, wrapping one hand around her hip as he used the other to guide his erection between her thighs.

"I don't like it this way," she protested feebly. He surged forward, and she bit back a moan as he dragged himself back and forth in her juicy slit, sliding against her clit, nudging himself against the wet folds.

"Why not?" he asked, moving his hand up to cover her breast.

"Because," she half moaned, trying to ignore the pleasure long enough to form a coherent sentence. "It's dirty, like you're an animal who doesn't even care enough to look at my face." He moved again, the thick ridge of his erection awakening every nerve ending with delicious friction. Despite her protests, she found herself leaning farther forward, tipping her ass up in an effort to entice Joe to stop all the teasing and fuck her like he meant it.

"But if I fuck you like this," he said as he worked his cock inside her, "I can watch the beautiful way your back arches." He rocked his hips, going so deep she felt him at the base of her spine. "And I can touch you like this." His middle finger drifted back and forth over her clit in perfect rhythm. Taylor moaned and arched her back, pushing against him as she sought to increase his pace. From this angle, he was huge, thick, stretching her wide as he drove impossibly deeper.

"Look at us, Taylor," he whispered against her neck before sinking his teeth into the sensitive curve. She opened her eyes, startled to realize she had an unobstructed view of them in the mirror over her dresser. Immediately she snapped her eyes shut, not wanting to acknowledge the truth she saw in her reflection, the reality of herself, the pale skin of her body flushed with desire, her lips parted as she moaned like a porn queen. "We're beautiful together," he murmured, drawing himself almost all the way out before sinking back in. "How can anything that beautiful ever be dirty?"

At his words, she opened her eyes, unable to look away, even though the primitive sexuality unnerved her. Behind her, Joe looked huge and dark, his tan body a stark contrast to her milky curves. His hand was so big it spanned the width of her belly, his shoulders and chest so broad in contrast to her narrow frame. Yet something about them together, like this, looked so right it shook her to her very core.

He urged her up, sitting on his heels so her knees straddled his thighs and her back pressed against the hair-roughened skin of his chest. Gone was the urgent, aggressive lover from before. Now Joe held himself still, buried deep inside her as he took advantage of their position to explore every smooth patch of skin he could get his hands on. He rained hot, sucking kisses on her shoulders and neck, pinched and cupped at her breasts, making them both moan as she clenched and writhed on his cock.

She became transfixed by their reflection, watching his big, hard hands move over her body with exquisite care, knowing exactly where and how to touch her to take her to the very brink of climax. Finally, unable to stand it any longer, she released her grip on his thighs and grabbed his hand, guiding it firmly between her legs. In the mirror she watched his finger press against the gleaming bud of her clit. He circled once, twice, and she was coming, pulsing and clenching around him as he drew her orgasm out.

She collapsed back against him, her head resting against his shoulder. Tipping her chin back, he took her mouth in a lusty, tongue-thrusting kiss before urging her forward. Once more she braced her hands against the footboard and tilted her hips up, open and willing to his heavy thrusts.

His hands closed over her hips as he pounded into her, his balls slapping against her ass with every stroke. To her shock, Taylor felt herself tightening around him as another climax built deep in her core. She slammed herself back against him, meeting him in a harsh counter-rhythm as she felt him swell even bigger within her. Her pussy tightened and throbbed around him as she came in a blinding wave, even more intense than before. He uttered a muffled curse as his cock pulsed and jerked inside her before he collapsed on the bed.

Wrapping his arm around her waist, he rolled them to their sides, spooning her from behind. "Told you you'd like it," he murmured sleepily.

She smiled ruefully in the fading evening light, searching her brain for an appropriately witty comeback and coming up empty-handed. "You win," was the best she could do.

Joe had won the battle, but not the war, as became evident the next morning over breakfast. "My sister's having a barbecue this Saturday," he said without preamble, "and I'd really like it if you would come with me."

Her coffee cup froze halfway to her lips, and his gut clenched as her mouth formed a tight, apologetic smile. "I can't. Our senior partner is having a party at his house, and there's no way I can miss it." *And no way would I ever choose my boy toy fuck buddy over anything work-related.* Though she didn't say it, Joe got her message loud and clear.

Still, he must have woken up with a masochistic streak this morning because he couldn't stop himself from asking, "Maybe Sunday, then, we could go out to dinner." Just to be sure he was crystal clear on what was going on, he named a restaurant that was well known as a hangout for local venture capitalists and Silicon Valley's technology elite. He didn't miss the panic that crossed Taylor's face before she blew him off with a, "Maybe. We'll see."

He left shortly thereafter, unwilling to sit across the breakfast table like some chump, pretending nothing was wrong, pretending he didn't want something more. His head was screaming at him to end it, to cut her off before he wasted any more time waiting around for whatever crumbs of affection she deigned to throw his way. And yet, there was something under that snobby, image-obsessed surface that drew him in and wouldn't let go. A funny, sexy woman who for some reason was terrified to show that side of herself to the rest of the world. Something loving and protective in him wouldn't let him give up on her, needed to show her that it was okay to let the rest of the world see the real Taylor Flynn.

He left for work that morning no closer to a decision. The only thing he was certain of was that he was damn sick of being Taylor Flynn's dirty little secret.

12

Taylor sipped her white wine and made small talk with Marc Spellman's wife, Kathleen. A pretty brunette about Taylor's age, Kathleen was busy making sure everyone felt welcome. Though the event was called a barbecue, the Spellmans had clearly spared no effort or expense. The food was beautifully catered, and the wrought-iron tables placed around the pool and on the lawn were perfectly decorated like something out of a Martha Stewart magazine. "Your house is beautiful," Taylor murmured, "and I especially love your outdoor kitchen."

"That's my brother's work," Kathleen said, unable to keep the pride from her voice as she stopped a server so Taylor could get a crab cake. "He's a genius. If you ever need any landscape design, you should talk to him."

"Taylor actually has an amazing gardener." Taylor turned to see Jenna, who hugged Kathleen like they were long-lost sisters. Suddenly, Taylor's polite handshake seemed rather cold. "You should see him work." Fortunately, the lascivious tone in Jenna's voice was lost on Kathleen.

Their conversation continued, and Taylor tried to stay engaged as Jenna asked Kathleen about her children's summer activities. But her thoughts kept wandering to Joe, wondering what he was doing right now. If he was having fun at his sister's. She tried to imagine what his family was like. Close, probably, sharing an easy camaraderie and lots of laughter. Her gaze wandered over the guests, most of whom either invested in or worked at high-tech companies. They were clumped in small groups, mostly segregated by gender. The men discussed business, latest technology trends, and which company was about to either implode or go public. Taylor knew she should make her way over to them and impress them with her charm and knowledge of the industry.

Joe never cared what she had to say about the IPO market. In fact, Joe didn't even know what company she worked at. Still, they never ran out of things to talk about, and she always got the sense that, unlike a lot of the men at this party, Joe was really listening when she spoke. Taylor was nearly overcome by the intense desire to see him to share a sunny weekend afternoon with him, to be laughing with him instead of trying to impress her colleagues and their wives with her perfect manners and business acumen.

"Hey, sis." Taylor almost thought she had conjured his voice.

"Speak of the devil, there he is now," Kathleen said, snapping Taylor out of her reverie.

She turned, and to her intense delight and horror, there was Joe. His smile faltered, then widened as he recognized her. "Taylor!"

The bottom dropped out of Taylor's stomach as Kathleen looked back and forth between them with intense curiosity. Jenna sipped her wine, eyebrows raised, lips quirked in a smile that said she couldn't wait to see how this all played out.

"You two know each other?" Kathleen asked. "How?"

I've been spent every night naked with him for the past

month. Taylor knew she needed to seize control of the situation before the truth spilled out. Joe opened his mouth to reply, but before he could speak, Taylor said, "We're neighbors. Joe, as it happens, lives right next door to me." She looked at him, pleading with her eyes for him to stay silent about the rest.

His smile remained fixed, though his eyes went flat. "There's a little more to it than that," he said, sending a bolt of panic down Taylor's spine. "I also just finished redesigning Taylor's yard and patio."

Taylor nearly wept with relief and somehow managed to say, "Yes, and he did an amazing job. Now I know why I was so impressed with your landscaping."

Joe and Kathleen quickly settled into a discussion about their family, giving each other updates on parents, siblings, nieces, and nephews, leaving Taylor and Jenna with nothing to contribute. Jenna started up a conversation with an attorney who worked closely with their firm, while Taylor awkwardly hovered on the fringes of Joe's conversation with his sister. He was clearly trying to block her out, even going so far as to position himself with his back to her. But Taylor couldn't risk leaving him alone for fear he might spill all to his sister.

Finally, Jenna physically grabbed her by the arm, whispering, "Leave them alone. I need you to help me convince Spellman to fund this new idea." Judging from Jenna's firm grip on her arm, Taylor wouldn't be able to resist without some sort of physical altercation. And that would cause a scene, which Taylor of course wanted to avoid at any cost. She allowed herself to be dragged away. When Jenna cornered Spellman, Taylor obediently nodded in agreement and uttered meaningless catchphrases at Jenna's urging.

But her attention was focused on Joe and Kathleen on the other side of the lawn. From her vantage she could barely make out their expressions and had to rely on body language. Once, she thought Joe glanced her way as he shrugged. He kissed his sister on the cheek and squeezed her around the shoulders before joining the nearest group of men in conversation.

Taylor's mind raced with panic, wondering what he had told his sister, but at the moment, four people, including Jenna, were staring at her expectantly, waiting for her to weigh in with her opinion on Jenna's proposed business model. She gave it, and excused herself to get another drink.

As she made her way to the bar, her gaze was continually drawn to Joe, who seemed to move around the crowd with enviable ease. The men laughed and joked with him, the women flirted benignly. In his button-front shirt, khaki slacks, and expensive watch, only his tanned face and perfectly honed body hinted that he wasn't just like the rest of these men.

"God, he's gorgeous," she heard a feminine voice say. "Maybe I'll hire him to do my yard. I'd have a *Desperate Housewives* moment with him, no question," said another, making Taylor's stomach clench. She wanted to turn and scream at them that Joe was more than just a pretty face and hot body. That he was smart and kind, funny and loving like no man she'd ever met. But she continued to the bar, saying none of these things, knowing if she did, they'd look on her with amused scorn before spreading the gossip like wildfire.

As she reached the bar, Joe appeared at her right and held out his own glass for a refill. "Don't worry, I didn't say anything to Kathleen. I didn't let her know you've been slumming it with your gardener." The disgust in his voice was enough to curdle her blood.

"Thank you for your discretion," she said coolly, looking around to make sure no one was listening.

He let out a scornful laugh. "Don't worry, Taylor, no one here is going to find out your dirty little secret."

Defensiveness rose within her at his tone. "What did you expect me to do, announce to your sister—my boss's wife—that I've been sleeping with her brother for nearly a month?" The bartender raised his eyebrows and backed away discreetly. "I don't want to talk about this here," she whispered through gritted teeth.

"Well, when you put it like that, it does sound pretty sordid," he said, turning to skewer her with his icy glare. "But I guess I had myself fooled that there was something more going on, that you were deep enough to stop caring about what I do and focus on who I am."

He walked in long strides across the yard, curtly nodding as people greeted him, and disappeared inside. Taylor followed at a discreet distance, slipping inside with the excuse of finding a bathroom. She looked in five rooms before finding him in what looked like a game room, complete with a pool table, widescreen television, and full-size arcade game. Joe stood staring out a window overlooking the side yard.

Taylor's throat was tight. "Joe, I'm sorry I hurt you—"

"So am I." He whirled around. "But what I'm really sorry about is that I let you hurt me. I stupidly let myself believe that there was something better underneath the surface you show the world. I convinced myself that there was someone in you worth knowing, and worth loving."

Every word poured through her like acid, and she held her hand up, but he wouldn't stop. Didn't he understand, she could never let go of the disguise? If she did, he'd see the ugliness of her past, the hopelessness she'd worked so hard to escape. He'd see that she was nothing but poor trailer trash, constantly polishing herself to keep the stains from showing.

"I told myself that the connection we had meant something, that I couldn't possibly be interested in someone so shallow."

She wrapped her arms around herself as though she could protect herself from the onslaught of pain. She'd tried to keep her roots hidden from the world, but he could see through her mask to the real Taylor, and she couldn't bear it. "Joe, please stop—"

"This whole time, I've been patient, waiting for you to open up, waiting for you to give me a chance." He stared at her, the disgust on his face nearly sending her to her knees. "You think I'm not good enough for you, Taylor. But the truth is, you're not good enough for me."

Something shriveled inside her with the knowledge that he was right.

"You have got to be the stupidest woman I've ever met." Jenna stormed into her office the following Monday. Slamming the door, she threw her arms up in exasperation. "Seriously, Taylor, you blew it. Big time."

"Did the deal fall through?" Taylor asked, trying to sound like she really cared. But since Joe had walked away on Saturday, she couldn't seem to drag her mind away from him and the awful feeling that she had made the worst mistake of her life.

Jenna's face knit into a disgusted frown. "Deal? I'm talking about Joe, and the fact that you let possibly the most perfect man in the universe slip through your fingers. No, wait, you didn't let him slip through, you practically strapped a jetpack to him and pushed him out the door."

Taylor's throat tightened and she went on attack to prevent herself from dissolving into tears. "You were the one who encouraged me to have a fling with him, to use him as my transition man before I was ready to date."

"That was before I met him," Jenna said, flinging herself into a chair.

"Just because he's gorgeous doesn't mean it could ever work," Taylor said, trying to convince herself as much as Jenna. "It never would have worked," she repeated.

"Okay, let's put looks aside. He cooks for you. He's smart too. I talked to him at the party, and he's a lot smarter than most MBAs I know." Taylor tried not squirm at her pointed look and didn't argue Jenna's point.

Tears burned the backs of her eyes as Taylor struggled to maintain control of her emotions. "He's nothing like us, nothing like me. If everyone found out—"

Jenna cut her off with a raised hand. "Taylor, I've known you for about a year now. And despite some major personality quirks, I really like you. So I'm going to tell you this for your own good." She leaned forward intently. "You care way too much about what people think of you. And people would like you a lot more if you cared a little less."

Taylor started, her preoccupation with Joe momentarily subsiding. "What do you mean? Don't people like me?" Of course she realized she wasn't best friends with everyone she worked with, but she'd always assumed she was well liked, at least on a professional level. Which, until now, was the only one she thought mattered.

"You don't let anyone get to know you, Taylor. The only thing anyone besides me knows about you is your professional track record and that Stanford MBA you mention within the first five minutes of being introduced. When I first met you, even I thought you came off as cold and potentially ruthless."

Taylor swallowed heavily at Jenna's portrayal. *Uptight bitch.* Joe's words knifed through her heart. All this time spent trying to morph herself into the perfect female executive, only to find out it was holding her back personally and professionally.

"You're so bent on showing people only what you want them to see, that people have a hard time trusting you," Jenna said softly.

Taylor stared blankly at her desk, pens and papers blurring as she blinked back tears. She didn't know how to respond to Jenna's harsh assessment of her, didn't know how to begin to explain herself. Jenna could never understand the drive to escape her past, to remake herself and her life into what Taylor considered the epitome of success. Somewhere along the way,

Taylor had convinced herself that there was only one path to success, and straying from it would result in an express ticket back to poverty in the trailer park.

"Well, thank you for your candor," Taylor said simply, proud that her voice barely quivered.

"Taylor," Jenna said beseechingly, "I'm sorry I was so harsh. I just hate to see you throw something amazing away because of some nonexistent ideal that no one else really cares about."

Taylor's shoulders slumped, and she met Jenna's sympathetic gaze. First her jaw clenched, then her lip trembled. Taylor opened her mouth to speak, only to choke on a sob. And finally, the tears she had been holding at bay since Joe had walked away from her burst out in a wave of despair of such grand proportions even Jenna looked scared.

"How do I get him back?" Taylor finally sniffled. "I've been so awful to him; he has every right to hate my guts."

Jenna rolled her eyes. "He may be mad at you, but I'm sure he doesn't hate your guts."

"He said I was shallow," Taylor said, spawning another round of sobs.

"Taylor, whatever he said, I know he loves you. And trust me, feelings like that don't just die after a few days."

Taylor honked into a tissue. "Really, you think he loves me?"

Jenna looked at her like she was an idiot. "Are you kidding? The way he looks at you? Taylor, I dream of having a man look at me like that someday."

"How does he look at me?"

"Like he's the luckiest man alive just to be in the same room with you."

As she'd been the luckiest woman alive to be with him. And she'd blown it. "I have to convince him I love him. And more than that—that I'm proud to be with him."

Jenna sat back with a satisfied smile. "I'm sure we can come up with something. The sooner you get him back, the sooner you can focus on me and the company I want to start."

Joe wiped the last bit of shaving cream off his chin, trying to muster up the necessary enthusiasm to spend tonight, Saturday, the same way he'd spent every night for the past week. Out with friends, having a few beers, playing a little pool, surveying the local single scene, trying to convince himself he didn't miss Taylor. That he didn't really love her and that he didn't feel like he'd been walking around with a giant hole in his chest where his heart used to be.

Suck it up, he told himself. *Taylor was very clear about what she thinks about you, and there are a lot of women out there who, unlike her, would be proud to be with you.*

After several nights out, though, he still didn't want any other woman. But, it had only been a week. He knew it would only be a matter of time before he found someone to catch his eye and his interest, before he forgot all about Taylor Flynn and the savage blow she'd dealt to both his heart and his pride. But so far, all the women he'd met were not quite attractive enough. Or they were too young, too immature, and too irresponsible. They giggled hysterically even though he knew they didn't really get his jokes. Compared to Taylor, they were all boring, vapid. Shallow.

Sighing, he pulled on boxers and jeans and wondered—not for the first time—if he shouldn't just stay home, regardless of what advice his friends offered. He was searching through his closet for a shirt when his doorbell rang, a full half hour before his buddy was supposed to pick him up.

But it wasn't his buddy. His mouth dropped as he opened the door to Taylor, looking as gorgeous as an old Hollywood movie star, smiling uncertainly as he schooled his face into an expressionless mask. Her pale hair was pulled back in a sleek knot. Her creamy shoulders were bare above her strapless dress, her skin pearly against the dark blue fabric of her gown. A wide belt cinched in her narrow waist, and the slightly full skirt stopped just at her knees, giving him a mouth-watering view of her legs as she teetered on lethal-looking high heels.

Somehow he summoned the will not to heave her over his shoulder and carry her up to his bed. Instead he crossed his arms forbiddingly over his chest and leaned one shoulder against the doorjamb. Striving for the coolest I-don't-give-a-fuck tone he could muster, he asked, "What do you want, Taylor?"

Her cool blue eyes raked covetously over his bare chest, and her tongue darted out to moisten her already glossy mouth. His cock thickened against his fly as he imagined her hands, her tongue tracing the same path. Blinking, she seemed to remember her purpose. She took a deep breath and said, "I owe you an apology."

A tiny kernel of hope tried to take root in his belly, but he ruthlessly squashed it, reminding himself that she thought him beneath her. He raised a discouraging eyebrow.

"You were right about me. I'm a snob. A terrible, awful, shallow snob who worried what people would think if they found out I was dating a landscaper who was younger than me. You deserve better than that, Joe. You were amazing to me, and I wouldn't give you a real chance."

She continued, words pouring out of her as she revealed the truth about her background. Living in poverty, watching her mother hook up with an endless stream of losers. She shook her head absently and said, "I realize now how stupid it was, but when I first met you, I somehow convinced myself that you were like them."

In that moment, all the layers of her perfectly constructed façade fell away. All of it—the desperation, the hopelessness, the driving need to escape and become a completely different person—was there in her eyes, in her voice.

His heart felt bruised as he fought the urge to take her in his arms, to tell her it was all okay, that he would love her no matter what.

But it pissed him off that she lumped him in with all the deadbeats from her past. Just because she was telling him the truth now didn't mean she was giving up on the ridiculous idea that the only appropriate mate for her was some kind of super yuppie. And he'd be damned if he would wait around, sniffing up her skirts while she was on the lookout for someone "better." "You thought I was like those unemployed slobs? Thanks a lot, Taylor." He pushed himself back from the door, not sure he wanted to hear the rest of what she had to say.

Her hand closed around his forearm, and even as angry as he was, he couldn't deny the jolt of heat that rushed through him at the first touch. "Wait," she said, "that's not what I meant." Removing her hand, she pressed her hand against her eyes as though to hold back tears. "I don't know what I meant. When I was growing up, I only saw one path to success, and I thought if I did everything right, if I followed all of the rules and married a man who did the same, I would never have to worry about going hungry or having people dismiss me as white trash." She rolled her eyes, blinking back tears. "And then I started spending time with you, and it felt so *good*. Not just the sex," she continued, almost as though to herself. "It was everything. For the first time in a long time I was excited to get home after work. I was excited to see you. But I was too caught up in my own bullshit to let myself think I could really have a relationship with you. I got so caught up in my idea of the right man, I didn't realize that you were the right man. For me."

He ignored the warmth that started to trickle from his heart like a slow bleed. "That's all really nice, Taylor, but I'm not interested in hanging around until you get tired of slumming it with the hired help."

Tears welled in her big blue eyes, and the uncertain tremble of her lips made him ache. He steeled himself, unwilling to give an inch, wary of opening himself up to her once again. She'd thought he was inferior, beneath her. Her less than ideal childhood was no excuse for the blow she'd dealt his pride. She'd have to go further than a simple apology to convince him to give her another chance.

"Do you want me to beg?" she said, her voice catching on a sob. "Because I will. I'll get down on my knees." She started to kneel down, then paused. "Okay, maybe not in this dress." He rolled his eyes, laughing helplessly at her innate prissiness that she couldn't suppress, even at a time like this. "Please, Joe. I know I don't deserve it, but I want another chance to show you how much you mean to me, to tell the world how lucky and proud I am to have you at my side."

He had never seen her look so vulnerable. Finally, she was letting him see the real, flawed woman underneath that perfect exterior. For the first time since he'd first laid eyes on her, she was hiding nothing, stripped bare, looking at him with her whole heart in her eyes. She reached out shaky hands and grabbed his. "Please, Joe," she implored. "I love you so much. Give me the chance to show you how much. Give me a chance to show that I'm good enough for you."

Taylor's blood froze in her veins as for several moments, Joe said nothing. This was a horrible, ridiculous idea that she and Jenna had concocted. She should have known better than to try to salvage this relationship after so brutally pummeling Joe's pride.

The frown never left his lips, but he cupped her face in his hands and closed his mouth over hers. The kiss was angry, punishing, but she could taste the mingled love and lust underneath the anger and hurt. His tongue thrust against hers, taking her, claiming her. His hands threaded through the hair at the nape of her neck, sending hairpins flying as he ruined her perfectly sleek chignon. "I love you, too, Taylor Flynn," he whispered, not sounding very happy about it. "I'm probably the world's biggest idiot, but I think I loved you from that first night when you came over. You tried so hard to keep it together, but I could see the flesh-and-blood woman trying to get out. It's taken a while, but I think I finally know who she is. And now I love her even more."

He kissed her, and in that one touch she felt all the love and lust that simmered inside. Her lips parted on a sigh, a sound of mingled joy and relief as, for the first time in a long time, Taylor felt completely at ease. Like she'd finally figured out who she was supposed to be.

The brief, discreet honk of a car horn startled her, reminding her of her excuse for showing up on Joe's doorstep.

He looked over her shoulder at the stretch limo parked in front of her house. "Got someplace to be?"

"Actually, we do—that is, if you're okay with that."

His smile took on a bemused cast as she retrieved a garment bag from where she'd draped it over the porch railing. "Every year Apex hosts a table at the Cancer Foundation benefit in San Francisco," she said.

He nodded. "My sister will be there."

"Right. As will most of the partners and their wives. I was hoping that you'd go inside, put on this tuxedo"—she held up the garment bag for emphasis—"and be my date."

"You're sure I'll be an acceptable companion?"

He was teasing, but shame speared through her as she realized that even a week ago, her answer might have been different. Clutching his hands, she said, "I will be the luckiest woman in the room."

He tugged her inside his entryway and closed the door behind them. She wasn't sure, but she thought she caught the sheen of tears in his beautiful green eyes before his lips closed over hers. It started sweet, but his kiss soon turned lusty after a week of being apart. She eagerly sucked his tongue into her mouth, and her hands swept greedily up and down the bare, silky skin of his back.

"I don't suppose we can skip this thing," he groaned. "I know how hypocritical this is going to sound after all the hell I gave you, but I really want you all to myself tonight."

"We'll leave right after dessert, I promise."

He went upstairs while Taylor repaired her hairdo.

Five minutes later, he was holding her hand to help her into the limo she'd hired to take them to the city. Determined to stay on good behavior for now, she sat on the bench seat opposite him. At the benefit, he ignored his sister's confused reaction as he arrived with Taylor. As she watched him confidently move from one conversation to the next, charming both men and women, Taylor again marveled at her own stupidity in thinking he would never fit into her world.

She watched him greet Jenna, who hugged him enthusiastically and gave Taylor a thumbs-up behind his back. Jenna leaned up and whispered something in his ear that made him laugh and nod vigorously in response.

"What did she say to you?" Taylor asked as they sat down to dinner.

"She wants to know if I have any friends I can hook her up with," he said, eyes gleaming with satisfaction. "Says she's tired of all these boring business types and wants a real man."

Under the table, Taylor slid her hand up his hard, muscled thigh and settled her hand over the rapidly growing bulge at his crotch. "Can't say I blame her."

Deliberately casual, Joe slid his hand over her knee, up her skirt. Hot color crept over his collar as his fingers traced the lacy tops of her thigh-high stockings. He nearly choked on a bite of steak when he discovered she wasn't wearing any underwear.

"We just have to make it through dessert," she whispered, as eager to escape as he.

She'd barely swallowed a mouthful of chocolate mousse cake before he all but carried her out of the ballroom. Taylor had no illusions that people didn't know what they were up to, but for once in her life, she really didn't care what anyone thought.

Once he'd loaded her into the limo, Joe wasted no time in raising the privacy partition. He pulled her into his lap and shoved her skirt up around her waist as she frantically unfastened his tuxedo pants. She was already drenched from wanting him. As soon as he rolled on the condom, she sank down on his cock, her moan mingling with his as he kissed her. Cupping his face in her hands, she sucked at his lips and tongue, tears rolling down her face at the exquisite perfection at having him inside her again. And to think she had come so close to never sharing this with him again. "I love you," she whispered, rising and falling on his thick erection as she tried to convey everything she felt with every move, every caress.

Studs sprayed here and there as she pulled his shirt open, needing to feel his skin. His hands tangled in her hair, pulling it awry as he held her still for the probing thrust of his tongue. His hips thrust up as he ground himself deep inside her. "I missed you so much," he murmured.

Even though it had only been a week, their bodies reacted as though coming out of a months-long sexual drought. A few more strokes, and Taylor was shuddering around him as Joe held her hips still to meet his final, frantic thrusts.

When they arrived home shortly after, Taylor gave the driver points for his seeming obliviousness to her now-Medusa-like hairdo and the red whisker burns that decorated her chin, throat, and upper chest. Joe walked her to her door, but before she could step inside, he scooped her up in his arms and carried her in.

"What are you doing?"

"Practicing." At her confused frown he said, "Carrying you. Over the threshold."

Rock Solid

Bonnie Edwards

1

His cell phone rang and vibrated, burning a hole through his dream. Shit, it was a good one, too, all heat and womanly body parts. Jake MacKay slid his cell phone out from under his pillow and flipped it open.

"Wazza matter?" Anyone who called at four A.M. had to have an emergency. Dread clenched his gut.

"Jake MacKay?" A woman's voice ghosted through the line, husky and feminine. Not his father. He sucked in a relieved breath, while his mind went muzzy.

"I'm sorry, did I wake you?" Her voice, honey velvet and hollow, stroked through his chest and down to his cock, curling around his shaft with a heat he strained toward. His body woke while his mind headed back toward sleep.

Half dreaming, half wakeful, he stretched out on his back to let the voice play him.

Rock hard, he closed his eyes. Pulled up the pictures from the dream he'd been having. The kind of dream that made his balls ache. Images and sensations flashed back to life as the voice stroked and pumped his shaft.

He knew the voice, had heard it all night long as the dreams had come in waves, rushing and receding. Crashing into him and carrying him along on crests of release.

"Who is this?" He tried to pull his mind to wakefulness, but the dark of predawn stayed with him. The woman's voice soothed in his ear, but the words didn't make sense. Insistent energy gathered in his sac, rolled up to his belly, hovered, then dropped to his cock again.

The phone slipped from his hand, forgotten, while the voice murmured inside his head.

A whole night of dreams. He was seeing more action than he'd had in months. *Make that years.*

"I need your help," the woman said smoothly, clearly. "My house needs your expert care."

"House?" He bit back a moan as his cock flexed once. Twice. He pulled his control back into place, tried to rouse, but his brain was addled and his cock was in charge. "Where are you calling from?"

"I'm in Fremont. It's part of Seattle these days."

"How did you get my name? I'm in Florida." Every word pulled against the tide of dreams.

"You were recommended, Jake." The way she said his name spiked his arousal, tweaked it, played it. So hot. The voice was heated honey, ravishing with sensuality. "Word is, you have the touch. And I need a man with just the right touch." The word *touch* sent a shiver through to his spine. "And only the best will do. And you're the best, Jake, the very best."

Her heat around his shaft tightened, squeezed, released, pumped. He moaned with more flexes. Could a man dream this kind of sensation? It felt like a blow job without a mouth to go with it.

Reining himself in, fighting for control against the mind-numbing need she created, he ground out, "I don't travel for work. Call someone closer to you."

"No one here has the touch. Not the way you do, Jake," she purred in a voice that conjured more stimulation. He groaned. "It's you I need." Pump, pump. Slide up, slide down.

Intense. A kaleidoscope of color rolled behind his eyes. He groaned and finally allowed a heated release with outrageous come to the end.

With the last of his spasms came a clearer head, but he still couldn't rouse himself to full wakefulness. He tried, but something blanketed his thoughts, made them heavy and slow. "I can't leave the jobs I already have. I'm not the kind of man to leave clients in a lurch." *I can't leave my father.* He *wouldn't* leave his father. Not now. The old man wasn't ready to be alone.

"I know," she soothed, all warmth and understanding. He wasn't sure if she agreed that he couldn't leave his clients or if she meant he wouldn't leave his father.

Either way, his mind eased, worry drifting away.

"You're rock solid, Mr. MacKay. That's one of the reasons I'm calling you."

Even though he'd dropped the phone, he expected to say good luck and so long, but she went on. "I wish there was something more I could do to entice you."

His cock filled again, insistent and throbbing.

"Your father will understand; he'll want you to take this job." *He'll take care of the clients, see the jobs through while you're gone.*

The thought wasn't his own. But it was certainly in his head. He struggled to get control of his mind, but she was still there. The voice in the predawn dark held him in thrall.

Entranced, all he could do was listen.

Something of the responsible man he was stirred in him. Rebelled and tried to rise. Jake never dumped his work on the old man. Especially not now. Jed MacKay needed his son at home, taking care of business. Jake never let anyone down.

"But your father always encouraged his sons to follow their

hearts, did he not?" Her whisper came warm and cozy in his ear. The heat on his cock intensified.

"If you know my father, then you know he's had a rough time. He needs me here more than I need a job in Seattle." The sucking on his cock started again, and he thought he heard a sigh of satisfaction and arousal.

This time he even felt wet heat on his straining shaft. Wet heat and suction.

A tickle of air blew across his balls, and he shut his eyes, letting hot licks of desire settle in the small of his back. He arched into the seeking wet heat and fell back into the dream.

"You really need to come to Perdition, Mr. MacKay. And you will."

For two more hours, Jake MacKay had the wildest dreams he'd ever had. Sex and seduction, push and pull, man to woman. He saw himself fall, grasping a woman he'd never seen before, his arms on fire as he held her, loved her. A burning touch seared every part of him connected to her. He broke into a sweat he barely acknowledged.

When he woke up at six A.M., he was freezing cold while his blood boiled with a need to follow the voice.

Straight to perdition.

By six-fifteen he was on the phone booking a flight to Sea-Tac Airport.

By seven, he was showered, dressed, and had the coffee on. He reached for a mug off the rack he kept beside the machine and caught the time. Made a rapid calculation of the time difference between Miami and Seattle.

Who the hell called for a carpenter's estimate at one A.M.? No one he'd ever heard from. Until last night. Odd, though, he could barely remember what she sounded like. Although she had seemed acquainted with his father and, more importantly, how Jed MacKay had raised his sons.

He hit number one on his speed dial, and his father answered on the second ring.

"Got a call last night from Seattle. You know a woman named Grantham?" He thought that was the name she'd given him, but it was fuzzy now.

"No, got a first name?"

"I can't recall. It'll come to me later."

"Grantham," his father repeated. "No. Don't know anyone by that name. Why?"

"She's got a Victorian mansion in Seattle she wants me to take a look at. Calls it Perdition House."

"That's great, son. When you leaving?" No questions about why he'd go that far. No doubt that he'd want the job. That was Jed MacKay.

His father was so set on his sons' happiness and success that he even refused to fault Jake's brother, Jared, for his useless decision to drift aimlessly around the Caribbean on his charter boat, the *SandJack*. So now, it was nothing for Jed to encourage a cross-country trip just to do an estimate.

Jake frowned because this was exactly the way the woman had said the conversation would go.

"I've booked the first flight out. Remember, we've got the Jameson place to start today, the Mitchell's renovation to finish, and three quotes to do this weekend alone." He couldn't offend Jed by asking if he was up to handling all of it, because in spite of everything his father had been through, he was one helluva contractor.

"I'll take care of everything," Jed assured him. "At least go look at it. Talk to the woman," he said with a ring of impatience in his tone.

His father was so damn proud of Jake and his reputation that he'd do anything to promote more business. The impatience cut him, though. Jed had been chafing at Jake's hovering presence lately, and his father's next words proved it.

"Go. And, Jake? Cut loose a bit while you're there."

The idea of cutting loose held more than a little sway. Maybe if he hadn't been living like a monk for the past three years, he wouldn't have succumbed to the woman's voice and influence so easily.

Shoving aside guilt that was deep as a new foundation, he caved. "I'll see you Tuesday at the latest. Hold down the fort."

"No problem, son. Have a nice flight and a good time."

His father hung up before Jake could protest.

Free.

He was free for the first time in three years.

He called the number for Perdition House he'd already memorized and spoke to a Faye Grantham to arrange a time for a meeting.

"Mr. MacKay? You're calling about restoring Perdition?" She seemed surprised to hear from him so quickly.

"Yes, we spoke earlier?" She didn't sound anything like the voice he remembered.

"Earlier than this? Oh, hold on, please." Her tone was brisk, kind of pissed off, even. But then, it was still only four-thirty her time.

He heard her muffle the phone.

After a moment, she came back on the line. "You were talking with my aunt Belle; she's a night owl." He heard exasperation, and a lick of doubt crawled up his back.

"I've already booked my flight." He wasn't normally impulsive, but today was proving to be a day full of change.

"Of course you have, Mr. MacKay," she said, sounding amused. The exasperation must've been for her aunt. "I'll see you when you arrive. You don't have to worry about a hotel. There's plenty of room here. It might be helpful to get a feel for the place by sleeping in it."

"Great."

Next, he called Jared on the *SandJack*. "Hey, bro, I've got to be out of town for a few days. Can you fly in?"

"Where you off to?"

He explained about Perdition House and the way their father jumped in to cover for him. But he didn't say a thing about the odd voice and the odder dreams.

"Does Dad need my help?" Jared asked. "I'll be there if he does, but to tell you the truth, Jake, I've got a business started. I was planning on letting you know next time you and Dad decided to fly in."

They managed to get together for some deep-sea fishing whenever business allowed. Jake and Jed flew in to hang out with Jared three or four times a year.

Finally! A business. No more drifting aimlessly. He'd been worried about Jared. Damned inconvenient to have a change of heart just when Jake needed him here, though. "What kind of business?"

"Honeymoon charters. Business has taken off. I'm booked solid."

Jake blew out a breath. "Glad to hear it." At least he hadn't turned pirate, although he looked like one these days.

The line went silent for a long moment.

"It's been three years, Jake." Jared's voice roughened. "I think it's time we let him be alone."

He bit back a retort. Bristling at Jared was always useless.

Their father may not fault Jared for drifting for three years, but Jake did. He didn't know how Jared could be so irresponsible when their father needed them both. "If you won't be here for him, then at least check in."

The voice from the night drifted through his mind, clouding his thoughts. *Your brother needs this time alone and apart, just as much as you need to spend time with your father. Jared has the touch, too, and he'll learn to accept it just as you will.*

"Dad'll be pissed, but I'll check." Jared chuckled. "And, Jake, see if you can get laid while you're out there. You need to lighten up."

Lexa Creighton surveyed her appointment schedule with satisfaction. This spring was way better than last. Business had picked up considerably since she'd done the Proctor's garden. Mrs. Proctor was giving her great word of mouth.

Still, as good as things were, she was thrilled to get a call from Faye Grantham at Perdition House. The mansion's grounds were the perfect setting for the heritage gardens she loved to create.

Working with heritage plants like hollyhock and American Pillar roses gave her a sense of continuity. What was once long gone was revived in the cottage gardens and formal Victorian designs she loved most. Thankfully, home owners were beginning to agree with her.

She drove up to the mansion's front gate for her initial appointment, climbed out of her pickup truck, and pushed at the wrought-iron gate. It swung inward silently and easily.

The driveway was lined with thirty-foot weeping cedars on each side. They hadn't been pruned in years, and the boughs touched in the center of the narrow unpaved drive.

No way would she leave the boughs like this. They were overgrown to the point of hiding the rest of the property; she could work her ass off to produce an incredible garden, and no one would ever see it.

To Lexa's mind, the point of landscape design was to highlight a house and add to curb appeal. No one would want their home hidden behind eighty-year-old hedges.

Luckily she hadn't yet been able to invest in a new truck, so it wouldn't matter if she poked the nose of her old one through the boughs. New scratches would hardly be noticed on top of all the old ones.

She inched her way through the gates. In an optical illusion, the trees seemed to sway open to let the truck pass. She slammed to a halt. Blinked. No, the boughs were still there, covering the drive.

She rolled forward again. The illusion continued. She could swear the boughs separated just ahead of the truck hood, then closed up again behind her.

Freaky weird.

As was a sudden stab of sexual arousal. It was so intense she shifted in her seat as heat crawled under her skin, down to her belly, up to her breasts, along her neck, behind her ears. Heat and want and need that she hadn't felt in too long flowed through her veins, right out to her fingertips. Spicy and delicious, she closed her eyes to enjoy the deeply moving sensation. She flexed her fingers around the hard smooth steering wheel, felt the firmness warm in her palms.

She blossomed with moisture. Her labia plumped, her clit rose, juices flowed down her channel.

Welcome to Perdition House. Maybe the family legend was true. Maybe the place really was haunted by salacious ghosts.

Maybe the very walls were imbued with sexual memory. The gardens too.

At this point she didn't much care; the feelings were so intensely delicious, all she could do was ride them out. She rolled her head back on the headrest as her fingers skimmed her crotch. She hadn't felt an urge like this in months. Maybe it was time to see to some neglected business.

Closing her eyes, she touched and teased. No one could see, as the boughs surrounded the truck front and back.

She couldn't recall her last date. Sex? She remembered vowing to have it sometime this year. Yeah, oh, that was good. Her fingers rubbed harder, lining the seam of her denim shorts along her clit.

Her breathing picked up, becoming deep and shallow at the

same time that she panted and rubbed. Her hips rolled toward her hand, legs splayed as she worked her pussy.

She moaned, needing more than her own hand, needing stronger fingers, a bristly chin . . . a man.

Oh, yes! A man—that was exactly what she needed. Breathing harder, deeper, she continued to reach for her pleasure.

2

A sound crashed through her own heaving breaths, and Lexa opened her eyes. Startled by more rustling and footfalls, she slid her hand away from her crotch to her thigh, where it warmed her flesh.

Her pussy wept and pulsed with the denial of her need. Her cheeks heated as she saw movement in her driver's side mirror.

"Hello, need some help?" A man walked alongside her truck and looked in her open window. His gaze, mere inches from hers, was electric blue, like the hottest flame, and surprise filled his eyes.

"Ah, no." *Yes, do me, do me now.* She licked her lips, fought back the urge to place her palms on his cheeks to drag his mouth in for a kiss. Tasting a mouth like his would be heaven. Thin, straight lips that twitched into a lopsided smile at her startled face drew her toward the stranger. "No, I don't need any help. Why?"

She glanced down his body.

Hot.

Hard.

Built.

His blue eyes were killer, set against black eyelashes and thick curly hair.

Oh, man, the guy had *delicious* written all over him. Mouth watering, she felt invisible fingers pluck and pull on her nipples, distending them. She crossed her arms, then decided what the hell, let him look. Her vow to have sex this year rang through her mind. If this guy was involved, she'd get her wish today.

"Looks like your truck's dead." He set down an oak-colored leather duffel bag and walked toward the truck hood.

She hadn't been aware of turning off the engine, but obviously she had. She leaned out the window. "No, really, the truck's fine. I was just thinking."

"In the driveway?" A quizzical arch of his eyebrow made her think of pirates and booty and, oh, dear God, rapacious lust.

"Yes, it's a good place to gather first impressions." She was so turned on she could barely concentrate. She pulled her mind back to the conversation. "I'm here to discuss a project with the home owner."

She poked her head out the window to watch his ass as he bent over to grab the handles of his duffel bag.

The man was hot with a capital *H*. Low-riding jeans, tight, hard butt. Fabulous arms, strong and muscular.

He read the sign on the side of the truck. "Creighton Landscape and Design." She knew she needed new lettering. Needed a new truck, too, but all that would come with time—by the end of the summer, if business continued the way it had been going.

He turned to survey the green wall of cedars and scratched his head. "I can't see a thing but green. That's my first impression, but then I'm not a landscaper."

And I can't see a thing but you. "My point exactly. These

cedars are overgrown. But I like them. And I'm a landscape designer," she corrected.

He turned and the gleam in his eye said he knew exactly what she'd been up to, landscape designer or no. Ridiculous to think that a woman would stop on the way to an important meeting for a moment of self-pleasure. Where would he get such an idea?

But the tent in his jeans said he was in the same state of need that she was.

Interesting. Must be the ghosts of Perdition, because it couldn't be from first sight of her. She looked like shit this afternoon. No makeup, her hair was tied back with an elastic band she'd pulled off a stack of mail, and her shorts were cutoffs that were nearly worn through.

But she had good breasts, if she did say so herself. To make certain he noticed, she stretched her arm along the back of the seat. Her high round breasts perked up and out when she gave a slight stretch.

And like every red-blooded male she'd ever known, he noticed.

"I'm Jake MacKay," he said with a brisk step back to the truck window. He stuck his hand inside, offering it in greeting. His fingers extended toward her taut left nipple.

She clasped his hand, gave it a brisk shake. An arc of electrical charge snapped from where they touched and went up her arm and into her heart. She slammed back against the seat, and he jumped away from the truck.

"What the hell?" he said. He shook his hand several times, then rubbed his arm from wrist to shoulder, finally smoothing his square palm across his chest over his heart.

"Wow! You felt it too?" Her heart thudded while her whole arm sparked. She flexed the fingers of her right hand. They felt okay now, but her arm still buzzed. "Wow!" she repeated. "I've never had that happen before, have you?"

He stared hard at her, like a drowning man reaching for a life preserver. "No, never."

"I'm Lexa Creighton," she managed. "Are you staying at the house?"

Jake MacKay, electric man. Apparently close to stunned by the charge they'd sparked in each other. He was still staring at her as if she'd done something outrageous like cut out his heart.

Eventually, he pulled himself together and glanced down at his bag. "I'm here until Tuesday. Giving an estimate on the interior of the mansion. I specialize in restoration."

"Want a lift? I'm not sure how long this driveway is; could be quite a walk." The odd buzz still ran under her skin, but at least it didn't hurt anymore.

She watched him cross in front of the truck while she started the engine. He climbed in beside her, careful to put the duffel bag between them. She glanced at it and smiled. "Good idea. Whatever that spark was, we don't need another one."

He snorted. "You can say that again. It snapped like a live wire."

"Hot, though," she said as she put the truck into gear.

"Very," he agreed, but the glint in his eye was anything but agreeable.

Lexa and Jake got their first look at the mansion as she followed the circular drive to the veranda. She parked and they both leaned forward to peer out the windshield, straight up the front wall.

Three stories of Victorian splendor stared back down at them. "Faded glory," she said.

"But great bones."

She glanced at him and caught him looking back.

Heat sparked between them. She covered it by opening her door and climbing out. He followed suit and got out on his side.

He stood with his hands on his hips and surveyed more of the grounds. "She's got acres here."

"And they all need work," she said with glee.

He nodded. "For a long time. Got a big crew?"

She shook her head.

"Just you and your husband or boyfriend?"

She gave him the once-over, not that she needed to—she just liked the view. "Jake MacKay, are you asking if I'm available?"

He moved so that he stood directly in front of her. She came up to his shoulder, so there was nowhere else to look but up into his expressive face. "I wouldn't want to have to break a man's heart."

She laughed. "Because you're going to steal me away?" She chuckled again but thought better of touching his chest. She was none too sure that zip and zing was gone. "And what? You don't care if you break a woman's heart?"

"I wouldn't do that." His expression heated, and she had the distinct impression those jeans of his were tented again.

"Right," she said, not looking south of his massive shoulders. Carpenter's shoulders, used to heavy work; carpenter's hands, dexterous and knowledgeable; and a carpenter's head for angles and design. This guy was the whole package. "You don't break hearts."

"Never yours." He grinned. "I'm glad you understand me."

She tried not to roll her eyes but failed. She needed to get the conversation to safer ground. Sex with Jake MacKay was one fabulous idea, but having her heart involved was dangerous. She had no time for *involved.* Her business held her captive, and she loved it. Time for ground rules.

"I'm taking Creighton Landscape and Design in a new direction, and the season has taken off for me. The business sucks up all my time." In other words, don't expect more than a good lay.

196 / Bonnie Edwards

Curious to see more of the gardens, she turned toward the far side of the house and followed a weed-choked brick path around the veranda, confident he'd follow.

Around the corner, she could see what was once a vegetable garden. "Here's where they got their fresh produce."

"I don't see anything but raspberry canes."

She pointed out the old vegetable beds, lined up and squared off with the same brick used for the walkway, crumbling into dust but still visible. Raspberry canes had overgrown the patch.

Trees encroached on the lawns.

His heat burned up her back as he loomed behind her. He was a big square man and made her feel small and very wanted. Temptation rose from her lowest belly in response. She glanced over her shoulder and saw him slide his gaze down her back.

He liked what he saw.

He wanted what he saw.

And she wanted him back. She tilted her backside infinitesimally toward him, then swept her gaze up to his to make sure the action registered.

It did.

"Are you staying at the house?" His tone said he hoped so.

"I haven't been invited. I live in Bellingham, though. It's a fair drive."

"Who called you in?"

"A Ms. Grantham."

"Faye?"

She straightened and turned fully toward him. "I don't exactly recall the first name. I was half-asleep at the time." More than half-asleep—she'd been pulled from a wildy erotic dream. A dream that started up again as soon as she answered the phone.

Odder than odd.

"What was her voice like?"

"Hot." She wanted to bite off her tongue. "I didn't mean,

you know, that I found her hot." She eased closer to his chest. She dropped her voice to an intimate, confidential level. "I'm not into women."

"I am," he said, as if she hadn't seen his interest. "Tight, athletically built women turn me on." He let his gaze trickle down from her eyes to her perked nipples to her trim waist and her too-short cutoffs.

She bloomed all over again.

"Women with burnished brown hair, wide smiles, and intelligence and wit."

She felt her cheeks go hot at his description. The man was a turn-on, no doubt about it.

His gaze pulled at her. She wanted to fall into him.

"And I love a man in a tool belt," she said, all warm and ready. "All that leather, the tools, the large belt buckles."

His hearty surprised laugh boomed out across the grounds. "I didn't know women noticed belt buckles. I always think the weight of the tools make my jeans droop and turn me into butt-crack man when I bend over. I hate that."

She smiled. "You'd be surprised what women like. And, no, you shouldn't worry about being butt-crack man." She let her gaze slide down from his broad shoulders to his hard flat belly. "You don't have the build for it." Invisible bands of desire tugged between them. She leaned closer. He took a step toward her.

"Hello!" A call came from the corner of the veranda. A woman leaned over the railing, waving at them.

They turned as one to face her.

"What year is this?" Jake asked while he waved pleasantly back to her.

"According to what she's wearing, nineteen fifty-something."

"Does she look like—?"

"A blond bombshell? Yeah. Wow." Lexa smiled and waved at the woman. They matched pace as they walked toward the veranda. Jake's shoulders took up most of the brick pathway, but it was his scent that called to her. She hadn't noticed before, but he smelled fresh and crisp. Clean and healthy. Virile.

Oh, yum.

His jaw was just showing some afternoon bristles. They were still short enough to scratch, but in a few hours, they'd be silkier, easier on her tender flesh.

Where the hell was her mind? And her control? She was about to make a first impression on Perdition's owner, and all she could think about was getting down and dirty with Jake MacKay.

3

"You must be Lexa Creighton and Jake MacKay." Even the woman's lipstick color was Marilyn Monroe red. A shoulder-length cloud of platinum-blond waves wafted like silken ribbons around her face.

"That would be us," Jake confirmed.

She turned her wide blue gaze to Lexa. "Your great-grandparents met and fell in love at Perdition House." Her smile turned private as if at a personal memory. "I'm Faye Grantham."

Her voice warmed in welcome, but it was not the voice Lexa remembered from the late-night call.

Jake was first to clasp her hand in a firm handshake. Lexa watched closely but saw no zap or electrical jolt at their contact. It was a normal, gentle clasping of hands. Perfunctory, even. No more eye contact than you'd give any stranger. Feminine pleasure spiked through her. Jake's interest was focused on her, in spite of the blond's rare beauty.

Lexa offered up her own hand, smiled, and released, pleased with what she'd seen so far.

"Please, come in," Faye offered with a wave up to the veranda. "I have coffee and warm muffins in the kitchen."

Jake's fingertips cupped Lexa's elbow as she grasped the railing of the veranda stairs. Another burn sizzled straight to her heart from where he touched. He dropped her elbow a second after contact, but the sparklers continued. He flexed his fingers.

"Did you feel that one too?" she whispered. Apparently his zing was reserved for her. Even more pleased, she climbed the four steps to the top.

At his worried nod, she smiled. "Now it's your turn to see what you've got to work with here, so stop frowning. It's going well so far," she said in a whisper just for him.

They followed Faye through the front door.

Lexa took a breath and stepped inside.

Perdition House. "The house of family legend." She released her breath and took it all in. "It's so grand!"

A double-wide staircase rose to a square landing, then turned to the second story. The next floor up had an open hallway that looked over the entrance. Several rooms opened off the hall, like an old hotel.

She could just make out a second set of stairs that led to the third floor. "Are there rooms up there too?" she asked.

"My private suite. It used to be Belle's, the original madame of Perdition."

"Madame? So the family stories are true?" Annie Creighton, Lexa's great-grandma, had been a prostitute.

Faye turned and smiled gently. "I'm aware of the stories, but your great-grandmother didn't work here as one of the girls."

"No? The family just assumed the whole story about her parading around as a boy was a cover-up."

Faye laughed. "As sweet as Annie was, she wasn't as polished as Belle wanted her girls to be. Besides, it suited everyone's purpose to have Andy, the name Annie used as a man, work on the building. She had to pretend to be a man to learn what she needed for building and design. She was beautiful when she cleaned up." Faye eyed Lexa critically. "Yes, quite a beauty. Much like you, she was athletic and toned, with fine elegant features."

The inspection continued for a moment. "Yes, you look like her around the cheekbones and eyes. You have prettier hair, though. Annie kept hers too short."

"You must have a ton of pictures of her. You talk as if you know her."

"Do I?" With that, the mistress of Perdition turned and walked into the dining room, dismissing the subject of Annie/Andy.

But Lexa, fascinated as always by the great-grandmother she'd always felt a kinship with, refused to let the matter drop. "I'd love to see whatever photos you have," she said. "There's something about Annie and Matthew's story that fascinates me."

Faye seemed more interested in showing off the dining room. But she went to a sideboard and opened a lower drawer. She brought out a small black photo album. "Here, study them at your leisure. I'm sure Annie would be pleased to know you're so keen to learn more about her."

"Thank you." Lexa took the album and opened it to the first photo. It was a studio portrait, very formal, of Annie and Matthew. Typical of the times, she was sitting, with Matthew standing at her shoulder. There was a tilt to her head that spoke of energy held in check, as if she was impatient to move and get on with her day. Lexa smiled, aware of countless times she'd felt the same way. Her days were normally so full, she couldn't afford to sit for even as long as this photo had taken.

Another connection to an ancestor whose genes she carried. Was workaholicism passed down through generations? "I can see where we look related. Even in this straight, long-waisted dress, she has curves like mine."

Faye glanced at the photo. "I believe you inherited more than just the physical from Annie and Matthew. You have their drive, ambition, and work ethic too."

"I was just thinking the same thing." The smile they shared warmed. Faye could be a friend, not just a client. "I'd like to look at the rest of these later, if you don't mind."

"Of course. I believe this is the only formal photo. The rest are of picnics, dances, and family occasions here at Perdition."

Jake listened to the female chatter with half an ear. His arm still buzzed and sparked from touching Lexa. It had happened twice now, and it scared the hell out of him.

Once he could dismiss. But twice? His belly sank.

All he could think of was what his mother had told him when he was a kid. His gut puckered in memory.

He'd asked his mother if he could marry his kindergarten teacher when he grew up. She'd said no and explained the curse of the MacKay men.

Although, now that he thought of it, his mother had called it a blessing. At five, the idea of love at first touch seemed completely logical. Just the way his Transformers toys were logical. If a robot could change into a truck with a gun turret, then why couldn't the touch of a pretty girl turn him into a husband?

It wasn't until he was in his teens that he thought of it as a curse. As he tried to get into the pants of every girl in high school, he was terrified that one of them would catch him with an electrical charge that, once applied, would never let go.

An electrical charge like the one he shared with Lexa. He wondered if he should call the old man, just to be sure.

He couldn't call Jared. His brother would laugh his ass off. He'd never believed in the curse and had married a woman he thought would suit him. No zip, no zing, nothing but like minds, he'd said.

That had been a disaster.

Maybe Jared should have waited for the burn and snap of love at first touch. If he had, perhaps he wouldn't have divorced three years into a marriage. Perhaps Jared wouldn't be drifting through the Caribbean on the *SandJack*. Perhaps his brother would've shared the responsibility of keeping their old man sane after their mother's accident.

Maybe having this burn and snap was the blessing his mother always claimed. Ignoring it hadn't done a damn thing for Jared.

And Jake always learned from his brother's mistakes.

He looked keenly at Lexa one more time. His heart swelled at the sweet expression of awe he saw in her eyes. Perdition House was impressive, and she couldn't hide her reaction. He wondered if she'd show the same kind of open honest response when he touched her in passion.

He got hard just thinking about it.

He shook the buzz out of his palm, then rubbed his arm to his elbow to displace the lasting spark.

Shit, he was in trouble. Impossible trouble. An image of his father flashed through his mind, but before he could grab on to it long enough to anchor himself, remind himself of his responsibilities, a whiff of Lexa's scent destroyed his concentration.

He ran his fingers through his hair, across his chin, trying to recall what he'd just been worrying about. But the thought was gone, swept away by her scent.

A movement caught his eye. Both women stared at him, obviously waiting for some kind of response.

Faye—blond, wide-eyed, and dressed in a quirky ode to the fifties movie queens—looked hot but amused by his confusion. The woman oozed sex through every pore, and she'd be impossible to resist, if not for Lexa and the power of the curse.

A damned inconvenient curse. But then, he'd never heard of a convenient one.

Lexa, beside Faye, was short, dark, and inspiring. Inspiring him to fantasies of lifting her to his lap and bouncing her on his cock. Her wet depths could suck the life and heart right out of him.

And from somewhere deep in his chest, he understood that was exactly what he wanted from her.

Oh, shit.

He was doomed.

A certain humor in Faye's expression told Jake she understood he was busy inside his own head. She took pity on him and covered his lapse of attention. "We can discuss the condition of the wainscoting later, after you've seen the rest of the house." She turned and led the way through a heavy swinging door.

He'd missed a whole discussion about the dining room walls while he'd been swallowed up by worry about his damn curse.

Lexa gave him a curious glance, then followed Faye through the door into the kitchen. He caught a whiff of the muffins and coffee Faye had mentioned earlier. His stomach growled.

The filler airlines called *food* was long gone.

Faye poured coffee and popped muffins out of a pan while Lexa stared out the kitchen door at the side yard, giving him time to think.

Just because he understood and accepted his curse didn't mean Lexa would. He couldn't explain it to her either. That kind of thing tended to make smart women run like hell in the opposite direction, and Lexa looked plenty smart.

What woman would believe in the curse of love at first touch? And accept that it had happened to *her*?

Aside from the problem of making her believe in the curse's existence, he understood all too well the demands of a new business. He would never ask Lexa to walk away from everything she'd worked for. She'd lit up like a light standard when she'd been looking at the old vegetable patch. She was obviously itching to get her hands dirty and bring her talents to the property.

Besides, the little he knew of gardens told him that transplanting her knowledge to Florida would be impossible. Every bit of practical knowledge she had would be useless there. His gut twisted. No, he couldn't ask her to sacrifice years of work.

He forced his ragged thoughts away and tried to focus on

the real world again. The muffins oozed berries and smelled rich and homey. The coffee was strong and delicious. The first sip tasted like heaven. "Thanks, I needed the caffeine, and the muffins hit the spot." He took a second, because he knew one wouldn't hold him.

Faye looked pleased. "I love a man with appetites."

Lexa looked amused. "I like a man who shoots sparks." They locked glances while he chewed the rest of his muffin.

To avoid steaming up the room with their sizzling looks, he walked around the kitchen.

A quick estimate of size set it at forty by twenty or so feet. An industrial-kitchen-length island sported hanging copper pots overhead. They were huge and obviously well used, although dusty. He noted a cobweb or three stringing between a frying pan and a large colander.

The cabinets were aged pine, with white enamel knobs on the doors. The knobs all had spider-vein cracks, giving away their age. Decades of use had taken their toll on the kitchen, but the wood was in great shape.

"This house has great bones," he repeated.

Lexa smiled and nodded, remembering his previous comment.

Faye gave him an enigmatic glance. "I like it," she said. "The house is old and large and probably drafty in the winter, but she's mine. The old girl deserves to shine again, don't you think?"

"Yes, she does," he said, dazzled by the enthusiasm he read in Lexa's expression. She was wildly turned on by the prospect of working on the house's gardens, while he was turned on by working on *her*. He shook his head to clear it.

Faye smiled at Lexa. "I hope you don't mind sharing a bathroom? The house was finished in 1911, so at the time, one bathroom for two bedrooms was the epitome of luxury."

Lexa flashed him a look hot enough to scorch. "No problem, Faye. We'll share. I didn't think I'd be staying the weekend. I need to go home to get some things for overnight."

"I have all the clothes you'll need. I own a vintage clothing store in Fremont. We specialize in Hollywood castoffs." She waved a hand down the front of her outfit. "I'm wearing Jane Russell's blouse and Betty Grable's shorts. I'm guessing something of Sophia Loren's would do for you. Your coloring's similar to hers. Being blond, I don't often wear clothes from my Sophia collection. The red she wore wasn't right for me."

Lexa blushed an intriguing pink. "I don't think I could fill out one of her blouses."

Jake clicked his tongue. "Sophia Loren? You'll look great—better, in fact." His mind was already on the possibilities presented by a shared bath and memories of the hot and sexy Sophia in a soaking wet blouse.

"If you spend the weekend here," Faye said, "you'll come to understand the house and its needs. It makes sense to have my interior restoration coincide with the new landscape design. The house and grounds should flow one to the other, don't you think?" She lifted one corner of her mouth in a private smile. "Like people in a pure fire attraction, the outdoors should draw people out while the indoors should pull them in. In and out, push . . . and . . . pull."

Lexa and Jake nodded as one. She shifted closer to him. The delicate heat from her arm seared the skin of his. Her scent wafted to him, and he felt a rage of desire flow from his chest to his cock.

Faye looked pleased by their ready agreement to stay the weekend. "We've just opened a new location for TimeStop, and I'll be at the store most of the time. I'm sorry I won't be around much, but you'll have free use of the house. I hope you make the most of your time here and enjoy the place as much as I do." Her eyes sparkled with humor. The private smile had turned into a full-blown private joke.

Thing was, Jake thought it must be at his and Lexa's expense.

"Great, I'll give you a full report of what I see needs to be done," Lexa said.

"Fine. I'll be sure to be home on Sunday evening."

"I'm looking forward to digging around out there to see what plants were original to the garden."

Jake nodded agreement. "You'll have my estimate then too."

"Your rooms are ready, and the kitchen's well stocked, as is the liquor cabinet in the front parlor. Enjoy yourselves and the house. Perdition has a lot of interesting stories to tell, but don't be surprised if you hear things; the house is old and drafty sometimes. In spite of that, it's a pleasure living here. I hope you make the most of it." The way she said the word *pleasure* put thoughts of hot dirty sex into his mind.

Lexa's glance was eager and feverish. All he wanted was Faye out of here so he could have Lexa to himself.

Faye chuckled while her eyes cooled to appraising. "I see you understand me, Mr. MacKay. I believe my aunt was right. You do have the touch."

With that, she nodded and left them. The door was still swinging at her exit when a steady, thrumming throb began in his cock. The hair at the back of his neck rose, and a chill filled the room.

The creak from the hinges died away, leaving the room silent and strangely expectant.

Lexa licked her lips. "Ah, why do I feel we've just been left the keys to Paradise?"

"And that there's more going on in this house than Faye Grantham will admit." He ran a fingertip from her shoulder to her wrist, tracking her warm flesh in a heated tracery. Sparks flowed from his fingertip to her muscles in a caress of promise. "I think the key to Paradise is in this snap and crackle we feel when I touch you."

She closed her eyes and leaned her head toward the side he stroked, like a luxuriating cat. "I can feel the heat, but it doesn't hurt now," she said.

Her nipples beaded, and the sight made his mouth water.

Would they be creamy in his mouth or ripe and tangy against his tongue? Did her skin heat and flush quickly, or was she a cooler breed, slow to rouse? With those hot glances and luscious lips, he bet she was quick off the mark, ready for anything. Her hips flared to perfection, and he wanted, needed, his hands on her soon.

"It feels good," he said. "You feel good."

She opened her eyes, and he read acceptance in them. "Let's have a look around first," she suggested.

The word *first* made need pulse through his body so fast he had to shift his weight from foot to foot to keep from grabbing her.

This was not the way he operated. When he met a woman he wanted, his normal procedure was to talk, get to know her, find out enough to satisfy his curiosity about her before jumping her bones.

But this was different. Lexa was no ordinary woman. She was *the woman*.

The one.

His.

He was already halfway to acceptance, and it scared the shit out of him. Lexa walked through the swinging door with a glance over her shoulder that sent fresh heat roaring through him. His head spun with the onslaught, and he had no choice but to follow.

Do her. Here. In the dining room. She wants it hard and fast on the table.

He shook the wild thought out of his head.

Lexa hesitated by the head of the table and trailed her fingers over the fine china place setting. Elegant and refined, the table was set for two at this end. Their hostess wouldn't be joining them for dinner.

They really did have the keys to Paradise.

4

Lexa's nipples were so hard, her soft cotton bra felt scratchy and too hot against the tender nubs. The china pattern at her fingertips was older than any she'd ever seen, the cut crystal water goblets elegant. Too elegant to sweep off the table so she could offer her body to Jake.

Offer herself? Here? On the table? It was nothing but a crazy hot impulse she refused to act on. But the refusal cost her in nerves.

The idea of sex on the table took hold and sent a gush of moisture to her panties. Warm, so warm. She fanned herself with the photo album, but all it created was hot fluttering air.

"We should walk through the downstairs first," she suggested, trying like hell not to think about what might happen when they got to the parlor. The breakable china had stopped her from making a fool of herself in here, but she figured a sofa or love seat would be impossible to resist.

"There's that word again."

"What word?"

"*First.* You say it as if it's a foregone conclusion we'll be doing something after we look around." The look he gave her burned through her clothing. "What is it you think we'll be doing afterward?"

Heat bloomed in her chest, then crept up to her cheeks. She didn't normally blush, but now she wondered if she sounded like some skank who took sex for granted.

She shuddered at the idea of stretching out, naked, opening her legs and letting him do whatever came to his mind. Or hers. And since her mind didn't seem to be under her control right now, that meant any damn thing imaginable.

Not trusting herself to speak, deciding his question didn't deserve an answer because he knew damn well what she was thinking about, she didn't reply.

Instead, she walked on unwieldy legs around the dining table and through the front hall past the staircase. The front parlor was jam-packed with heavy Victorian furniture. In the crowded room, every tabletop was filled with figurines or a lamp. Lace doilies covered most surfaces. Taking in the decor gave her a chance to dispel enough of her arousal so that she could think again. She found an empty spot on a marble-topped drinks table and set down the photo album, reminding herself to find it later.

She'd been fantasizing about giving herself to a total stranger, a man she knew nothing about, for pity's sake. While the thrill of the fantasy might call to her, she was still a practical kind of gal. Even in her flights of fancy, she needed to know more about him than just what she saw. Yanking her good sense back into place, she asked, "Where are you from, Jake?"

"Florida."

"That's a long way away." A very long way. Too far to think about, really. Whatever happened between them would be here and now only. There wouldn't be a next week or a next month. Just this weekend.

A weekend in Perdition. Suddenly the flight of fancy took

an easier path. Jake would have to be crazy to expect more than this weekend.

Hallelujah!

The man in question focused on her face as if he could read her joy at his answer. "We don't see many real Victorians in Miami. Most of the restoration work I do is on Streamline Moderne." His lips turned down at the corners.

"Don't like that era?"

He smoothed a palm down the dark wainscoting. "Not as interesting as this." His hand, broad with square-tipped fingers, fit him, and the sight of the stroke of his hand on the burnished wood brought a new fire.

"If you haven't worked on a lot of Victorians, then why did they call you?" Her area of expertise was perfect for Perdition House's gardens, so calling on her made sense.

He shrugged. "No idea. Maybe they got my name from someone, but if they told me, I can't recall. Both Faye and the woman on the phone mentioned I have the touch." He looked at his hands, flexed those long strong fingers that could wreak havoc along her nerve endings.

"Maybe it's got something to do with the burning sensation I get when you touch me?"

He faced her straight on, and something in his face stilled and went serious. His gaze caressed her face, and she wanted to close her eyes, tilt her mouth up, and beg for a kiss. He stepped close. "The burn's all yours, Lexa. I've never felt it with anyone else before."

She nodded. "Me neither. It's kind of scary." She paused, crazy with delight at the idea that this was a private, intimate sensation they shared only with each other. "Don't get me wrong," she said when he looked surprised. "It excites me too. I like it," she confessed so he'd know she wanted more of the sizzle and crackle.

"I'm glad." He looked happily satisfied with her answer.

"So, tell me, if you were to find yourself in a completely different climate, different soil, seasons, and so on, would you be able to transfer your skills? The way a carpenter can? Building is building, after all."

"Good design doesn't change. It's much like architecture. What works here will work anywhere as far as layout goes. And soil composition is highly erratic. You can have heavy clay in spots and light soil in others, even in the same garden."

He nodded. "Sounds technical." He frowned.

She could go into more explanation, but he obviously wasn't a gardener, and boring him to death was a surefire way to kill his interest.

In the wide bow window, Boston ferns in heavy oak stands stood next to a window seat covered in plush purple velvet. A gold tassel hung beside thick red velvet drapes.

On an impish impulse, she tugged the bell pull. A distant chime came from the kitchen. "They used this to call the maids for help or food."

An ornately carved fireplace mantel filled with knickknacks and bric-a-brac provided a focal point on the far wall.

"Faye's aunt said she insisted on the best of everything. I guess that meant service too. This place is like a living museum."

Jake wandered over to the fireplace to inspect the mantel. "This solid cherry is in immaculate condition." He muttered a soft curse and stared hard at the carvings. "I've never seen anything like it. Come over here and take a look." His glance brought fever to a whole new level.

She hurried over to where he stood in shock.

Carved into the cherrywood were naked sultry women sucking the hugely erect cocks of well-muscled men, while the men had their faces buried in pussy. The head-to-tail trail of people started at the floor and continued up each side to meet in the middle of the top cross beam. "Often you'll see cherubs or horses and hunting dogs carved into mantels, but this is unique," he said, his voice a hot, hollow shadow of its usual vibrancy.

She moved in closer for a better look. "Wow, am I crazy or does it look like they're writhing in sexual ecstasy?"

She blinked but the moving illusion continued—the men's cocks strained toward the slightly orgasmic faces of the women, while women moved their hips in demand for more tongue, more pressure, deeper cunnilingus. The whole mantel was as hot as anything she'd seen in a porn flick.

He leaned in close, the heat from his body sending her own into the stratosphere. She pulled her cotton shirt away from her chest to let cooler air flow around her.

A pulse of sexual energy beat in her pussy, then moved up, increasing in tempo until it reached her chest. She tilted her head back, closed her eyes, and let the pounding beat surge around her heart in a throbbing rhythm. She set her feet apart, dazzled by the sheer sexuality racing up from her depths. Needing help to stay upright, she braced her hands on the mantel, cupping the faces of two of the women giving head. Magnificent, sensually delightful head.

"God, you're hot," Jake said in her ear.

"Yes, hot," she whispered as the orgasms careening through the carved women roiled inside her. She rode out one, then the other as she moaned and rolled her hips in supplication.

Her lips parted, and he took the hint with a rapacious growl that sparked a fire inside.

Jake took her lips in a kiss that seared from her mouth to her spine and down to her tailbone. Mouth against mouth, she writhed with need and desire. She wound her arms around his neck to hold him tight and close and let him eat at her lips, taking and holding and increasing her need for him.

With each hot swipe, sparkly heat vibrated between them, and she lost her hold on reality.

Primed by a force of sexually heightened awareness, Lexa gave Jake all he sought in the kiss. Heat burned and coiled deep in her belly, melting and puddling into her panties. His palms molded her backside and tugged her close and hard into his erection.

And erect he was. Hard as iron. She squirmed against his hips, pushing her softer flesh toward the heat she needed so desperately. *In. In. In. InInInInIn,* she pleaded silently, echoing a voice she heard only in her head.

"In," she said between ravening kisses. "I need you inside."

She pulled at his shirt, dragging it out of his jeans. Her hands found heaven when she palmed his belly, then moved up to his lower ribs. Hair! Oh, she loved a man with hair on his chest. She skimmed her hands up to cup his pecs. She tweaked his nipples between her thumb and forefinger, then tugged. She rolled her thumbs across them, delighting in his response.

"I want inside, too, but I didn't bring condoms."

She groaned. "I don't have any either. Aren't we just Mr. and Mrs. Responsible," she said in a quickened breath. "Suggestions?"

Jake moaned and slid an exploratory finger up the right leg of her shorts. "We'll manage without them," he ground out.

Trails of heat followed each light stroke of his finger. Without a thought to stopping, she widened her stance and bore down, seeking his fiery touch on her sodden panties.

He found her, wet and straining with need. He slid the wet cotton away from her clit while she silently egged him on for more. Her clit was a plump full packet of screaming nerve endings that pulsed until he pressed a finger, hard and fast against the throb. She took the press and roll from his thumb into herself and held it, hard and tight inside while she allowed pleasure to roll in liquid waves up from her deepest belly. She rolled her hips and pushed toward the pad of flesh he used against her.

She loved what he was doing, loved it and embraced every

aching slide of his thumb. While it bathed her in pleasure, it also served to create more need.

Her belly clenched low and hard as she rode his thumb, until she cried out, unable to hold back from confessing. "Fuck me, Jake," she panted against his mouth. Her belly collapsed in on itself in a writhing bundle of desire.

"You're so wet, and hot," Jake growled in a low burr that rumbled from the delicate, receptive flesh behind her ear down to her hips.

"I'm burning up." She wrapped one leg around his hip and pressed as close as she could while his hand continued its exquisite explorations from her clit to her inner lips, which opened in need. But he didn't press in.

"Scorch me, then. I need your fire."

She bucked and rolled against him, while her mouth sought his; her fingers pulled and tugged on his nipples, and she danced on the knife edge of orgasm.

Finally, finally, she felt the tip of his finger penetrate lightly. She rocked and bore down, seeking more of him. Needing. Needing. Needing.

Up, up, up she went until she could go no higher. The world tilted, and she fell off the edge, gushing moisture into his palm as she came and crashed against him, a safe haven in the storm of her flying apart.

Jake lifted her so Lexa could ride his hips while he carried her out of the parlor. He got as far as the staircase before her nibbles and kisses made him falter. Whatever the hell was going on with this curse of his, he was up for it. He'd never been so hard, so hot, so ready.

He'd never had a woman shatter in his hand the way Lexa had. He'd barely touched her and she shuddered and shook and cried out in her release. She'd drenched him with her creamy hot juices, the scent of her making him wild.

His cock was on fire, full and so ripe he could hardly walk.

She wrapped both legs around his hips, and his cock strained for entrance. She nipped the skin of his neck between her even white teeth, and he lost all thought. He'd never make it to a bed. Between the sparks that flew from his body into hers and the images that invaded his mind, he felt like one big firecracker ready to explode. "I have to have you now. Here," he demanded, and set her down on the fourth stair.

"Yes," she replied, reaching for his belt buckle. She undid the clasp, then started on his fly.

"Careful. I'm so hard, there's no room to unzip."

She laughed and grinned, her eyes a hot swirl of need and salacious delight.

"Sounds delicious," she said on a breath of deep, hot desire. Her legs were splayed open, so he could see the wet spot on her crotch where she'd gushed with her come.

He'd never seen anything so arousing. "Get your shorts off."

He took over the work on his fly, taking care not to catch his burgeoning cock on the teeth of the zipper. He eased his jeans down, then kicked off his shoes. By the time he got naked from the waist down, she was too.

5

"You're beautiful," Jake whispered, hardly able to breathe through the hard pounding lust that gripped him.

Lexa spread wide to let him look his fill, and for a long moment, all he registered was the thick slide of juices that filled her delicate slash of deep pink flesh. Her clitoris peeked out of her hood, firm and in need again.

He set a fingertip into the slick heat of her, and she blossomed open, exposing the base of her pearl and her deepest, darkest flesh.

He pressed his finger inside, up to the last knuckle.

She reached out for his cock and wrapped her delicate hand around the base. The pressure from her palm and fingers on his shaft nearly blew his head off. Lexa squeezed drops of pre-cum from his head while he barely controlled his urge to buck. She slicked the moisture around the head while he plunged his finger in and out of her juiciness.

He slid his finger out and ran his tongue along it, tasting her salty sweet inner moisture. Fresh and hot, her cream enticed his mouth and nose. Nectar.

"So sweet," he said. Her eyes flared as she watched him lick her wetness from his hand.

She tossed her head back to rest on the next stair, and he knelt crosswise so he could see her pussy up close. So lovely and pink, musky with need. His cock throbbed at the sight of his rough finger sliding in and out of the delicate, clinging slash between her legs. The slick pull of her inner muscles as he slid a second finger into her drove him wild, but he needed to see more before he took her over the edge again.

A third finger went in while he pressed his thumb to her straining clit.

She jerked harder on his cock in response. Her belly quivered and she moaned encouragement.

"Yes! Yes, do that, but lick me too. Eat me, Jake. I need your mouth." She released his cock so he could move between her legs.

Settling in, he chuckled and nuzzled her with his nose, lips, and tongue. He nipped the inside of her knee with his teeth. She crooned when he licked the spot he'd nipped, then slid his tongue higher. He found the hollow crease between her pussy and her thigh and licked her there.

When she whimpered, he drove his tongue deep between her inner lips. He flicked his tongue against her while she rose as high as she could to press her pussy to his mouth, but he held off giving her what she craved.

If he truly was cursed with love at first touch, then he had to do everything in his power to make her want him just as much. Even if it killed him.

So he left her clit out of the equation.

For now.

"Do you want to come now, Lexa? Do you need to come?"

"Yes," she panted, arching toward him. He pressed the pad of his thumb hard against her full, rubbery clit. His mouth watered as her scent rose to him. He'd never come across a sweeter arousal, a wetter pussy, or a meatier clit. She was a marvel of aroused flesh and needy woman.

He couldn't resist one more question. "Do you want to feel my tongue deep inside again or are my fingers better?" With that, he pressed all three fingers in hard, then tried to spread them open, stretching her. He set his tongue to her clit and sucked gently, rolling the nub with the tip.

She grunted and sighed and pleaded for release. He tongued her clit with a long, wet stroke as she cried out on a flood of juice. The slick sound of his fingers plunging in and out of her made his cock flex once. Twice.

He removed his fingers in a quick jerk and buried his tongue inside before her lips could close. He'd never been so deep. He felt the flavorful burst of juices on his tongue and speared into her, tasting and lapping as he worked her into insanity.

He felt the inner contractions almost before she did as she rose to another orgasmic release.

He allowed her to ride it out to completion and held her gently as she sagged against his mouth when she finished.

"Mmm, your turn," she muttered with a greedy edge.

Thank God.

He rolled to lie back on the stairs, offering his cock like a flagpole. The stairs at his back softened to comfortable support as he watched Lexa strip off her T-shirt and bra. Her breasts bounced fluidly as she found her position on the floor in front of the stairs, settling between his knees.

Her lascivious expression aroused him even more. Her gaze went carnal as she set her elbows on his knees. "My turn to torture you," she said with a grin that made his cock throb in anticipation. His belly tightened as he felt the rake of her nails along the inside of both thighs.

He wasn't sure what his little vixen had in mind. "I want you to open wide and slide that luscious dripping pussy down my cock to the hilt. I want to be so far up inside that I'm banging on the door to your heart."

"No condom."

"Shit, you're right. Then I want to be so far down your throat I'm banging on the door to your heart."

"Either way, you'll be inside."

The roar in his head from that idea stalled his heart. He didn't think it would start again.

She centered home and clasped his sac in all ten fingers. The squeeze, when it finally came, was exquisite. "Do that again and I'll spurt in your face."

"Mustn't have that now," she murmured. "Not before I get a taste."

She closed her eyes and dropped her head to his dick, her hair swirling and heating the flesh of his belly. He ran his hand through her hair to hold it out of the way so he could watch. Her wicked pink tongue peeped out and touched the tip of his penis. The single eye wept a tear of pre-cum, and she lapped it up, making a show of savoring the flavor. "Mmm, as delicious as I expected."

Her eyes opened and took on a dreamy quality as she tilted her head and opened her lips to lick his sac. She drew it into her mouth, hot and wet. He moaned with the intense tightening of his scrotum as she laved and suckled his balls one at a time.

"Work it," he moaned with a shudder that ran from his ass to the back of his head.

"That's all I do is work. I'd forgotten how much fun this is. I love giving head." She grinned. "I've missed giving head."

"Good. You can make up for lost time."

She settled more comfortably and continued her ministrations for a lifetime of agony and teasing. Her eyes glazed with desire as she nibbled and sucked and licked at his tight hard sac.

He threw his head back against the stair the way she had, desperate to hold on. His dick flexed and jerked with each sucking stroke of her tongue. "Take the shaft! All of it," he demanded.

"It's about time you spoke up. I've never seen such control," she responded lightly.

She rose to place her lips on the tip of his head, and in one long, deep slide dropped her mouth to the base of his cock, taking him in full to the hilt. He felt the back of her throat open to accommodate his girth and groaned aloud at the slick, hot sensation of her mouth.

The small of his back tightened into a knot as a climax built to a roar. His thoughts whirled as she rode his cock with her mouth. She swirled her tongue around him until he spurted, full out, into her mouth. She moaned and lapped and took all of his offering.

The head of his cock burst with a full shot of semen as he rose off the stairs and came.

No sooner had his cock stopped spurting than she climbed up his body to ease her pussy to his face for more tongue. Boneless and unable to move, he obliged her, letting her ride his mouth to another glorious orgasm on his face.

She rattled and shook around him, her thighs quivering as she pressed her delicious cunt to his mouth and lips. His tongue pierced her slit, and her juices burst across his taste buds, familiar and hot.

"Sorry, I enjoyed sucking your cock so much, I got horny again. Had to have some more," she said as she climbed off and stretched out across the stairs above him with a soft sigh of complete satisfaction.

"We need to get some rubbers. I'm not going a whole weekend without fucking you."

She chuckled. "I wouldn't let you. We'll make a run to the store together." She sighed, and he felt as sated as she sounded.

"Wow, look at that ceiling!"

He followed her gaze and did a double take. A mural above

them depicted exactly what they'd just done on the staircase. He blinked because the circus performers depicted in the mural appeared to move and arch and sway as if in the throes of orgasm.

"Maybe this house is bewitched."

"No, it's haunted by the ghosts of the hookers who worked here."

He turned to look at her, fully expecting to see a hint of humor in her eyes. There was none. She was serious. "Haunted? Forgive me if it'll take more than great sex to convince me," he said.

She rose to an elbow and looked down her nose at him. "Honest. It's a family legend. My great-grandparents met here when the house was a brothel. We thought Annie was a hooker, but according to Faye, she just worked here as a carpenter's helper during the construction of the house itself and then a couple of additions. Her husband, Matthew Creighton, was the architect builder for the conservatory. Which is out front on the right corner of the house. I guess you weren't paying attention when Faye and I talked about Annie earlier."

"So, what you're saying is, the hookers are having their way with us?" He eyed the mural again. The action had eased off, and the faces and bodies looked still and serene. Satisfied smiles grinned back down at him, mirroring his own sated condition.

"You might say that."

Which meant Lexa would never believe his curse existed. Would never believe he was already halfway in love with her. She'd say this whole thing between them was because of the ghosts of Perdition.

Perdition House. Haunted by horny pernicious ghosts.

Shit. Lexa may never believe what they had could last.

This was getting more complicated by the minute.

6

The heated sparklers from Jake's touch along her outer thigh went to all of Lexa's hottest spots. She quivered, but he barely noticed because he was completely focused on the mural over-head. Her desire simmering nicely, she stretched out along the stairs and enjoyed the languorous feeling three orgasms had produced. The mansion oozed sex right out of the walls. The mantel, the mural, even the stairs themselves. "I need a shower. Did Faye mention which rooms were ours?"

"No, but I'm guessing they won't be hard to find." He rose, all six feet of him, his cock dangling juicily below his belly. Such a lovely penis. Versatile and delicious.

She grinned and allowed him to help her to stand. "We'd better take our clothes up with us. We wouldn't want Faye to come home and find them."

He frowned and retrieved her shorts and panties for her. He handed them over, then got his own clothes and shoes. "I have a feeling Faye knows exactly what happened after she left. She's been living here a while, soaking up the atmosphere." He flicked a glance toward the lascivious ceiling.

"You seem ticked off that the place is haunted. I assumed you just wouldn't believe me."

He grinned and traced a fingertip down her cheek. "It's inconvenient."

"What's inconvenient about a house that oozes sex? I've never been more free. I'm not usually so hedonistic." She palmed his belly, grinning when he sucked in a harsh breath. "I don't fuck strangers, Jake. In fact, I've hardly thought about sex in months."

"Seems like neither of us has had much fun lately." He blessed the tip of her nose with a kiss that warmed her through. Affection glowed in his eyes, and her belly thrilled to it.

And that was not good. "Um, with you in Florida and me building a business here, we won't be able to have more than this weekend. You're okay with that, right?"

"If you are, I'll have to be." He busied himself with his clothing.

"Right, then." Not as convinced by his tone as she ought to be, she turned on her heel and headed up to the next landing. "Let's find our rooms."

She got no farther than the landing when another thought struck. She stopped and looked at his serious face. "Did you notice something odd about the stairs?"

"No, they were comfortable." He arched his back and stretched. "No kinks."

"Exactly. We should be bent out of shape after what just happened. We both stretched out as if we were on comfy pillows."

He frowned again. "Damn house." Then he reached for her hand to hold it. "Do you still feel the sparks?"

"Yes. Like low embers. The heat rises with every skim of your fingers. Those ghosts sure know what they're doing." She grinned and led the way up to the second floor, knowing he was checking out her bare ass. She gave herself some extra sway to encourage his attention.

Which she got halfway up when he grabbed her around the waist and planted a nip and kiss on her left ass cheek. "Oh, you sexy beast!"

She giggled and held still while he explored the other cheek as well. Curious fingers slid between her legs. Yes, the spark and crackle still fluttered along her most sensitive nerve endings. She looked at him over her shoulder and wondered how she was going to survive the weekend. Her legs were already weak from coming, her mind was fogged by the electric snap between them, and she wanted to lose herself in Jake's laser-blue eyes.

She gave him more room between her legs, then caught her breath on the invasive swipe on her clit. "Are we going to make it to our rooms?"

"If you think you're sleeping in another room tonight, you're wrong."

His words sent a thrill up from her belly to her heart. "Okay. I'm wrong."

"We'll find our room, and then go outside so you can see the rest of the grounds. Maybe if we get out of the house, we'll be back in charge."

While it seemed odd that he wanted to wait to have more sex, she could see his point. Her own behavior had taken an unexpectedly salacious turn the minute she'd pulled through the gates. "As soon as I saw you in the driveway, I wanted you."

He nodded. "And out by the vegetable patch, I wanted to stretch you out in the raspberry canes. I saw you out there, legs open, ready to take me in."

"But we were able to control ourselves."

"Until things got out of hand when we were left alone," he said. "Inside."

She glanced up at the mural again, thought of the writhing bodies on the mantel. "You're right; we need to get out of the house."

She headed up the stairs, sorry to feel the loss of his fingers on her pussy. But it was the only way to gain any semblance of control. When she got to the head of the stairs, she pulled on her panties and shorts.

His expression said he was as sorry as she was that they'd decided to cool off.

"We're onto you!" she called out to the house. To Jake she said, "Think they heard me?"

"If they did, they probably don't give a damn." He turned right. "I'm betting Faye put us at the front of the house."

She followed him to an open door. A beautiful early twentieth-century-decorated bedroom waited in sun-dappled glory. The bed had a wrought-iron headboard and footboard.

A nightstand held a Tiffany bedroom lamp, with crystal teardrops dangling around the circumference of the shade. "Think this is an original Tiffany?"

"Only the best for Perdition House," he replied absently. He was busy checking out the closet, which she judged to be ridiculously small. Then he went through another door.

"Jake? Don't leave me in here alone," she said as she scurried after him. "The bathroom. How quaint."

She ran her fingers along the cool enamel top of a claw-foot tub. Rose petals lined the bottom, with more sprinkled around the pedestal sink. "Nice touch. Faye really knows how to lay out a welcome."

Another door led to a second adjoining bedroom. This one hadn't been cleaned or dusted.

"Faye expected that we'd be sleeping together," she said as she pointed through the door to the dusty furnishings.

He leaned in close to her to look into the bedroom. The hum of electricity cranked up her libido again. "Stand back, please. I can feel the spark off you, and it's making me wet." She skimmed a hand across her nipples, already hard. He caught the gesture and nodded.

But his eyes, oh! They burned with desire so fast and hot she felt the scorch of his need from where she stood.

He stepped back and the sensation of heat eased. "We have to get outside. We need to talk."

They each took a brisk shower, then kept at least four feet between them as they headed back downstairs, through the kitchen and out the side door.

Lexa breathed a sigh of relief when the cool air from the bay eased her overheated body. Her nipples softened and her legs felt less wobbly. "That's better. I'm still hot, but it's manageable." A cold breeze tickled her back, like icy fingers, then receded. She shivered. "Drafty out here."

"I felt some of that in the house. Isn't that supposed to be a sign of spirits in a room?"

She shivered again, this time from nerves. She ran her hands up her arms to ward off the gooseflesh.

"There's a gazebo—might be better out there." He stepped off the side porch and made for the white and green structure.

"It looks familiar," she said, trying to remember where she'd seen it. The memory was no more than fog wisping through her mind. "I can't recall exactly when I saw it."

She walked across the lawn, dragging her mind back to her purpose for being here. She noted the number and types of weeds. "This lawn needs care for sure, but I won't need to resod. We can handle the weeds with natural methods."

"Seems I read somewhere they take longer."

He was right, but she was determined to preserve as much as she could. "Did you get a time frame for completion?"

"No. I'll give Faye my estimate, then check out some other restoration companies in the area. I'll find someone I think can handle the job, then make a recommendation. I'm too busy to come all the way from Florida to handle the work myself." He stopped walking and stared pointedly at her, his jaw flexing so hard a muscle jumped in his cheek.

"You look like you want to say something. Spit it out."

"Later," he said, and took off at a fast pace toward the gazebo again.

The man had a fine ass in his jeans. And out of them. Broad shoulders tapered to a trim waist.

"I want to see you in your tool belt." Shirt off, jeans hanging low.

"What?" He turned but kept walking, backward, his quizzical expression making her laugh.

"You heard me. I think tool belts are hot. All that leather and the big buckles. Makes me squirm just thinking about you." She did a hip swivel to emphasize her point.

His eyes glazed as he watched her hips roll. She'd never had this kind of effect on a man before. She liked it and refused to consider that the ghosts were responsible. Ruined the fantasy.

And she really didn't want this fantasy ruined.

She trotted toward him, noting how he watched her breasts bounce with each heavy step.

"Naked," she said when she got close enough to touch him. "I want to see you with nothing on but your belt."

"I don't know if I packed it."

"Of course you did," she pronounced. "What carpenter would ever go anywhere without it?"

He grinned and took her breath away. His hair got caught in a breeze and lifted, showing her a cowlick just left of a narrow widow's peak. His eyebrows were two black slashes that set off the blue eyes he used to such great effect.

The man had no idea how gorgeous he was. So beautiful it hurt to look at him. Hurt more to think they had so little time.

She gripped a support beam on the gazebo and used it to

swing herself up the two steps to the floor inside. Low benches with thick pads covered in yellow gingham ran along the sides.

Suddenly gripped by images of people waltzing all around her, she spun, trying to catch glimpses of their faces, their clothes, their shoes, but she couldn't hold on to anything but flashes of shadow. "Damn, they're here, too, but I can't make them out. They're nothing more than shadow."

Chilled air swirled around inside the structure, but the trees that ringed the lawn were still and quiet. There was no breeze out here today. Not so much as a hint of one.

Jake came up behind her and ran his hands down her arms from her shoulders to her elbows in an attempt to warm her. Trails of heated electricity tracked along each stroke of his palms.

She leaned back against him. "Do me here, Jake. I want you." And she did, with a ferocity she'd never felt before, not even in the house.

He turned her to face him. "First, we talk."

7

"I don't believe Perdition House is haunted." It was the best place to start, Jake figured. He had to get the idea out of her head. Because if he didn't wipe away her belief that ghosts were creating this heat between them, she'd never accept the curse as the proof of their destiny.

"But I just saw—"

"Nothing but shadows; you said it yourself." But he'd seen them too. Apparitions of people dancing and twirling in each other's arms.

"How do you explain the mantel with the moving figures? When I touched it, I felt their orgasms like a battering ram, Jake. I know I did."

"If you'll recall, I was touching you at the time." He didn't remember exactly, but he was betting she wouldn't be certain either.

She tilted her head and studied him curiously. "You think it's normal for people to jump on each other the way we did?"

"I don't know about your sex life, but I've been too busy these last three years to think about mine." And he was only counting back to his move to Florida. He'd tired of one-night stands and quickies a while ago. Now he knew what he'd been waiting for.

Lightning.

And he thanked the ghosts of Perdition for bringing it to him. He didn't want to deny their existence, but he couldn't see any other way out of his predicament.

She looked uncomfortable with his admission. "Let's say you're right and this is simply a case of two people turned on by proximity, convenience, and a very high level of need. What's with the snap and crackle when we touch each other?"

It was on the tip of his tongue to spill the beans, but she was still thinking of ghostly influences and wasn't ready to hear about the MacKay curse. Passed down on the male side of the family, the women often had a hard time accepting it. His own mother hadn't figured it out until after she'd married his father.

He raised his hand, let it hover near her cheek, cupped so she could take the next step and rest her silky skin in his palm. Her eyes closed on a sigh. She wanted the lightning as much as he did. The heated thrum was addictive, and he wasn't sure if he'd ever get enough.

In truth, he never wanted to get enough. "Do it," he said.

She tilted her head toward his hand, began to lower it.

He watched anticipation flit across her perfect delicate features as millimeter by millimeter she sought the feel of his palm.

A feminine giggle rang through the trees that bordered the lawn.

Lexa's eyes shot open. She twirled to see who was watching from the woods, and Jake fisted his hand in the suddenly chill air.

"Damn!"

"What the hell's with this house?" Jake demanded of Faye when she climbed out of her car. He'd waited on the veranda while Lexa took a long soak in the tub with the rose petals. For the last forty-five minutes, he'd been battling with himself over going inside to have her again. The sexual need had grown beyond bearable just as Faye's car pulled into the drive.

"What do you mean?" She walked to the passenger side and opened the door. She bent in, displaying a fine ass and fabulous legs that didn't do a thing for his libido.

Now he was sure he was cursed. Any man would want a piece of that. Any man not dealing with love at first touch, at least.

She pulled out several pieces of clothing on hangers. "I found a few skirts and blouses for Lexa to try on. Mostly Sophia Loren, but there's a sexy little corset in here from a seventies porn flick that'll show off her breasts nicely." She presented it to him with a flourish.

It was deep red with an underwire but with no material to cover the breasts; all he could see were Lexa's large distended nipples atop the creamy flesh of her tits jutting out of the laced-up corset. His mouth watered, and his semihard cock rose to complete attention.

Faye's chuckle brought him back to the conversation. "You have a fuckability about you, Jake. I like it, but I'm involved elsewhere, and something tells me you're all about Lexa."

He wasn't sure but it seemed that her right hand was sliding across her pussy behind the clothes she was holding in front of her. Her eyes slid shut, and her mouth pursed into a sexy, plump moue.

"About this house," he began, trying to remember what it was he needed to say.

Her eyes opened, arousal rising in their depths. "Yes?"

"Lexa thinks it's haunted."

"Does she? And what do you think, Jake?" Her hand swished again, faster this time.

"I know it is." He couldn't believe he'd accepted it so readily, but there you go. If a guy could be cursed, why couldn't a bordello be haunted? "And that's fine, but the spirits are messing me up with Lexa big time."

"Aren't you enjoying yourself?" Her hand slowed again, but her chest rose and fell in quick pants.

"Never had better sex, but then, I'm in love, so that makes sense."

"In love?" Arousal fled from her gaze, replaced by shock.

"It's the family curse. Love at first touch. As I understand it, when a MacKay male touches *the* woman for him, there's an electrical charge he can't resist." He also liked Lexa's humor, her ambition, and he respected her passion for her work. Accepting a haunted mansion was easy in comparison to accepting that love had hit him and wouldn't let go.

"How delicious. Does his woman feel this love touch too?" Her eyes widened as her interest was piqued.

"Always. It's hot and burns under the skin. Takes a few years and a couple kids before it eases back to comfortable. Makes the sex happen fast and takes it into the stratosphere, sensationwise."

"Really? This *is* interesting. Did you feel this burn when you shook my hand?"

"No, but it turned me to ashes the first time I touched Lexa. You're hot, don't get me wrong. If it wasn't for Lexa, I'd be all over you, but now . . . I'm already crazy for her. Will be forever." He scrubbed his hair, still shocked at the speed and ferocity of his feelings. "I have to make her see that love can happen this fast. Right now, all she sees is the lust this house keeps slamming us with."

"So? Lust can turn into love. That's what happened with Liam and me." She smiled, pleased.

"The ghosts are fucking me up. She won't believe in love at first touch if the ghosts are making us so randy we can't climb the stairs without making meals out of each other."

"Oh, I see," she said on a breathless whisper. Her hand moved faster. "The mural?"

"Oh, yeah. And the mantel. You've got some interesting carvings on there."

"I do like them." Her voice went breathy.

"Can you get these spirits to back off for a bit? Let nature take its course, so to speak? I've only got tonight and tomorrow left. Lexa's smart. She'll never believe I love her this quickly." His heart clenched. He had no idea what would happen if the right woman denied the curse. As far as he knew, it had always worked out. But none of the other men had this kind of interference working against them.

Desperation settled behind his heart. He palmed the tightness in his chest.

"I'll try to convince the spirits to tone it down, but you have to understand sexual arousal and release is just about the only physical sensation the spirits retain. They've got decades of unwanted abstinence to make up for."

"They feel our orgasms?"

"And enhance them."

"No shit."

Her hand shifted into high gear, and all semblance of hiding the action disappeared. "If you'll excuse me?"

"Go to it," he said as he rose from the top step of the veranda to join Lexa upstairs. As he opened the front door, he heard a quick sigh of satisfaction, but tempted as he was to watch the lady get herself off, there was another one upstairs waiting for him.

Lexa stood at the window watching Faye by the car. The blonde's hand slid beneath her skirt and traveled up her thigh to her crotch. Jigging and rubbing, Faye spread her legs and worked herself into a frenzy of arousal. Her eyes closed and her face tilted to the sun.

She'd never seen another woman carry herself to orgasm before. Surprised at how hot Faye looked, Lexa enjoyed watching; knowing that Jake was on his way up to her only added to the anticipation of having him again.

She'd heard the car tires crunch on the gravel while she was climbing out of the tub. Now, wrapped in a towel, still wet from the bath, she enjoyed the wildness of Faye's self-pleasure.

The blonde dropped the clothes she was holding and speared a finger from her other hand into her pussy. Lexa could almost feel the wet flesh on her own hands and fingers. If this was what the spirits could do, she was all for it.

Her belly tightened in need as she heard Jake's footsteps enter the room behind her. He came and stood at her shoulder, and she knew that no matter how aroused the spirits made her feel, or how much they interfered with her libido, it was Jake she would remember from her time in Perdition.

"Watch," she said, pointing out the window to the driveway. "Faye's going to come any second." She groped for Jake's hand and slid it to her aching pussy under her Egyptian cotton towel.

At first touch, the thrum and humming charge from him centered on her clit and buzzed up to her chest, making her heart stutter.

"You're dripping wet," he growled low in her ear. She could feel him unzipping behind her; then the smooth head of his heated cock slid between her thighs.

"Move," she begged, arching backward to present herself for him. She placed each hand on the center window frame and leaned forward. His cock slid back and forth along her trench, the bulbous purple head whispering a touch to her clit with each pass. As gentle as the touch was, it still raked her soul with passion and hot desire. Her delicate bundle of nerve endings pulsed and rang with the need for release. She groaned and arched more greedily.

Below, on the driveway, Faye hiked her skirt to her waist

and put her foot up on a tire while both hands slid and rubbed at her pussy. Her hands moved faster and faster, in time with Jake's rhythm.

Flavors burst on Lexa's tongue as she watched Faye. Even without mouthing him, the spicy taste of Jake's cock and precum warred with the salty flavor of her own juices in her mouth.

Faye's hand plunged into her channel in an outrageous display of feminine need and demand. Her eyes opened as she raised her face again. The distance between Faye on the driveway and Lexa in the second-story window collapsed, and Lexa read the desire-befogged glaze of arousal in Faye's eyes.

The intensity of sensation from Jake nibbling her neck, sliding his cock along her trench to her hottest button, and seeing Faye rock herself into a climax combined to take Lexa into a screaming, mind-blowing orgasm. She chugged and groaned and grunted with the shattering release.

Beyond thought, she allowed Jake to turn her and press her down to her knees. Tasting her own sweet juice on his cock made him more delicious as she sucked and licked him into a cataclysmic spurt. His hips jutted toward her, and his ass cheeks hollowed under her hands, tight and hard.

His first spurts hit the back of her throat as she worked and milked him with long strong strokes of suction.

A chill breeze floated past her from the window but couldn't distract her from the joy of taking Jake to heaven.

He groaned in his throat as she took all he offered. "God, I love this, love you," he said.

8

A figure of speech, that's all it was, Lexa convinced herself. Jake hadn't meant to say he loved her. That would be impossible. They'd just met. No one fell in love on four hours' acquaintance.

They had only a couple more days together. He was here until Tuesday morning, but she had to get back to work on Monday.

That gave them less than forty-eight hours, by her reckoning.

She put his come-induced comment out of her mind. But it lurked in her heart just the same.

Faye had finally come into the house and handed off a few skirts and blouses and one hot corset Lexa couldn't wait to put on for Jake before disappearing into her room to prepare for a date. A lawyer, she said with a sparkle in her eye.

How she could look so flushed and aroused after working up to a great orgasm out on the driveway was beyond Lexa. Must be the hookers. No matter what Jake said, she was convinced the house was inhabited by the girls who'd once worked here.

The old family stories were too realistic to be anything but true. Trapped between lives as working girls and finding their one and only loves caused the girls' spirits to get confused. Something about needing to tell their stories before moving onto their rewards. It was all kind of vague now, because she'd heard the tales as a child from older cousins who'd thought to scare her.

Instead, the stories had taken on a life of their own inside Lexa's head. She'd embellished each one and turned them into short stories she'd used to amuse herself.

If she'd known most of the stuff she'd fantasized had actually happened, maybe she'd have stopped. But then again, as she'd advanced into her own sexual life, she'd come to rely on the made-up stuff to get her through some pretty ho-hum sex.

Ho-hum until Jake. She'd never experienced the touch of a man in quite the way she felt Jake's. It bit and tore through her, then soothed and eased and especially teased. The anticipation of touching him again, of having him touch her was already building.

It would be easy to say it was the spirits of Perdition that caused this reaction, but if she was just horny because they made her so, it wouldn't matter whether it was Jake's touch or someone else's.

But it mattered that it was Jake whose touch fired her soul; it mattered a lot.

What she needed to do was talk to Faye to try to figure out what had brought her here. Or, rather, who had brought her here. It hadn't been Faye's voice on the line in the wee hours asking for an estimate.

The voice had been hollow and lusty. Desire had curled into Lexa's belly as soon as she'd answered the phone out of a heavy slumber. Hours later, sated by orgasm after orgasm, she'd surfaced from her sexual delight, excited at the prospect of working on the gardens here.

What she couldn't figure out was why the same voice had summoned Jake. He had no connection to Perdition House that she could figure.

But he sure had a connection with *her.* An electrical connection that sent her through the ceiling when he touched her.

She loved the way his touch made her body hum and buck with a surge of power and sexual need.

She could do with a lot more time than a weekend. And a lot more of Jake.

The man with the riveting touch was having a shower, and while she was tempted to join him, these few minutes could be put to use talking with Faye.

Maybe she could get an audience with the spirit who'd summoned her to Perdition. She had a lot of questions to ask. And she needed answers now, today. Before she lost even more of herself to Jake and his wild touch. She shivered at the thought of his hands trailing sparklers to all her secret places and headed straight for Faye's room.

She knocked quietly, because she could hear Faye talking, presumably on the phone. She turned to leave, thought of Jake's determined stance that the house wasn't haunted, and stalled out.

She had to know the truth.

How wrong would it be to tap again, then poke her head in the door? She needed to speak with her right now, without Jake.

If Faye's flustered aroused expression meant anything, it was that once she left for her date, she wouldn't be home until morning.

And *anything* could happen at Perdition between now and tomorrow. Nothing evil; she had no concerns about the typical haunted mansion horror flicks. She wasn't a woman to head into the basement with nothing but a candle to light the way.

She grinned.

Perdition House, for all its weird sexiness, was not scary. *Homey* was the word that best described the house, big and drafty though it was.

She tapped again, then opened Faye's door just enough to stick her face in. She plastered on an apologetic grin and nearly choked on it when she saw Faye.

Faye was talking all right, but not on the phone. An almost mirror image of Faye *hovered* in a staircase that led to God knew where. The roof? Maybe.

"Who are you?" she whispered.

The hovering image blinked out, just like that. *Pfft.*

Lexa stepped all the way into the room. Held the door handle at her back. "That was the spirit interfering with Jake and me, wasn't it?"

Faye rolled her eyes. Then she crossed to a dresser and picked up a brush. "What do you mean?"

"I saw her, Faye. She looked just like you, but she wasn't . . ." She groped for a way to say what she saw. "She wasn't of this time. Her clothing, her hairstyle. She was dressed like my great-grandmother Annie when she bothered to wear a dress."

Faye's shoulders slumped. She opened her mouth to speak, but the image returned in full body, clearer now than before.

A lustrous green appeared in her dress, her hair went shiny blond like Faye's, and her shawl deepened to a rich black.

"You tell her," Faye said to the image.

"I'm Belle, Lexa, a friend of Annie's and Matthew's." She floated toward the bed.

Lexa blinked. Yes, *floated* was the right word.

"My great-great-aunt," added Faye. "I think there may be more *greats* in there."

"Annie wanted you here, so I facilitated things," Belle said in the voice Lexa remembered. A wave of the long-dead madame's hand bade her sit on the bed.

Lexa sat.

Her great-grandmother Annie Creighton had orchestrated this visit. How weirdly comforting. "Why did Annie want me here?"

"She's afraid for you. You've shut all the joy out of your life. You're so driven to succeed, you've denied yourself the pleasures of life."

Her ambition must have touched something in her great-grandmother. She warmed at the idea.

"It's more than ambition, Lexa. Annie's stubborn drive to work the way she wanted to work nearly ruined her chance at love with Matthew. If he hadn't put aside all his ideas about women and their place in society, they never would have had a life together. She doesn't want to see you make the same mistake. You must make room in your life for love with a good man."

"There's plenty of time for that," she said. "I'm only twenty-seven, and there are plenty of fish in the sea."

Faye gave a light cough while Belle's eyes widened. "In my time, twenty-seven was over the hill."

"Times change. I'm sure Annie thinks the way you do, but believe me, my business won't succeed if I don't buckle down." Setting aside the whys of her summoning, she had some questions. After all, it wasn't every day a girl got to chat with a woman born over a hundred years ago. Especially not a woman with Belle's experiences.

"Why can I see you?" Lexa asked. The spirits in the gazebo had been too shadowy to see clearly.

"You're family," Belle explained with a gentle nod that seemed designed to ease Lexa's mind. It didn't.

"And?" she demanded.

"When those horrid cousins of yours tried to frighten you

as a little girl, you turned everything they said into wishes and dreams. Why shouldn't we show you the truth?"

Lexa smiled, remembering her fanciful daydreams. "Annie and Matthew watched over me." They brought Jake here too. For her.

"Love doesn't stop with death; it's a living, breathing entity. It was their love that watched over you, that encouraged you to see beyond the frightening ghost stories."

"You were receptive, Lexa," Faye added. "So was I as a child."

Lexa tore her gaze from Belle to look at Faye. "That's why you live here," Lexa concluded, "with the spirits of Perdition. Does that make you a guardian or a gatekeeper?"

Faye laughed. "To the underworld and beyond? No, I'm more like an enabler. I'm trying to keep the house going so each spirit will have a chance to tell their story, then move on."

"How many are there?"

Faye bit her lip. "That's up for discussion. Belle is not as forthcoming as one in her position should be." She gave her great-aunt a stern look.

Belle arched an eyebrow. Then she faded to beige, all color gone. Her expression dulled into disapproval.

"Ooh, looks like she's miffed," Lexa pointed out, quickly picking up on the quirkiness of the other women's relationship.

"You catch on fast." Faye laughed, a tinkling seductive sound of amused indulgence.

"I saw you in the driveway." Lexa warmed at the memory of Jake having her while Faye pleasured herself, each of them watching the other.

"I know." Faye leaned against the dresser, arms folded. "Perdition oozes sex. The walls, the floors, the beds, the very grounds themselves are imbued with memories. And"—she shrugged one smooth round shoulder—"I like sex. I love orgasms. I indulge in them often."

"Because the spirits entice you?"

"When I first moved in, I had no control, but now I'm in charge. It's the only way to stay true to myself."

Lexa nodded, wondering how much of what was happening between her and Jake was real. "Will Jake be able to see you too?" she asked Belle.

"Jake's dealing with something else at the moment. But he does have an open mind."

She decided to keep it to herself that Jake denied the house was haunted.

Belle allowed a celery green to appear in her gown, but it was still a far cry from the emerald she'd been wearing before.

Lexa figured she enjoyed talking about men and that her stormy mood had lifted. "How do you mean, true to yourself, Faye?"

"I had two lovers for a time."

"You *needed* two lovers, you mean." Belle's colors deepened to grass green and smoke gray in her shawl. "I enjoyed them as much as you did," she said. Her mood was definitely improving.

That was a good sign. A powerful spirit in an amenable mood would be more likely to answer questions.

Faye gave Lexa a slight upturn of her lips in acknowledgment.

Seemed the still living were well in synch here.

Lexa sighed in relief. "And?" She brought Faye back into the conversation.

"By the time I figured out how to block all the sexual suggestions, I'd figured out I wanted to work on my love life as opposed to my sex life. Now I'm in a committed relationship with a wonderful man who fully understands the needs of the house."

"Needs of the house?"

244 / *Bonnie Edwards*

"Without a solid income, Perdition would fall to ruin, and we're not sure what will become of the girls."

Lexa nodded. "So, why spend money on the gardens?" There was that ambition again. She didn't want to lose this contract.

"Belle's idea, not mine. I don't think we can afford you at this point, but she's determined to have nothing but the best for Perdition, just as she did during her lifetime. Belle built the house, so she knows exactly how it should look."

"You have a great store, though. TimeStop, right?"

"Two locations and I'm hoping for more. But I still don't think we'll have enough income. Perdition House is heading for the century mark, and with the last few years of neglect to contend with, there are a lot of repairs to be done."

Lexa's dream of a showpiece garden went up in smoke.

"That's why we're going into a new venture," Belle piped in.

Lexa waited. Belle's expression glowed with enthusiasm, and emerald shimmered through the dress, making her shawl glow black again.

A happy ghost was a chatty ghost. "We're going to hold bachelor auctions for wealthy women." Belle's announcement brought a smile to Faye's face.

Lexa didn't need any more explanation. Both women wore identical expressions. Salacious smiles lit their faces while images of straining, writhing bodies all over the house woke up Lexa's libido. Her pussy twitched awake, and she squeezed her thighs together. Heat rose into her chest, bringing her nipples to a peak, hard and fast.

"Yes! It'll be just like that," said Belle with a bawdy grin.

Faye rolled her eyes. "Stop it!" she called out, then swiveled to glare around the room. "Someone's putting thoughts into Lexa's head. Now is not the time!"

Chilly air raced through Lexa time and again, each swipe

raising her internal temperature while cooling her skin to the point of gooseflesh. The sensation created a thrilling arousal.

"Oh, God, I've got to find Jake." She stood and made for the door. Roiling with liquid need, she walked away, aware of each clenching muscle in her thighs as she took each step. Every sinew attached to her groin, each ligament, every muscle tightened, drawing her cradle into a clenched ball of sexual need.

Her lips and clit plumped; her inner channel filled and dripped with wetness. Heat suffused her whole body to the point of pain.

"I . . . I . . . I'll come back soon," she managed to mutter as she opened the door.

"Have fun with Jake." She heard Belle speak, but the sound seemed to come from inside her head, not from the room behind her.

She closed the door and heard footsteps downstairs. She leaned over the open railing that ringed the second floor. "Jake! I'm up here. Hurry!"

She pressed her mons to the hard smooth railing to ease some of the pressure. Soon, he'd be here soon.

One look at her face and he'd know. He'd take care of her. He'd plunge inside so hard and fast her muscles would rejoice and release sweetly all over him.

9

Jake heard Lexa's cry of need and dropped his clipboard and notes on the dining room table. He ran to the staircase to see her at the railing above him. Blood rushed at the sight of her. She glowed with an aura of sexual need. Her beautiful face yearned; her hair seemed alive as it flowed across her breasts in teasing swirls and tendrils.

He knew then and there he'd lost his heart completely. He could hold nothing back.

He took the stairs two at a time, hit the landing, and shot over to her.

"Baby, what's happened?" Her cheeks were flushed, but under the red, her skin was pale and white. She burned in his arms, but her flesh was chilled. "Never mind, I can feel it."

And he did. Her painful arousal, the chilly rushes of air, her burning need. He had to get her out of harm's way.

Before he lost all control.

He swept her up and carried her back down the way he'd come. She clung and mewled in his arms, clasping and needy.

The need to take her here, *now*, grew and grew, a monstrous ball of writhing lust.

Fighting himself, and every other spirit who lusted, he made his way downstairs. The front door stuck; the knob slipped out of his grasp, but he kept on, muscles straining, determination gathering with every setback. Finally, the door gave way, and he wrestled his way outside with her, into a headwind that threatened to knock him on his ass. "We've got to get away. We've got to think for ourselves."

"Jake, oh, baby, please. Touch me where I need it. Touch me where I hurt for you," she pleaded and cajoled, squirming in his arms. "I'm wet for you ... need ... you ..." She kissed his neck, sucked his earlobe. Hearing her cries was the worst of it. They called to the man he was, the man who wanted to drive into her, come with her, be man to her woman.

But a roar in his head forced him to keep moving. The need to protect his woman overrode everything and kept him fighting.

His heart pounded, his own blood and hers racing through every artery and vein. He could feel it all, while the roar to keep her safe gathered strength. His pulse thumped as he set her on the passenger seat of her truck, then rounded the hood. Each step away from her felt like stumbling in a quagmire. Invisible hands tugged, thoughts of possession and deep plunging sex pulled until exhaustion threatened. If he turned back toward her, all resistance would disappear and it would feel as if he had wings on his feet. Nearly seduced into giving up, he tried one more headlong lunge and pulled himself around to the driver's door.

It took all his strength to open the door wide enough to hoist himself into his seat. "Hold on, Lexa, we'll be off the grounds in a minute."

But she didn't seem to hear, swallowed as she was by lust and rapacious need. Even as he spoke, she climbed onto his lap, crotch to crotch. Her body burned his, his cock raged, his lips itched to kiss and bite and hold while he plunged.

Resistance ebbed until he felt the sparklers from her thighs bracket his hips. If he lost this fight, she'd never believe that they had what it took to build a life together. For her, this weekend would always be about great sex and wild spirits.

He turned the key in the ignition, relieved when it caught. Dodging Lexa's lips was tougher than escaping the house. But with his love for her spurring him on, he slammed the truck into gear and sent up a spit of gravel from the tires. The truck took off with a lurch around the driveway. A sense of victory egged him on as he barreled down the straightaway to the gate. He plowed through the cedar boughs that blocked his way.

"Lexa, get off me!" Words he never imagined saying in a million years. "I can't see around you." His hard-on pulsed against his zipper, sending rolling black through his vision.

She crooned and cajoled, oblivious to her surroundings. Her eyes glazed to unseeing; her scent rose as need swallowed her. She was beyond knowing.

When the open gate came into view through the overhanging boughs, he gave a silent thank-you to Faye for leaving it open. He didn't have the strength of will it would take to climb out and open it. Moving away from Lexa at this point would be impossible.

With a final push, he shot through onto the quiet street. No maelstrom of need here, no headwinds, no quagmire holding him back. Blessed peace.

Once free of the entrance, he slammed the truck to a halt, unable to drive any farther with her on his lap. The truck idled while he clasped her face gently.

"What?" Lexa's eyes widened, cleared. She looked around, surprised, then crawled off him. Her face and neck were red, flushed with sexual arousal. "How did we get here?"

He wanted her so much he could taste her. Her silken mouth, her soft skin, her wetness. He squeezed the steering wheel and eased the truck to the side of the road. As it rolled to a stop, he rested his forehead on the wheel to let his racehorse-paced heartbeat slow.

"I had to get us out of there. I'm sorry, babe." His heart still thudded in the silence, but his pulse no longer pounded in his ears. For now this was as peaceful as it would get.

She slid her palm to his cheek. "Don't be sorry; you were right, Jake. Something had hold of me. I couldn't resist." Her chest heaved with each breath. "Thanks for getting us out." She placed her hand on his thigh, her touch burning through to his balls.

"Don't touch me," he said. At her wounded look, he explained, "I've just had the fight of my life, and I don't have the strength to fight you too."

Her eyes danced with understanding, and she pulled her hand away. Scooting over to her side of the truck, she clipped her seat belt into place. Way over on the passenger side where there would be no mistaken touches. "This okay?"

"Thanks." If he was going to win her heart for the lifetime he wanted, she had to know him as he really was. There was nothing he could do to stop the burning sparklers when they touched, but he could sure as hell ease the sexual influence the ghosts exerted. "We need to spend time away from the house. I want to learn who Lexa Creighton is outside the bedroom."

"You're admitting the house is haunted?"

"This is more than spirits having fun. More, do you understand?" He hoped that would help pave the way for his explanation of the curse. He put the truck back into gear and pulled out onto the road.

"Where are we going?" she asked.

"Anywhere away from here."

Anywhere ended up being a neighborhood of funky shops and restaurants off the expressway. "Do you know where we are?" Jake asked.

"No, never been here before, but it doesn't matter. I feel more like myself now, so I don't care where we end up." Her glance was warm but brisk.

He grinned. "I hear you. I . . ." If he knew what to say, he'd say it.

She was busy looking out her side of the truck for a parking space and didn't realize he'd halted. "There's a spot. We could go for a stroll around that lake." She pointed to a public pathway filled with walkers, cyclists, and skateboarders.

He parked and ran around the truck to open her door. She blushed prettily at his action, and he had to wonder how the previous men in her life had treated her.

"Surprised?"

"You're very gallant, considering we're driving a fourteen-year-old Ford pickup that has seen better days." But she held out her hand so he could take it and help her down from the truck's high seat. The snap and hum gathered steam between them, but she tucked in close. He looped his arm around her shoulders. She placed hers around his waist, letting the buzz settle into a gentle heat where they touched.

"This is nice," she said. "I need this calm quiet." She patted her free hand to her chest.

Dusk gathered around them, and already some of the strolling parents with children were heading out of the park. He'd soon be out of time. "We need to talk about something. You may not want to hear it."

"Did Faye tell you she probably won't be able to afford us?"

"No, we were discussing something else in the driveway. But after my shower, I took a good look around downstairs. I don't understand why they called me. There's next to no repair needed. The wainscoting is in excellent condition."

"Maybe they wanted you here for another reason," she suggested.

"If you think of one, let me know." He shrugged. "But even to my untrained eye, the grounds look like a disaster."

"The gardens need serious help, but if Faye can't afford me, all I can do is make suggestions." She looked sad at the prospect of limiting her involvement so severely.

"Let's walk while there's still daylight. Then we'll grab dinner somewhere close." His cell phone rang. With a stab of guilt, he flipped it open. He'd hardly thought about his father since he'd climbed on the plane this morning. His caller ID gave him a sharp reminder.

"Dad? What's wrong?" He turned away from Lexa and plugged his other ear so he could hear every nuance. He'd become good at reading between the lines over the last three years.

"Hi, son. Nothing's wrong. In fact, things are great. I just wanted to know how it's going on your end."

He glanced at Lexa with a grin. "Never been better."

His father laughed. A full-bodied laugh Jake hadn't heard in far too long. "What's so funny?"

"Sorry, son, I'm just in front of the Mitchell's house. Had a good day here. Very interesting."

"Did the locksmith show up?"

"Sure did." He heard a grin in the old man's voice, a lightness in the tone Jake hardly recognized. "So did the lady they hired to stage the interior for the open house."

"What's going on?"

"Nothing. I gotta go. Oh, and I'm shutting off my cell, so don't bother trying to reach me."

And with that, he was gone. "He shut off his phone."

"Who?"

"My father."

"He probably doesn't want to be disturbed."

"You're right, but that's what disturbs me."

Lexa pointed out that his dad was an adult, but Jake wasn't listening; he'd already hit another button on his cell. The concern in his face warmed her. It was sweet to see a man accept family responsibility. In her family, the women tended to carry that burden.

"Jared? Have you checked with Dad?" Jake said into his phone.

No one used a brusque tone like that with anyone other than family. She touched his sleeve. "My brother," he whispered to her unspoken question.

She nodded. It was hard not to hear his half of the conversation since he stood not five inches from her.

Since the dash through the gates at Perdition, her curiosity about Jake had taken off. Soared. She wanted to know everything about him. A voracious interest consumed her. As wild as the sex had been, so now was the need to learn about him. A veil had been lifted the moment the gates were behind them.

Sex with Jake had been the best of her life, but she wanted other things now: more and deeper knowledge of him, the man. Wanted it to the point that it scared her a little.

An overwhelming need to have his focus on her kept her attuned to his mood, tone, and glance. So, ignore this conversation with a brother? Not on her life.

The veil at Perdition consisted of desire, lust, rapacious need. Without the spirits' influence, she could breathe again, think again, be curious again.

Jake was speaking into the phone. "You're in Miami? Good." He looked relieved. "Thanks for canceling your charters."

His brother had obviously stepped into Jake's role while Jake was in Seattle. Which meant he had a lot more than simple business to take care of back home.

Florida was a long way from Washington state. Dread grew as she considered the distance. Jake lived so far away. Her life was here. Everything she'd ever wanted with Creighton Landscape and Design was within reach.

But this snap and burn she shared with Jake was strangely

addictive. Every time it happened, she enjoyed it more. When he wasn't touching her, she missed it. Wanted the next jolt with an eagerness she found hard to deny.

"Who is she?" Jake asked. Silence while he listened to a long-winded reply. Jake's brows knit in consternation.

She touched her fingertips to his free hand in support. The tingle zipped around and through their joined fingers. She smiled at him when he glanced at her. The fiery touch between them had freaked her at first, but now it felt right.

This was the way things were supposed to be. The spirits, hot as they made her and Jake, could never duplicate this sense of heated belonging. She was as sure of that idea as she was of the taste of Jake's kisses.

Jake flipped the phone closed and stared at her. "My father's gone on a date; that's why he shut off his phone."

"That's nice, isn't it?" She squeezed his hand.

He nodded, then leaned against the back side of an empty park bench, propped his butt on the top, and settled there, head down while he thought.

She perched beside him. "So, he shut off his phone for a happy reason. Are you glad or disappointed?" She trailed a fingertip from his wrist to his elbow.

"Surprised as hell."

She stood in front of him. Nudging his thighs open, she leaned in close and gave him a hug. "I thought you brought me here to talk."

He snugged her up close to his chest, letting the heat buzz from his chest into hers. "I did."

She slowly brushed her breasts in tantalizing swishes across his chest. His eyes flared hot, and he finally settled his lips on hers, tongue diving in and sweeping her into a blaze of desire.

There was no spirit directing them, no murals guiding them, no influences but Jake's on her. She responded as fully as a woman could to the touch of her man in need.

Thought tuned out while sensation took over, and she let her body speak as she pressed close and opened her mouth under his. She tasted him, Jake MacKay, and gloried in the sweep of his tongue, the nip of his teeth on her bottom lip, the soft coaxing of this lips on hers.

She sighed into his mouth as she accepted him.

They'd been having wild sex all afternoon, but nothing they'd done could compare to the intimacy and deep connection between them now. Jake placed kisses on her cheeks, brow, nose, and chin. Each kiss crackled like fresh fizzy soda; each one blessed her with his undivided attention.

She craved more of this. Wanted all of him and no matter what happened back at Perdition House, these moments away from the raging hormones the ghosts created would be forever precious.

"I'll remember this for far longer than anything those spirits can conjure. You make me want so much more than what happens in the mansion." She couldn't believe she'd said it, but the snap and crackle seemed to add to the safety factor. Jake was safe to share with; she knew it down to her soul.

He grinned and sighed, dug his fingers into her hair, and tucked her head under his chin. She could hear him swallow, hear his heart thud in his chest, feel his relief trickle through him as the muscles in his arms relaxed. "Thank God," he said in her ear. "I feel the same way, Lexa. What we have is much more than what they gave us."

"Jake, I'm confused. We can't feel this way so soon, can we? You must be jet-lagged, wiped out. Maybe it's just exhaustion." They'd only met a few hours ago and most of that time had been spent naked, straining for sexual release.

Relationships didn't start that way, flings did.

"No jet lag." He grinned and cocked his head, considering. "I'm revved up and ready to spend as long as it takes to make you understand one more thing."

"That is?"

"I'm cursed. All the MacKay men are."

"Cursed? Right. What was that I just said about jet lag?"

He leaned his head back to look into her eyes. His were so serious, she was compelled to cock her head to listen. "Tell me, Jake. Tell me about this curse." She snugged her hips tighter to his.

"You'll think I'm crazy if I blurt it out. I'll get to it, I promise. But for now, walk with me; tell me about Lexa Creighton."

He wanted to know as much about her as she did about him. Confidence in whatever this was between them made her want to open up in the same way her body had.

She told him everything he might want to know. Her deepest thoughts, her harshest self-doubts, her needs, and, above all, her wants. She needed to learn to balance her career with making a home and raising children. But she also needed to work and build a business she could be proud of. The way Annie and Matthew had.

Through the whole conversation, Jake nodded, taking everything she said seriously, commenting rarely. When she exposed some of her deepest doubts, he frowned and looked ready to speak but held back.

Finally, he tugged her hand and led the way to shelter under a maple tree. He leaned against the trunk and held her loosely, his hands clasped around her waist. Lines of tingling sparks, like an invisible loop of energy, made up a belt of electric warmth.

She tilted her face up to his.

"Tell me about your last boyfriend, Lexa. Who was he?"

"Most new lovers don't want to know about past ones, Jake." Surprised by the question, she stalled.

"He wasn't important, was he?" His eyes gleamed with interest. "None of mine were."

She sighed. "His name was Dave, and he gave up on me when my business started to take off. Said my work was more important to me than he was." She felt rueful now, but at the time she hadn't felt much of anything.

"And?"

"That much was true. I didn't even bother to call him back when he left the message."

"Harsh."

"Yeah, well. He wasn't all that." She trailed a fingernail along his arm. He stepped back out of her reach. "Oops, sorry, I forgot." They were supposed to talk, not flirt, not turn each other on.

He yawned.

She chuckled in understanding. "Looks like the three-hour time difference is catching up to you."

"Not to mention all the sex. I need to hit the sack."

"While I need you," she said, allowing the snap and crackle to glow warmer. Odd how she could coax embers to flame now that she'd been exposed to the heat for a while. "Are you going to explain your curse?"

"Yes. But first, I need to get you into bed again. Then I need sleep." He ran his fingertip down her nose, his eyes full of affection and awareness.

She smiled and hugged him. "I'll forgive you if you fall asleep immediately after this time." She glanced around, saw that no one was watching, and slid her hand down the front of his jeans. The hardness she found brought an immediate slickness between her thighs. "Let's get back to the house. You haven't actually been inside me, and I need you in the deepest way, in my deepest places."

His eyes flared, and she would swear she felt his cock jump behind his fly.

"Let's hurry, Jake. I saw a drugstore in the strip mall across from the lake. We need condoms."

"Way ahead of you, babe." He gave her hand a tug and led her back along the lakeside trail. He walked like a man possessed, not like a victim of jet lag. Not by a long shot.

"Mr. Responsible to the rescue."

"Always." But he frowned as he said it.

10

Jake sat in the passenger seat of Lexa's truck, thinking about the date his father was on. Worry ate at him. Worry that hadn't filtered through while he'd been inside Perdition. Fact was, he'd hardly thought of the old man from the time he'd stepped onto the grounds until he'd left. The spirits had driven all his concerns from his mind. The only constant had been sex.

He was making up for his lapse now. Lexa's comment about him being Mr. Responsible rang true. He found it irritating that she'd pick up on his concern for his father so quickly.

This must be part of the curse as well. His woman being in tune with him, the way his mother had been tuned in to his father.

He was already aware of how important her business was to her, how much she needed to succeed. Her face telegraphed so much to him. Other women had been honest and open, but with Lexa, it was like he knew her deep down.

While she drove, he slid his fingers across the seat to clasp her hand where it rested on her thigh.

At the first tingly touch, his worry about Jed lifted. "Sorry

I've been quiet. Now that I'm away from the house, I'm remembering things I need to take care of. That happening to you?"

"Big time. I hadn't planned to stay over and here I am, frittering away all these hours where I could be working." Her eyes went wide. "Oh! I'm so sorry. I know how that sounded, and I didn't mean this time with you. I can't believe I said that."

He laughed. "Look, if anyone understands the demands of a business, it's me. It's hard carving time out for yourself."

"Maybe that's the point of this whole thing."

"What do you mean?"

"Annie and Matthew Creighton left Perdition and founded a huge business. They built a lot of banks, office buildings, commercial stuff. They worked together on everything."

"Are you saying they want us to join forces?" He couldn't see how. She couldn't transplant to Florida. And he couldn't leave his father.

His responsibility there was clear.

"I spoke to Belle, the one who called us." She stopped the truck in front of the closed gate, then turned off the ignition. She sat with her head on the headrest. She looked at him then, eyes wide. "She told me Annie and Matthew were worried about me. Wanted me to find love before it was too late."

"Too late?"

"Apparently, I work too hard to leave room for a man in my life."

"Are they right?"

"Maybe. Probably. Who knows? I've been so busy getting to where I am that I don't think about that stuff." She blinked and shrugged in a gesture that screamed confusion. "At least, not until today."

And he'd been consumed by family obligations as well as relocating his business.

She undid her seat belt and turned toward him. She blew out

a breath. "There's something on your mind. Spill." She glanced at the gates, and he saw the way her mind turned.

Once they went through to the grounds of Perdition, their minds and bodies might not be their own. "We don't have to go back in there," he suggested.

"How's this? If we feel anything remotely out of our control, we make another run out the gate and never come back. Agreed?"

"Yes."

"Now, what's on your mind?"

"My father's date."

"Uh-huh?"

"Apparently, the Mitchell's home stager showed up on the job site today, and my father fell over himself trying to impress her. Looks like it worked."

"That's what Jared said?" She smiled and gave his fingers a squeeze. She looked delighted and relieved.

He nodded. "He said they shook hands and Dad's face changed. Went from dark to light." His voice had sounded lighter too.

"That's a weird way to say it."

"Judging from the change I heard in his voice, I'd say it was accurate."

"Cool! Dating this lady could be good, Jake. How old is your father?"

"Fifty. No, wait, fifty-one." He waited for the explosion of disbelief.

Right on cue, her face split into a grin. "No way!"

"My parents married within days of meeting each other. He was just shy of twenty. She was eighteen. I was born right away, and Jared followed a year after me." The curse was a force of nature not to be ignored. But Lexa would understand soon enough on her own. Explaining it wouldn't help.

He wasn't sure how he felt about a woman stepping into his

mother's place. It wasn't something he'd ever thought of. He figured the curse precluded a second go-round.

He frowned. His reaction made him look and feel like a nine-year-old. He chuffed out a breath.

"What happened, Jake? Why do you worry about him? Is he ill?"

Not ill, but sick at heart. "My mother was killed in an accident with a patrol car. High-speed chase. She was in the wrong place at the wrong time. Nearly killed my father."

"Was he in the car too?"

He shook his head. "Might as well have been. She went out to pick up a book from the library, a simple errand that could have waited. But she'd been waiting weeks for the book to come in, and she got impatient. She was always in a hurry."

"How long ago?"

"Three years. My father claims he knew the moment it happened. Says he got cold, like the burn that he'd felt for her since their first touch had gone out."

She blinked. Blinked again. Then he saw her eyes fill and moisten.

He pulled her close and let the buzz and crackle soothe them both. It zipped around his chest, then lower as she rubbed her cheek against his shoulder. "I'm sorry, Jake. It's hard losing someone you love so suddenly."

"I've been afraid I'd lose the old man too. It was like a light went out behind his eyes. Jared ended up walking away from his marriage and a great career and headed to sea. He told me that just last month he set up a business taking honeymooners on charters in the Caribbean. Serious case of burnout and too much loss all at once." Saying it that way made it sound simpler than he'd thought.

Burnout, a terrible accident, a marriage gone cold. The blame he'd wanted to place on Jared slipped away. In his own grief, he hadn't seen the load of shit Jared had faced.

"You've been watching over your dad alone?"

"Moved my business to Florida and started again from scratch. Dad went black with grief. Dark and morbid. He scared the shit out of me. Jared too."

"Is this the first time you've left him since?"

"Yes." The only reason he'd come here was because of that voice in the night. "I'm glad I did; it was way past time. I wouldn't have met you if I'd ignored the call."

"I don't think either of us was able to resist." She brushed her lips against his earlobe, then down his neck. The buzz spiked a warning and blood rushed.

He gave her a light squeeze. "Thank God."

The zing settled back to a low glow as she snuggled against him. Seattle was colder than Miami, and he found the sea-laden air sharp and surprisingly refreshing. He hadn't noticed how little he enjoyed the Florida heat until he was away from it.

Through the trees that lined the drive, he saw clouds scud overhead, promising rain through the night.

He thought of keeping Lexa warm under the down covers at Perdition, his legs tangled with hers, his heart beating against her chest, her smooth soft breasts a cushion against him.

"I suspect your father can take care of himself. Besides, if he chose a good woman the first time, have faith that he'll choose well now. If this lady's not right for him, he'll know it soon enough."

"She made him sound happy; that's a good start." Besides, Jared was there. With his jaded view of romance, he'd spot trouble right away.

"We could turn around, Jake," she said with a nod toward the gate. "We don't have to let the spirits play with us again."

"I don't think they will. Not to the same degree anyway. We both know how we feel now, and that's more than anything dead hookers can bring to the table."

She grinned and the lighthearted glance she gave him eased

his load of worry about Jed. He climbed out and opened the gate to Perdition.

"Put on your tool belt for me, Jake." The heavy promise in her voice chased around his belly, then headed south. Blood rushed and he swelled.

"My tool belt."

She nodded while sitting primly on the side of the bed, hands folded in her lap. "If you want to see me in that sex-kitten corset Faye lent me, you'll strip to the buff and strap yourself into your tool belt."

Lexa in that corset.

Then Lexa out of that corset.

"Fair's fair," he said, and sent a silent thank-you to the spirit who'd goaded him to pack it. "With or without tools?"

"You did not lug tools across the country."

"I may have a screwdriver or two."

"No hammers?"

"No hammers."

She put on a dramatic sigh. Her chest rose and fell in a way that should have made her breasts jiggle.

"What are you doing?" she asked as he advanced toward her.

Without touching her flesh, he used one finger to unbutton her top two buttons. The woman wore denim well. She was practical; he'd give her that.

The third button popped open, and with the precision of a television detective with a pen, he widened the gap to expose the truth. Her breasts were held up by the eye-popping corset.

"Witch. You've been wearing this all along?"

She nodded slowly, her eyes heavy-lidded and sultry. The woman was in serious need.

"Then the least I can do is put on the belt."

Lexa watched as Jake dug into his duffel bag. He rooted for

a moment, then, with the panache of a sleight-of-hand artist, pulled out the wide leather belt by the buckle end. A double buckle, she realized. The man meant business.

Her heart picked up speed as she watched every inch of the heavy tan leather rise out of the bag. One pouch, a couple of loops for hammers, a smaller loop for a screwdriver. "Don't forget to strip to the buff," she said. His jeans hung seductively low on his hips. "On second thought, just take your shirt off before you put it on," Lexa said with a strain of desire that lashed them both. "You can leave your jeans on."

He tugged his tee up and over his head, giving her a perfect view of his sculpted chest and the V of hair that warmed her fingers when she played. He slung the belt around his hips, catching the buckle end. When he'd buckled both catches, he stood for inspection with his hands on his hips.

His eyes twinkled with humor, but his neck flushed.

Men really had no idea how beautiful they were. His forearms flexed, his shoulders gleamed, his belly hitched in a notch as he caught her expression. Which must, she realized, be pure lust.

"Oh. My. God."

He was man to her woman, male strength to her feminine, hard to her soft. She melted.

"Now," he said, "it's your turn."

In her lust, she'd forgotten she was even in the corset. "Fair's fair," she repeated, and rose. She slowly undid the last of the buttons on her shirt and slid the sleeves off her shoulders, letting them fall to the bed behind her.

The female core of her melted and opened, woman for man, and her mind followed. He was hunger, she was food, she was empty while he could fill.

Drawn by aeons of primitive awareness, they moved into each other and held on.

He tilted her head back while he looked his fill. Her heart

pounded in time with his. Jake. This was Jake, and he was everything she'd ever wanted or could want in a man.

Everywhere they touched, the spark snapped and popped between them, rising as the fire enveloped her.

Lexa pressed her hips to his in perfect alignment, the buckles of his tool belt cold and hard on the flesh of her belly below the corset. Her breasts, held up and out, speared against his chest.

She swished them in a back-and-forth motion he couldn't ignore. Reaching into the low-slung cups, he scooped her bobbling flesh into his hands.

When he finally lowered his lips to suckle her, she crooned and bucked toward his mouth. She lifted her chin to expose her neck, and he traveled up from her nipple to her throat and on to the sensitive flesh under her ear.

"Jake, I need you. All of you. Your hands, your mouth, your cock. Please, Jake. Now."

She reached for his belt buckle and began to work at it. The tool belt fell away, leaving his zipper available for plunder.

She made short work of his jeans and kneeled to take him full in her mouth, devouring and lapping.

She thought she heard a sigh of feminine need, but she ignored it. But he turned to look over his shoulder at the same time.

"Do you think we're alone here?"

"I know I'm in charge, Jake. What I feel for you is all me," she said, certain of it.

"Me too." He jutted toward her mouth, and she took him deep into her throat. He cupped the back of her head to encourage her. "I can't take much more."

"You won't have to," she promised. Both nipples puckered and ached as she swished her nipples against his knees. Anything to feel the delicious sparkles everywhere.

"Enough," he said, stepping free. He clasped her shoulders

and guided her to the bed. He followed her down into the soft comforter, making her sigh with the rightness between them.

"This is all us, Jake," she whispered. "And it's so right, it scares me."

"I love you, Lexa, and it's never been better."

For that shining moment between wanting and having, she believed him. And wondered if she felt the same.

Could she love this man? Was she as cursed by this burning touch as he claimed to be?

Heart hammering, her thoughts spun away, and she let herself drown in sensation. Jake. Jake. *Jake.*

Lexa spread her legs in a plea for his touch. He obliged and poked a finger up the leg of her shorts and found the string of her wet panties between her legs.

Tugging the wet material from her flesh, he pulled it taut and rolled it back and forth across her clit, making her moan and thrash.

"In, I need you in." Her whisper was barely more than a soft croak.

So wet.

So hot.

So his. All for him.

"I need you inside. Now!" She yanked at her shorts, struggling to slide them down her hips.

He unzipped her, then drew the denim down her legs. She kicked them off and opened her legs wide. She streamed from her slit onto the bed. "I've never seen a woman so wet or so open, Lexa. You're mine, even if you haven't accepted it yet."

"Jake!"

He pressed his palm to her mons and slid two fingers into her sopping channel just to ease the immediate need.

"Oh! I want you everywhere at once. In my mouth, in my pussy. I want your mouth on mine, but I need your tongue on my clit too."

Her fingers danced across his scrotum and squeezed gently, sending his cock into spasms. She slid her hand to the sensitive spot just below the crown and squeezed hard enough to hold back his come.

He brushed her mouth and fingers away and grabbed for a condom. With a snap of latex that stung and heated his already overheated cock, he was ready.

He rolled onto her, sliding between the cradle she eagerly offered. The moment she felt him settle, she clutched at his hips and pulled him close, grinding her pubis against his.

"Be inside me, Jake, please, finally, be inside me. I need you."

The plunge into her was slow and easy as he allowed every millimeter of sensation and heat to grip them both. Penetration at this agonizing pace made her blind with need. Her vaginal walls grasped and pulled at him, coaxed him deeper and deeper, clinging and releasing as he pressed in.

It had been forever since she'd felt this fullness. And never had she felt so complete.

With every slide, he penetrated more fully while she opened slowly, needfully, her acceptance of him rapturous and oh so natural.

She watched his face, heavy with concentration and connection. "I love you, Lexa, I do."

His cock slid home.

"I care for you too," she said on a whimper, feeling the truth rise up and grip her heart. Rocking up toward him, she sighed into his mouth in a deep, need-filled kiss.

He rode her slowly and gently while love spiraled from his heart into hers. She kissed his nose, each ear, and even his cowlick between smiles of joy and acceptance. "I can't believe what's happening to me, Jake. I—Oh! Jake!"

His eyes glittered, then closed as she felt his tight control slip.

Her orgasm gathered in a knot of need and tight nerves. Jake tipped his pubic bone hard against her, and she carried him along into ecstasy.

He groaned and gathered her close to hold her while his spasms blasted into her. The pummeling she took from the sparking heat and his tightening body rose inside her as she tipped over the edge and crashed.

She kissed him and tasted the salt of tears. His? Hers? Lexa didn't know, or care.

11

Their hearts pounded as one, each of them trembling. Jake held her close and tight, her arms and cradle a sanctuary he never wanted to leave.

Exhaustion hit him hard as he nuzzled the heated flesh between her earlobe and neck.

He rolled off the bed and lifted her. She weighed so little, and he was used to hard physical labor. Her head lolled against his shoulder, her expression sated and loose. "Is it crazy to feel this much for you this soon?"

"Crazy? Cursed? What's the difference? It's more real than either of us has ever had before."

She thought of her previous boyfriends and her lukewarm response to them. "You're right." She looked up at him as he carried her through the doorway into the bathroom. "You were right about the spirits too. What just happened was all us."

He took her into the shower and washed them both in the tight corner unit. Tempting images of a water-drenched pussy slid through his mind, but he resisted dropping to his knees to eat her into oblivion. She needed to rest, and he wanted to give her time to think. Pushing her now could backfire.

After the shower, he watched as she slid into one of his work shirts and quietly slipped out the bedroom door.

She was gone a long time, but tempted as he was to follow, he figured she needed her space.

He'd had a lot of years to ponder the curse, while she'd just been hit with more than any normal person should be expected to accept.

He rolled into position and sank into a dreamless sleep.

Lexa found the photo album where she'd left it. The marble-topped side table showed up clearly in the moonlight. The leather felt cool to the touch, but it would warm soon.

Crossing the hall, she slipped through the dining room and turned right into the conservatory at the front of the house. Octagonal, with high windows in every panel, the hush enveloped her and even her breathing slowed to calm.

Here was the spot, she knew. It was here that Annie fell for Matthew while they worked side by side to build this fantastic addition. She trailed her fingers across the panes of glass, imagining the plants and aviaries Belle would have put in here. All gone now. From what Faye had said, the elderly woman she'd inherited from hadn't been able to maintain the mansion.

But whispers and shadows showed her the way it had once looked. As if a curtain lifted, daylight filled the half-built conservatory and she saw a boyish-looking person in work pants sawing a two-by-four on a sawhorse. The lad removed his hat to swipe his sleeve across a sweaty forehead, and she knew it was Annie she was seeing.

Matthew, tall, lean, and handsome, was approaching from the cliff. He'd been swimming, and water still dripped from his sculpted body.

The look on her great-grandmother's face at the sight of her man stunned Lexa, and she knew what it was their spirits wished for her.

The images faded as the light retreated to darkness again. She settled in a patch of moonlight and opened the photo album.

The next morning, Lexa felt the bristle of Jake's leg hair, the knobbiness of his knee under her calf, and she reveled in the sensations that made up Jake MacKay. He smelled like desire and man with a twist of sex musk added to the mix. She nuzzled her nose next to his ear, felt him grin in response.

She tested her thoughts, considered her level of morning desire, and knew she was alone in her own head. Nice.

"Last night was fabulous, Jake." She replayed the way he'd taken his time with her. The first slide inside her had been so slow, so complete, she'd tilted into an orgasm the second she'd felt his fullness.

"Sorry I fell asleep. I wanted more." His voice was early morning rough, and she loved the sound.

"I didn't. It felt right to make love slowly, completely, knowing we were alone in our bodies."

He tilted his head to look at her. "This is good, Lexa. We have a good thing here."

He was right. This crazy thing they'd fallen into was unbelievably great, but she still needed to keep things light. Falling for a guy within hours was just about the craziest, least likely thing for her to do. "Tell me. Was it a witch or a gypsy who cursed you and all your male relatives?"

His chest rose and fell with a chuckle. "I don't know how it started. All I know is, when a MacKay touches a special woman, there's an electrical charge they can't escape."

"Like the one we share?" Her heart picked up speed. She lifted her head to see his face. She got a great view of his straight nose and strong jaw, but he didn't turn toward her. She settled back down and slid her fingers through his chest hair.

She palmed his chest over his heart and pressed. "Can you feel it here?"

He nodded. "Deep as can be."

"It runs under my skin like an itch . . . but travels lightning quick," she said.

"Does it settle into something softer?"

"Eventually. And it's always lighter after an orgasm." The need for which was building. He felt good and strongly solid in a world that had gone all kinds of wrong. Hell, so wrong she believed she'd actually spoken to a ghost yesterday.

"It lightens up for me then too."

"I'm not frightened by it, though. Not anymore." Intrigued, curious, comforted, but not frightened. "Should I be afraid?"

"Not unless you hate my guts."

She laughed. "That'll never happen."

He rolled to his side and cupped her cheek. The hum of heat trailed down to her low belly as she studied his serious expression. "It's more than touching a special woman, Lexa."

"More?"

"It's love at first touch."

She huffed out a ragged breath. Love. He'd said it before, during the throes of orgasm, but she'd been quick to deny it. She was quicker now. "You're kidding, right?"

He shook his head.

She skittered off the bed, falling on her ass in her haste. "No, not love. Lust," she said, needing his reassurance. "That's easy. Lust is easy." She nodded her head like a marionette, unable to stop. "I can do lust." She motioned from her chest to his. "We can do lust."

But her belly flip-flopped, and her heart hammered. He couldn't mean it.

"It's love, Lexa. For me it will always be love." He sat up on the side of the bed.

"But we live on opposite sides of the country. We have businesses to run." Damn that midnight vision. She wished she'd never gone downstairs, had never set foot in the conservatory.

"I know." He scrubbed at his hair, revealing his cowlick, and for a moment she saw him as he'd have been as a little boy. "No one ever said love was convenient."

Her heart cracked at the idea of Jake as a child. Having a child, being a father. A father for her child. The images refused to clear. Someone or something had put them inside her head. She raised her face to the ceiling.

"Stop making me think of these things!" she called, but got no response. The room was silently still. She whipped around to look at the window, but fluttering lace curtains was the only response she got.

It was Annie, her great-grandmother; she just knew it. Annie and Matthew had brought Jake here. For her.

To give her a chance to know love. Their kind of love. The forever kind.

She squeezed her eyes shut for a long moment. Popped them open quick as a wink. She spun in a circle but caught no movement, not even a shadow.

Her own family! Messing with her life. How rotten was that?

"What are you thinking?" Jake asked.

"Never mind. We need to dress and get out of here. I have to think." She glanced around at the walls again. "By myself, away from sneaky, pernicious ghosts with nothing better to do than mess with my mind."

"We're out of here," agreed Jake.

It was Saturday and playing tourist made sense while Faye put in some hours at her store. The likelihood of getting a contract to redesign the gardens was unlikely for this year at least, but she wanted to remain on friendly terms with the woman just the same. There was always next year.

They found Faye in the front hall, putting the finishing touches to the veil of her hat. "Liam loves me in these. He says I look mysterious," she explained. This Liam fellow was right—Faye looked like a '40s mystery woman. Faye studied Lexa, then turned her gaze to Jake. "Going out?"

"Will we be able to?" Lexa asked with a glance over her shoulder. Yesterday's mad dash seemed like an escape.

Jake held her close to his side, tensed and ready.

"Of course you can leave. There's nothing holding you here." Faye took one more glance in the mirror and smoothed the tight waist of her light wool jacket. This time she looked like a forties film noir star. The veil was the perfect accent. Beneath it, her lips looked moist and luscious, painted red and full.

Jake and Lexa brushed past quickly, taking in the amused chuckle of more than one woman. Neither of them looked back to see who or what else was watching them leave.

And laughing about it.

Hours later, they'd been to Pike Place Market, then walked the downtown Seattle area. They'd gone up the Space Needle, even ridden the monorail, a relic from the World's Fair.

All the while, he'd waited for her response to his L-word. Acceptance would come; he just wanted it sooner rather than later.

But for now he was content to spend the day with her doing nothing more than holding hands and talking. They ate ice cream, shared a pizza from a takeout window, and watched people everywhere they went.

Her delightful imagination intrigued him. Throughout the day, she'd created stories about the couples they saw. These people just met, that couple had problems, that guy was still in the closet and the wife didn't know.

Now, on the waterfront, the state ferries glistening white on the waters of Puget Sound, he dug out his cell phone and called Miami. Jed had been on his way to do the estimates he'd blown off because of his date last night.

The date Jake still hadn't asked about. Jed answered immediately.

"How'd it go?" Jake asked.

"Fine, son. Just fine."

"Did you get the estimates done?"

His father sighed. "Yes."

"So the electrician got the wiring done in the Mitchell's kitchen?" It was Saturday, but the electrician was backed up and had agreed to work.

"He's a pro, just like everyone else on the job. You hire the best, you get the best. Isn't that what I taught you?" The edge of anger in his voice was new. Jake hadn't heard it in so long, he'd forgotten the old man was capable of snapping.

"Yes, sir, that's what you taught me." Along with respect. And how to love a good woman. He cut Lexa a glance.

In profile, she was even more gorgeous. She had one of those well-defined jawlines that some women wore well. Delicate but sharp.

He asked a few more questions, and with each response, the old man's voice grew more exasperated until finally he blew. Another thing Jake hadn't heard in too long.

"Son, if you keep treating me with kid gloves, I'll kick your ass when you get back. On second thought, don't come back! Not until you've had a real vacation."

"What?"

"Look, Jake, I know I've given you cause for concern. Losing your mother nearly took me too. But this babysitting's gotta stop. I want my life back, and you need yours too. Go get laid or something. But don't come back here until and unless you're ready to let me be." Then he was gone.

He turned to Lexa. "He hung up on me."

She turned her face away, but he still caught the shadow of a smirk on her lips before she did.

"What?" He touched her shoulder, the snap between them sharp, like the crack of a whip. He drew his finger back. Maybe it was more than sexual awareness that brought the buzz to life.

Maybe the zing came from other emotions too.

She dropped her chin. Then she raised her head and turned to look at him, her eyes clear and edgy. "Whenever we get away from the house, our real lives intrude. I've been thinking about how I can help Faye with the gardens without it costing a lot, and you've been calling your dad. I counted at least seven calls in four hours."

Jake took a step back, releasing the grip on her shoulder. She rotated the shoulder he'd been touching, then smoothed it a couple times with her palm. "Thanks, that was a real burner."

"I've had a lot of worries with my father in the last few years. He used to be a crackerjack, but now—"

"But you make him sound like an invalid, Jake, and I can't let go of my work ethic long enough to spend a day away. How will we manage a relationship this way?"

"It's a step in the right direction to hear you admit we're in a relationship."

She grinned. "I want one with you. I just don't believe long distance can work for people."

"Another thing we agree on." But the invalid comment stung. He hadn't been treating his father like an invalid. Jed needed him. "A man's supposed to be responsible and dependable and be there when his family needs him."

"And that's one of the things I like best about you, Jake. You're rock solid."

He nodded, pumped that he finally had her admitting she

wanted a relationship and had noticed some of the things he took pride in. "So, if you were looking at us from a distance, what story would you come up with at first glance?"

Her lips tilted upward in a come-hither look that rocked his foundation. "Looking at us from a stranger's point of view, I'd say we could barely keep our hands off each other. That we were in the first blush of sexual heat but quickly moving into real intimacy. That we wanted to share the important things about ourselves."

"So we're in the getting-to-know-you stage." He nodded, happy enough. "And after a little more study?"

Her eyes crinkled at the corners as she considered. When she spoke, it was with consideration of each word. "I'd say we were trying to find a way to be together but had a lot of obstacles."

He had no response but to gather her close and set her head under his chin while he stared up at the cloud-studded sky.

"I looked at the photo album last night. Faye was right— after the formal studio portrait, the photos were of picnics and dances. They used to hold parties outside by the gazebo. I saw a Victrola in the background of one picture. The lawn was strewn with tables and chairs, the tablecloths fluttering in the breeze. What fun they had."

"Sounds great," he said, but he sounded distracted.

"Faye told me that Matthew Creighton had to rearrange his thinking completely before Annie would marry him."

"How so?"

"Back then, women weren't supposed to work in construction. Men didn't think they were capable of understanding design."

"Supposed to focus on the womanly arts?"

She grinned. "Something like that."

"He must have had a struggle coming to grips with a woman like Annie. Sounds like a helluva leap to make."

She considered that. And more. Like the way Jake had packed up and moved to Florida to start again when his father needed him. Leaving a thriving business was a huge decision.

Bigger than big.

But then, she was seeing that in Jake. The man had a huge heart and a rock-solid sense of responsibility. He could never leave his father for as long as Jed needed him. And to expect him to walk away from MacKay Construction was wrong.

But the thought of never seeing him again was tearing her apart.

Just as the spirits of Perdition knew it would.

They'd brought him here for a reason. They'd brought him here for her. Not for the sex they missed or for fun or sport.

For *her.*

"Jake, I . . . " She stopped, gathered her courage. "I know it's too much to hope that you'd consider moving here, so—"

"I would, if you wanted me to," he interrupted her, his voice firm, his words quick.

"But your dad, what about him?"

"You're right; he's not an invalid. He doesn't need or want me in his face."

"Did the date go well?"

Jake shrugged. "I hope so. But even if it was a letdown, he can handle it. Truth is, my dad's been okay for a while now. I'm the one who hung on too long."

He looked rueful. "Much as I hate to admit it, Jared was right. Dad didn't need me there every moment. What he needed was to grieve, then move on. Having me there might even have held things up on that score."

She hugged him tighter, wanting to comfort. "Don't be hard on yourself. You had a shock, too, and it's in your nature to take care of those you love. The way you're willing to move here for me." She sighed and nestled in under his chin, felt the steady thud of his heart, luxuriated in the low burr of heat they shared, steady now and ready to go from embers to conflagration in the wink of an eye. "That's something else I love about you, Jake. You give yourself completely. I've never been so cared for."

"Back up." He tilted her chin with his fingertip. "Did you just say what I think you said?"

She grinned. "What do you mean?"

"Say it."

She stretched up and kissed his chin. Then moved higher to buss his lips once. Twice. "I love you, Jake MacKay. And I think it's in spite of your curse, not because of it. I love you because you're you."

"Are you asking me to move here?" he asked.

"No. I've been thinking about Florida. About the challenge of learning everything I'd need to learn. I'm up for it if you want me."

His eyes glowed as understanding dawned. "You'd leave everything you've worked for?"

"That's my offer, Jake. What do you say?"

He laughed and howled, straight up at the sky. "I'm not asking. I'm telling you I want to move here. I love the feel of Seattle, the cool clean air, the misty rain. The dark green of the mountains."

Her breath caught. Held. Lurched to a start again.

"And I love you, Lexa Creighton," he whispered. "Marry me."

"It's been thirty-six hours, Jake. What took you so long?"

For an exciting sneak peek at
Cassie Ryan's next novel,
CEREMONY OF SEDUCTION
Please turn the page . . .

Chapter 1

Alyssa Moss floated into her recurring erotic dream with a sense of keen anticipation. "Stone?" The vibrations of her words echoed as if she were in a long tunnel. Misty fog drifted around her ankles, as she searched for the man who came to her each night.

Even though she knew he would appear, she was startled when strong hands captured each of her arms from behind. She inhaled the wild scent of sandalwood, woodsy and natural, with a masculine essence completely Stone. With just his touch, her body came alive. Her breasts grew heavy and moisture dampened the inside of her thighs. "Touch me," she whispered, leaning back against him, waiting for the moment his large hands would caress her full breasts. Anticipation in the form of white-hot electricity stung her nipples. "I thought you wouldn't come tonight. I've waited—"

He spun her around and silenced her with a kiss. His hands were everywhere, his tongue mating with hers, dipping and tasting her lips, her teeth, every part of her mouth. Her T-shirt swept along her skin, up over her head. He smiled that sinfully wicked grin that always made her toes curl as he flung the discarded shirt aside. His eyes darkened with desire and a feral growl rumbled deep inside his throat. Before claiming her mouth again, he laid her back on the feather bed. Her senses swirled and the bed dipped as he followed her down, anchoring his fully clothed weight on top of her.

"I'll always come for you, Princess. One of these days I'll find you and we can be together." His lavender eyes smoldered with lust as he stared down at her. "Will you tell me where you are, Alyssandra?"

She threaded her fingers through his silky mahogany hair and sighed. "I tell you every night. I'm in Phoenix, waiting for you." His hard cock dug into her stomach. She arched, wrapping her legs around his narrow hips, pressing against him, enjoying the way his rough jeans stroked and teased her wet pussy.

He shook his head. "I know not of this 'Phoenix', but I shall find it and when I do, we will be together at last." He stole her senses in a soul-searing kiss that hardened her nipples to taut beads beneath the touch of his calloused hands.

She arched against him, offering herself, begging for his touch. He chuckled and she captured the sound in her mouth. "My greedy princess." His hips thrust against her hot core, mimicking what she wished he would do in reality. She moved with him, each movement rubbing against her aching clit just the way she liked. He gently rolled her nipple between his thumb and forefinger and she gasped. When his mouth replaced his hand, she released a moan. Moist heat closed over her sensitive peak and lava burned from the tip of her breast straight to her pussy, liquid heat pooling between her legs.

Stone turned his attention to her other breast. She ran a hand over his hard cock and he shuddered and groaned. She cupped the hot length of him, stroking him through his jeans as he suckled her breast harder, teeth scraping over her nipple until she thought she would explode. She traced her fingers along the waistband of his pants and slowly dipped her fingers inside to feel the silky head of his cock, already moistened with pre come.

Stone's breath hissed out as he captured her hands in his, stretching her arms high over her head, her breasts thrusting upward. "You know I cannot let you touch me like that, Alyssandra. Not yet. You are not strong enough to give sustenance, only take. But soon, very soon."

As it happened every night, her hands were magically bound. She could neither see nor feel her bindings, which only served to heighten her arousal. Another rush of excitement dampened the juncture between her thighs and she squirmed against her restraints.

"I want to feel your naked skin against me, Stone. I want to take your cock deep into my mouth before you bury yourself inside my pussy, your balls slapping against my ass while we fuck." She smiled as Stone's features suddenly appeared strained. She hoped someday, she would break his control and he'd do all of the things she longed for.

"You are a witch." He smiled down at her, his features softening, obvious affection in his gaze. "And someday I will fuck you until you can no longer stand for teasing me so wickedly." His tongue traced a slow path down to her aching mound and she bucked against him, wanting him to taste her, to suck her clit until her world shattered.

Maddeningly, he took his time, tracing her thighs, calves and feet with his rough fingers and then following with open-mouthed kisses, nips and well-placed licks. Then, he pushed her thighs wide and settled between them, placing a pillow under her ass, opening her fully to him.

"You have the most beautiful pussy, Princess." He gently separated her folds and pressed a single finger inside her slit. "Slick and wet, as always." His moistened finger traced a path downward to tease around her tight rosebud and her breath caught in her throat at the forbidden sensation. When he slowly inserted one blunt finger, a long moan ripped from her throat. "One day, I will stretch this beautiful tight ass with my cock." Before she could reply, he dropped his head and laved her clit with his tongue, erasing all her thoughts.

"Stone, yes," she managed as he began to finger-fuck her ass hard while he caressed the sensitive underside of her clit with his tongue. Her inner walls tightened, ever tighter until she teetered on the precipice, and then he pulled back. "No," she screamed in frustration. "Please, Stone. Make me come. Don't leave me like this again. I can't stand it."

He only smiled and shook his head. "You need sustenance not completion. However, I will stay with you a little longer tonight. Not to worry, Alyssandra, we will not be apart much longer. I can't stand it either."

She thrashed on the bed against her invisible bonds. She couldn't go through another night of this frustration. Every day she spent with her entire body buzzing and ready, her breasts sensitive to every movement against even her softest bras and her clit and pussy lips so swollen with need, she could only wear skirts and not pants that rubbed against her sensitive flesh. Not to mention her daydreaming about the next time she could feel Stone's touch. "Please . . ." she begged. "You can't keep leaving me like this."

"Shhh . . ." he said before dipping his head to trace the swollen folds of her pussy. She willingly gave herself up to the waves of pleasure that coursed through her body at every swipe of his talented tongue. Then Stone did something he'd never done before, surprising her. He continued to lave her slit, plunging his tongue deep inside then carrying her moisture on his tongue to stroke her clit. Then he gently probed into her ass with two fingers, stretching her slowly.

Her eyes widened and she gasped as the new sensation zinged through her body, her nipples tightening painfully. She took a moment to allow her body to adjust to this new invasion, but then she bucked against him wanting more. He only continued the slow torture on both fronts. Each time she neared the edge, he would stop and whisper soothing words to her until the feeling would recede, just enough to keep her from coming.

Finally, after what seemed like hours, using his other hand, he inserted two fingers into her aching slit, filling her equally from both sides. She loved the sensations, but wished he would replace one of them with his hard cock. Sounds of his hands slapping against her flesh as he pumped his fingers into her filled the air, causing her breath to catch and come in choppy pants.

Suddenly, he removed his fingers, leaving her bereft and empty. Then he sucked her clit between his lips in long pulls, scraping it lightly with his teeth. Her arousal wound tighter and tighter and just before she found her peak, he dissolved away.

Her alarm clock began its relentless drone.

Alyssa opened her eyes to see her own room. "Damn him!" He had left her once again unfulfilled. She pounded the covers in frustration. Stripping off her T-shirt, the soft cloth scraping across her engorged nipples like sandpaper, she hissed against the sensation and headed to the shower. "Another wonderful morning, with a nice hard shower spray to get me off," she grumbled. "Whoever invented the handheld showerhead should receive sainthood."

Stepping under the hot spray, she wet her hair and reached for the soap. The scent of honeysuckle filled her nostrils when the soap lathered between her fingers. As steam drifted around her, she imagined Stone's large hands touching her body, caressing her as he had in her dream. She closed her eyes and spread the lather onto her sensitive breasts. She'd dreamed the touch of his calloused fingers on her body so many times, she knew how each caress would affect her. Tossing the soap back into the dish, she propped her left leg up on the side of the tub and took down the showerhead, adjusting the water to high pulse—her favorite.

She took a deep breath and in her mind's eye saw Stone's dark head between her thighs, his tongue buried deep, his thick fingers fucking her ass. Then she aimed the spray toward her aching clit. As arousal arrowed through her, she pictured his golden body naked and glistening with water. His massive cock driving deep inside her until she screamed his name. The thought sent her spiraling into an orgasm, which seemed to last forever. Energy zinged through her body, and then drained away as if it flowed down the drain with the water.

When the spasms finally eased, she sat down hard on the edge of the tub, exhausted, the showerhead still hanging limply from her hand. The sound of someone banging on the bathroom door startled her. She braced a hand against the wall as she lost her balance and fell forward in the tub. She caught herself just before tumbling headfirst.

"Alyssa! If you want a ride to work, then move your ass and quit masturbating in there. You're screaming loud enough to wake the dead!"

Her cheeks burned. "How fucking embarrassing. If Debbie keeps catching me masturbating, she's going to start checking my vision. Maybe I shouldn't have listened to my father when he said I wasn't smart enough for the driving test. If I studied hard enough and passed, I wouldn't be dependent on rides from Debbie anymore."

Chiding herself, Alyssa quickly finished her shower and dressed in her usual baggy oversized shirt, long jeans skirt, her favorite cowboy boots and a ponytail. She looked into the mirror and sighed at the sight of her pale freckles and plain face. "As usual, this is as good as it's going to get."

When she entered the kitchen twenty minutes later, Debbie was eating corn flakes and reading the morning paper. Alyssa studied her roommate and wished for the millionth time she could look more like her.

Debbie's silvery blond hair hung in a satin waterfall to her shoulders, her wispy bangs giving her a trendy look. Her perfect makeup, designer jeans and sandals showcased a tight athletic body, which would look equally at home on the pages of *Playboy* or in a modeling session.

Alyssa shook her head. She was pudgy instead of sleek and no matter how much weight she lost, she'd never look like Debbie. She had hips and breasts where Debbie had a tight trim body. That was probably why Debbie's room was a revolving door for all of the hottest guys in Phoenix. Alyssa had joked about installing a take-a-number machine on her roomie's bedroom door. Surely, she could steal one from the post office. But Debbie would just grin and say it would cost too much to keep replacing the numbers.

"Hey, you gonna eat before we go?" Debbie looked up from her cereal. "I'm sure all that whacking off helped work up an appetite." Her perfectly lined lips curved up in a smirk.

Alyssa ignored her and sighed. "I'll grab something at the bar. I'm training a new bartender this morning, so I have to be there early." She opened the side cabinet, which held all her medicine and took out the appropriate doses for the day. Ever since she'd turned sixteen, she'd been sickly and the doctors could find no cause. Instead, they treated her symptoms with no less than twenty different meds she had to take at various times throughout the day. Her adoptive parents often remarked that her real parents must not have been very healthy to pass on so many problems to their daughter. A familiar wave of pain spiked through her as she wished for parents who looked like her, acted like her, and understood her.

"Earth to Lyssa." Debbie waved a hand in front of Alyssa's face breaking her out of her thoughts. "Do you have your fucking pharmacy ready? We're going to be late."

Alyssa snapped her purse closed and stifled a yawn. It didn't feel like she'd slept at all last night. *Damned erotic dreams.* "Yeah, I'm ready. You're going to be able to pick me up at closing, right? I don't want to have to walk home that late."

"No sweat. I don't have a date tonight, so I'll cut out of work early and come get you. We can grab drive-through on the way home or something."

"Or something." She sighed. Debbie knew she wasn't supposed to have take-out. The doctors had kept her on a strict diet to try to minimize her symptoms. And even though nothing had helped, she did feel better when she didn't eat a constant stream of grease and French fries.

Alyssa looked up as a sly look crossed Debbie's face before she hid it. *Uh-oh, here it comes.* "What is it, Deb? You only get that look when you want something."

Debbie shrugged, trying and failing for nonchalant. "How 'bout you leave work early on Friday? I have someone you should meet."

Her mouth dropped open in shock and she turned to stare at her roommate. "You mean a guy?" Debbie always told Alyssa she wasn't attractive enough to have a relationship. And when guys did look at her, they were just staring because she looked like she needed a mercy fuck. So, why was Debbie suddenly trying to fix her up?

"Not a guy, a *man*," Debbie clarified. "Your twenty-fourth birthday is coming up, and I know this guy who is perfect for you." She stopped and looked Alyssa up and down. "He doesn't mind body types like yours. And since he has dark hair too, he probably won't mind your muddy brown."

Disappointment and hurt arrowed through her, tears burned at the back of her eyes and she blinked rapidly to clear them. She'd known her entire life she wasn't very attractive. If her family and best friend didn't even think so, then there was no use thinking anyone else would. *The only time I feel attractive is with Stone. I just don't fit in anywhere else.* She suddenly longed to call in sick and return to bed and to the comfort of Stone's arms—even if they were only in her dreams.

"About eight o'clock, okay?" Debbie continued either not noticing Alyssa's reaction or not caring. She bet it was the latter. "And try to wear something that hides your weight. I want him to like you."

Alyssa swallowed her embarrassment and slid into the passenger's seat. *Maybe I can get sick before Friday.*

"If I'm raped and murdered tonight, so help me, I'm going to haunt Debbie until her dying day!" Alyssa quickened her steps as the shadowed stranger behind her loomed closer. She searched the darkened street and closed shops in front of her for some sign of life, to no avail. The stifling Phoenix night closed around her like a shroud, heat still radiated off the cement and her footsteps clicked in time to her beating heart. The smell of stale grease from the Chinese restaurant permeated the air. *Why the hell can't something still be open?!*

"Damn you, Debbie!" she growled under her breath, and glanced over her shoulder to see the menacing shape of the man who still followed her. Debbie was probably off fucking some pretty-boy and forgot all about her promise to pick her up after work. *If I live through tonight, I'm taking that fucking driver's test. Even if I have to study for the rest of my life to pass it, it will be worth not having to wait on Debbie.*

Quickening her steps, she rummaged in her purse for her switchblade. Luckily, an extremely drunk Hell's Angel had run short on money and made a tip of the switchblade a few months ago. Now if she could just figure out how to use it.

A strong hand gripped her shoulder startling her and causing her to drop the knife, which skittered away over the hot cement. Time slowed and her self-defense training took over. *Thank God I didn't listen to my family and took the class any-*

way! She stomped down hard on his instep, the heel of her cowboy boot hopefully leaving a permanent imprint. Then she drove her elbow back into the attacker's midsection. A surprised "oof" of pain sounded behind her and she bolted forward out of his reach.

Before she'd taken two steps, he grabbed her around the waist, and all her air whooshed out in a painful rush. When she recovered, she realized he hadn't even broken stride and she hung over his arm like a sack of dog food. If she weren't so scared, she'd have to admire the man's muscle and strength. She screamed, but no sound came out. She took a breath and tried again, but it was as if she screamed inside a soundproof room.

"Calm down, witch," he said and slapped her on the bottom. "I haven't searched for you for ten years to have you feed me my own bollocks." The voice, which held a note of amusement, was so deep she felt the rumbling through his arms wrapped beneath her ass. There was something familiar about it she couldn't quite place.

"Put me down, you bastard!" Alyssa was surprised to hear her voice this time, although muted. She kicked and flailed to no avail. She started to bite him, but some deep internal instinct warned her not to push her luck. She could sense the aura of power that surrounded him without ever seeing his face. And she'd learned long ago not to ignore her gut.

"In good time, witch. You're almost home." He punctuated his remarks with another slap on her ass.

He knows where I live? Oh, God, I'm going to raped and murdered in my own shabby apartment!

She raised her head and was shocked to see her apartment steps come into view. Metallic panic rose in the back of her throat, and she renewed her struggles. As a single woman, she knew better than to let her attacker get her inside the apartment. Better to take a stand outside where someone could happen along or she had a hope of escape. But just as she took a breath to scream, he set her down in front of her apartment door, sliding her down his firm body until her feet touched the concrete. She startled when something about the sensation tickled her memory.

The scream died in her throat as she looked into the face of a familiar stranger.

Stone.

She'd know him anywhere since she'd dreamt of him so often over the past ten years, she hadn't ever bothered to find a flesh-and-blood man. To find him here now, standing in front of her, sent an erotic thrill racing through her body.

She shook her head, convinced she was dreaming again, but none of her dreams of him had ever taken place anywhere but in an ethereal bedroom. She took a moment to study him and compare him to her dream memory. He towered over her five-nine frame so much he would have to duck to walk through her apartment door. Broad shoulders stretched his black T-shirt taut across a well-defined chest, and his face resembled chiseled granite. When he smiled, the small dimple next to his mouth softened him, making him seem approachable. Unruly mahogany hair gave him a rakish air and liquid lavender eyes, the same color as her own, stared back at her.

His deep rumbling chuckle shook her from her reverie and she realized she'd been staring. "Do you see anything you like, witch?" His tone held a teasing warmth as he gestured to himself from head to toe. Following his hand all the way down, she noticed an extremely large bulge that tightened the front of his jeans.

She swallowed hard as she recalled her dream with him last night and liquid heat pooled between her legs and dampened her panties. Then fear and the remaining adrenaline brought her back to reality. How could a flesh and blood man invade her dreams? Could this man really be Stone?

"Who are you?" she demanded, ignoring his question.

"You already know who I am. The more appropriate question is who are you and why have I come to find you." He crossed muscular arms over his chest and grinned while he waited for her to ask.

An overwhelming curiosity had her inviting him in before she could think better of it. Her intuition was blissfully silent and she took that as a good sign. But her pussy screamed to be introduced more intimately.

Thankfully, her roommate wasn't fucking an entire football team in the living room, like she was last time Alyssa came home. She tossed her purse on the counter and grabbed two bottled waters from the fridge. She handed one to Stone who had already made himself comfortable on her couch. "So who am I?" she asked, as her fingers itched to trace the strong lines of his body. "Why did you come to find me? And who the hell are you?" Alyssa settled herself on the opposite end of the couch where she could watch him, and waited for him to dissolve at any instant.

He took his time studying her as she had him. Finally, he twisted the cap off the bottle of water and swallowed half in two large gulps. "You," he pointed toward her, "are Alyssandra de Klatch, first Princess of the Klatch. And I've told you for years, one day I'd find you and we could finally be together."

Shock traveled all the way to her gut. When she dreamed of him, he'd always called her Alyssandra or Princess. That was one of the reasons she'd always assumed he was purely a product of her overactive imagination. All of this was crazy, but something inside her knew he wasn't lying. But a princess? Not likely.

"Stone," she whispered. *I might be losing my mind, but if I get to be insane with him for the rest of my life, I'll take that over what I've lived for the past twenty-three years.*

He nodded, his lopsided smile making his dimple more pronounced. "Yes, you remember me." He looked pleased. "If you'd taken better care of yourself, witch, then you wouldn't have had to subsist on dreams. Since I'm here now, we can rectify that situation."

She blushed as she realized exactly what his definition of "rectify" was. "Stop calling me witch and just answer the rest of my questions!" *Or throw me on the floor now, and we can talk later...*

He shook his head. "Your heritage is very strong." He rubbed his stomach and chuckled. "As well as the rest of you. But you are a witch. A *Klatch* witch."

She narrowed her eyes at him. "You said my name was Alyssandra de Klatch. But that still doesn't make me a witch. And I was born Alyssa Moss."

"No, actually you were stolen from your true family by Cunts."

"Excuse me?" she demanded, shocked he would use the offensive term in front of her. "I'm far from prude, but I *hate* that word."

"As you should." He laughed, the warm sexy sound, which had melted her in her dreams, even now caused her nipples to tighten against her thin cotton top. His eyes zeroed in on her shirt as if he knew. She blushed and looked away. "My apologies. You have lived among the humans for far too long to understand my reference. Long ago, the Klatch had a civil war and split into two factions, the original Klatch and a new faction who called themselves Cunts."

Alyssa snorted in disbelief. "You've got to be fucking kidding me."

"As much as I'd like to fuck you . . . no. I do not joke about our history." He took another long pull of the water and she was fascinated by the way his throat worked as he swallowed. She resisted a sudden urge to run her tongue over the dip in his throat where his Adam's apple bobbed. His eyes glinted with mirth and she was afraid he knew what she'd been thinking.

Mercifully, he continued without mentioning it. In one fluid movement, he stood and pulled her to him, pressing her against the long line of his body. Her breath caught in her throat and every inch of her body screamed for her to rub herself shamelessly against him—or maybe just throw him on the floor and impale herself on his cock.

The sudden urge slapped her back to reality and she bolted from his grasp, putting the couch between them. He merely chuckled and continued. "The word 'cunt' is used as a slur because witches interact with humans and they pick up on our language. 'Cunt' has become synonymous with 'traitor' and 'outcast' to any witch. Although the humans use it in a slightly different way. Now come and kiss me, Alyssandra, I want to finally feel your lips in the physical world."

When he started around the couch after her, she held up a hand. "Wait." She gave her traitorous body a firm talking to, *this can't be real so work with me here*, and pierced him with her most skeptical stare. "What do witches have to do with this? You mean like Wiccans?"

He leaned forward resting his forearms on the back of the couch, causing the already tight black T-shirt to mold over the best shoulders she'd ever seen. Shoulders she knew she'd seen before—and felt before. She licked her lips at the sudden urge to trace each inch of his muscular shoulders with her tongue.

He continued, breaking her out of her thoughts. "Wiccans are humans who choose to practice a set of beliefs. Being Klatch is what you are." He shook his head and sighed. "I can see the Cunts withheld from you your heritage. This must be remedied." His hand snaked out to grab her arm and he pulled her to him across the back of the couch. When he cradled her in his lap on the couch, his strong arms bracketed around her, a sexual thrill zinged straight to her pussy. The fact that a very large bulge swelled against her hip only served to scramble her thoughts further.

He smiled, his eyes darkened dangerously. But a dangerous

she knew from ten years of dreams that meant wonderful sexual things, not anything to harm her. Every erogenous zone in her body rejoiced, drowning her in a sea of sexual energy.

She put her fingers against his lips when he lowered his face to hers. "Please, tell me about the Klatch." Anything to keep him talking until she could figure out how he evoked these feelings inside her.

"A Klatch witch is a being who needs sexual energy to survive. We also eat and drink, but in order to thrive, we must imbibe sexual energy." He kissed the fingers still resting lightly against his lips and then pulled one into his mouth. He sucked on the tip and swirled his tongue in a familiar pattern she remembered him using on the soft underside of her clit—which throbbed in response. She pulled her finger away, her breathing coming in short gasps.

His voice was a low rumble when he spoke. "Intercourse is the best and easiest, but any kind of sexual energy will do: masturbation, voyeurism, or even sexual dreams."

Alyssa found herself laughing despite the sexually charged atmosphere. "You're trying to tell me I'm some kind of sexual vampire?"

"Good God, no." He looked horrified at the suggestion. "You are no succubus, Princess. You are my betrothed and a full-blooded Princess of Klatch."

"Betrothed?" She gasped, and her mouth fell open. "As in engaged to be married?"

He nodded. "Yes, most Klatch never marry. They will either have half-breed children with humans or just feed from humans sexually their whole lives. But the full-blooded Klatch are betrothed at birth to another of full blood to retain the line and our heritage." He lowered his mouth to hers, but at the first jolting and very familiar touch of his lips, she squirmed out of his grasp and put half the room's distance between them.

Alyssa's mind whirled. When he was near her, it felt like all her circuits were on overload. She looked up into his darkened lavender eyes. The hunk of testosterone who sat across from her thought he was her fiancé? How lucky could she get? Her body immediately wanted to claim its conjugal rights. But then her overly logical mind weighed in and ruined everything.

"Look, I don't even know you. You follow me home from work, scare me half to death and now you're trying to tell me I'm some sort of witch who feeds off sex?" She paced back and forth in front of the coffee table. A large ball of lead settled in her gut and she knew at least some of what Stone said was true. She could feel it deep inside her. "Why did you wait until now to find me?"

"Alyssandra, I have searched for you for ten years. You were well hidden among the humans. When the civil war ended, they stole you as a bargaining tool so the king and queen would not hunt down the remaining Cunts. Then they slithered away to the human world to hide." He stood and laid a comforting hand on her shoulder. "I know you believe and I also know you don't want to. But tell me this. Did you fit in growing up? Are you like your parents or your siblings or even your friends?"

The awful truth hit her like a sledgehammer. She squeezed her eyes shut as tears burned at the back of her eyes. He was right. She'd never fit in and she never had any true friends. Her mother and father had fair hair and she had dark. Her pale lavender eyes had always been a topic of fascination or outright teasing and her early development of full hips and breasts had set her apart from her model-thin mother and sisters. She figured that's why she'd dreamt of a handsome man who made her feel as if she belonged. But now, with him standing so close, she could smell the woodsy musk of pure man, she knew better. "Are my adoptive parents . . ." She struggled with the word, "Cunts?"

He nodded and gestured to a family picture hanging on her wall. "The civil war came partially because of physical differences. The offspring of Klatch and humans who called themselves Cunts are fair of hair and skin and usually have thin bodies. The remaining faction of Klatch are dark haired, olive skinned and blessed with curves." He stared down at her body as if he could see through the baggy clothes. She thought he would devour her whole.

"The Cunts thought themselves more attractive, superior and better breeding stock, so they tried to overthrow the king . . . and failed."

Alyssa thought back over her life. Her family had always treated her more as a pet who wasn't very smart than a part of the family. College was never an option. Her father convinced her she just couldn't handle the higher learning and it wouldn't be worth wasting the money. The same thing happened when she wanted to get a driver's license.

So, she'd gone to bartending school. The pay was decent and she enjoyed interacting with the customers—most of the time. As for her personal life, her sisters still teased her about being fat and her long dark hair was always downplayed as less attractive than their lighter tresses. If everything Stone said was true, it made a lot of things more clear. *Go with your gut!*

"What exactly do you want me to do?" Her mind whirled.

"Your twenty-fourth birthday grows near and you will be coming of age. Because of your heritage, you'll be an extremely powerful witch in her own right. Come with me and meet your real parents and then you can decide."

She closed her eyes and searched inside herself for answers. Should she trust Stone? This entire situation was too crazy for words. She went with her gut. "Prove to me you are who you say you are, and I'll go."